MISSING
BUT NOT
LOST

RUSSELL WATE

CRANTHORPE
MILLNER

First published by Cranthorpe Millner Publishers (2022)

ISBN 978-1-80378-085-6 (Paperback)

www.cranthorpemillner.com

Cranthorpe Millner Publishers

This book is dedicated to my mother,
Florence Irene Wate

Foreword

This is a story about a detective, his skills and the process involved to investigate homicide. It shows us that detective as a man, his family and his life. The book is also a travelogue as seen through his eyes.

The investigation branch within the Foreign and Commonwealth Office described in this novel is fictional and is not currently or possibly ever will be real in the format I have described within the story. They do have very gifted police superintendents who work there on a seconded basis as liaison officers and they do all they can to support families and police forces. They work with a murder and manslaughter team within the FCO.

My absolute thoughts and wishes go to all those families who have lost loved ones abroad and the nightmare they face in trying to come to terms and understand and having to plan for their loved ones to be returned to the UK.

Chapter One

Alexander McFarlane, whilst sitting in his seat on the train, was smiling quietly to himself as he travelled from Ely to London. It was early Monday morning and he reflected on the wonderful weekend he had just had. The weekend had culminated on the Sunday with a fantastic family get together, which his mother Katherine had organised to celebrate his thirtieth birthday. He was also smiling because he was now definitely in a steady relationship with Hannah Tobias. Hannah was a barrister who worked in the same chambers in Cambridge as his grandpa, John McFarlane, who was a retired family court judge. Hannah had not been put off by the overexuberant attentions at the family gathering from his two married younger sisters, Aileen and Isla, who were both very keen for him to be in a relationship.

He looked across at his father, Gregor McFarlane, who was sitting opposite him on the train, who must have looked to anyone else looking at him in the train compartment as happy and content as Sandy was looking. Gregor and Sandy (which was the name his whole family and his friends used for him) were both travelling to London, where they shared a flat. Well, it was Sandy's parents' flat that he lived in during the week, for a very small monetary contribution. Sandy was a detective chief inspector (DCI) who worked for the Foreign and Commonwealth Office in Westminster, and his father was an accountant working for an international investment bank based in the City of London.

Sandy shut his eyes to try and sleep; he was now starting to feel the effects of jet lag due to a recent trip working in India. He had only returned the previous Friday and the adrenaline that had carried him through his busy family weekend was now starting to ease off. Try as he might, he was not able to sleep, and as the train pulled into Cambridge, they were joined by a large number of new passengers making an incredible noise. Many of them were carrying bags and cases and were taking an inordinate amount of time to get settled into a seat and for the train carriage to return to a more peaceful atmosphere. Sandy took a long sip of the coffee that he had bought at Ely railway station and picked up the morning newspaper.

On starting to read the Metro paper for that day, it had the headline: "Cop killer still at large". For any police officer and their family, this was a very sobering piece of news. Sandy had seen a few news reports about the shooting of Constable Joseph Foster whilst he was in India, but other than being immensely sad that a member of his wider police family had been killed in such a horrific manner, he did not know what had happened. The article said that in Derby city centre in the early hours of the morning almost ten days ago now, Constable Foster, whilst attempting to arrest two or three individuals for dealing in drugs, had been shot with a single bullet wound to his chest that had tragically led to his death. The individuals, or thugs as Sandy would have described them, had made off, and although Derbyshire Police had arrested four people, they had been quickly released on bail.

Gregor was also at that time reading with a concerned frown on his face the same article in the paper. He looked at Sandy and said, 'Son, isn't this awful! His poor family. When he left for work that day, I am sure they did not for one minute think that they wouldn't ever see him again. Heart-breaking!'

'It is so sad. He was only doing his duty protecting the public from thugs like them, who I have no doubt will not have the slightest bit of regret or remorse that they have snuffed his life out,' Sandy said, agreeing with his father.

'Looks like they have caught them though. The article says they have arrested four people and they are on bail.'

'I wouldn't read too much into that news, Dad, as they have probably only arrested the most likely suspects. A senior investigating officer might sometimes do this to shake the tree and to see what falls out.'

'Sandy, can you understand now why your mum and I were always so worried when you were a uniformed police officer out on patrol, especially at night?'

'I am thirty years old, Dad. Surely you don't worry about me still, do you?'

'Unfortunately, yes, I am afraid to say we do.' Gregor said to his son, 'However old you are, parents always worry, but we worry a lot less now that you are not working on the beat.'

Sandy presumed this was what all parents felt about their children. He decided to try and have a nap before they got any closer to King's Cross railway station as he knew this would be when his busy day would begin. Long before they got into London, people were getting out of their seats and collecting their belongings to enable them to get a quick getaway off the train once it arrived at the station. Sandy's heavy sleep-filled eyes had no alternative but to open as the noise continued to rise in the carriage.

∞

The underground train that Sandy was taking to Victoria was full of people. The crush of people on the platform in King's Cross was almost overwhelming and to compound this, on that June morning the weather in London was already quite stiflingly hot. Sandy wasn't helped either because as well as his briefcase, he also had a suitcase with his belongings in for his week's stay in London. He forced his way onto the train, pushing people out of the way; he had to do this to stand any chance of getting on at all.

The sun was shining as he left Victoria station and walked along Buckingham Palace Road, and the further he went away from Victoria, the more the crowds started to thin out. However, as Sandy got closer to the corner of Buckingham Palace, he knew that this wouldn't be the case when the time moved towards the Changing of the Guard at the palace. The Changing of the Guard is a ceremony where the Queen's guard hands over the responsibility of protecting Buckingham and St James's palaces over to the new guard. Sandy knew that this was one of London's most popular tourist experiences and the crowds who watched it were often huge. A lot of this was down to the pomp and ceremony of it all, with military bands playing and the marching precision of the drill. Sandy had seen it a few times and never tired of the wonderful tradition of it all.

The walk through St James's Park was very pleasant that morning as the crowds that were often there had not yet built up, so this made it easier to move swiftly through the park. The grey squirrels were extremely active that morning, scampering across the paths and racing up and down the trees. At the end of the park, he crossed Horse Guard's Road and went down King Charles Street. Sandy walked into the imposing Foreign and Commonwealth Office, which is housed in a beautiful building dating back over one hundred and fifty years. Sandy always marvelled at the architecture and he felt honoured to be working in such a beautiful building.

The area where the investigation team, within which he worked, was already full of team members. As soon as Sandy walked in, there were questions from everyone present about his trip to India. This was his first day back in the office since he had returned. India had been an incredible experience and a place he had in fact visited four times during the last few months whilst investigating the death of Robert Smythe. One of the detective sergeants who had been with him to India on one of those occasions, Juliet Ashton, was particularly pleased to discuss the details of the trip with him.

The boss of the team, Detective Superintendent Jane Watson, appeared in the corridor and motioned to him with her finger to follow her. Jane was a lady in her early forties who was always extremely smartly dressed. Today she was wearing a dark grey trouser suit. Jane was one of the most dedicated and hardworking people Sandy had ever worked with. He had nothing but admiration for her. He now felt that he had proved himself to her and was truly a trusted member of her team.

As soon as they entered Jane's office, she said, 'Two things, Sandy. Don't forget you have a meeting this afternoon with Mr James Peveril, the member of parliament for the Hope Valley. His son George is still missing in Manitoba, Canada. He says he is available from one p.m. in his offices at the Houses of Parliament. Please don't be late and make sure you get there early enough to allow time to get through security. Also, Phil Harris has flown to Brussels this morning to do some work on the use of European arrest warrants, now we have left the European Union, so I need you to lead the team meeting this morning and deal with the outstanding work.'

Sandy only had the opportunity to say, 'No problems,' because Jane's phone rang almost as soon as she had finished talking. It was all work with Jane, and Sandy now realised that there was to be no easy start to his working week and no allowance made for any possible jet lag. 'Just get on with it, son,' he muttered to himself as he went along to the office to make a start with leading the team meeting.

The morning seemed to go by quickly and before he knew it, the time had come for Sandy and Detective Sergeant (DS) Ashton to make their way to the Houses of Parliament to see the Right Honourable James Peveril MP to have a chat about his missing son. Sandy knew nothing about Manitoba other than he thought the state capital was Winnipeg, so he was interested to find out where in Manitoba George had gone to.

∞

They walked together into Whitehall heading towards

Parliament Square and the Houses of Parliament. Juliet was really excited as they walked along, telling Sandy that she had just booked flights for her family to visit her parents in Barbados for three weeks in August. Juliet had come to live in England with her parents and younger brother when she was very young. Even though she had lived in England almost all of her life, she still regarded Barbados as her true home.

Even before they had reached Parliament Square, they could hear the loud noise of a demonstration that was taking place. As they walked into the square, Sandy and Juliet saw that there were hundreds if not thousands of people, shouting and screaming loud chants. A number of them had banners that clearly showed this was a far-right political protest, which followed on from a Black Lives Matter demonstration, which had been held there earlier in the month.

Sandy, when he was a young, uniform police officer in London, had been involved in policing demonstrations, none of them were as volatile as this one looked likely to develop into and he had never policed a demonstration in this wonderful space, Parliament Square. Without all of these people in it you would be able to see that the square had a large green in the centre, with the Houses of Parliament on one side. Opposite this was the Middlesex Guildhall housing the Supreme Court. The other two sides had Westminster Abbey on one and part of the Treasury buildings on the other. There were also twelve statues, which were of several British prime ministers, including Winston Churchill, but also statues of Abraham Lincoln, Nelson Mandela and Mahatma Gandhi. It was unfortunate that the view of these statues was blocked by all of the people in the square.

Sandy and Juliet showed their police warrant cards to the security guard at the entrance to the parliament building. This allowed them to walk past the queue to the front, where Sandy told the people at the reception that they had a meeting with Mr James Peveril MP. The receptionist, after looking at her computer screen for a few moments, told them that they had come to the wrong building and that as an opposition MP, Mr Peveril did not have an office in the Houses of Parliament but in the nearby Portcullis House situated around the corner on the Embankment. Juliet started to giggle and said, 'It would appear that you didn't check where we were meeting, did you, Sandy?'

'How was I supposed to know there was another building with MP offices in?' Sandy said sheepishly as they left quickly to walk round to Portcullis House. They were now going to be late, which was something that Sandy tried never to be. Juliet and now Sandy were laughing about it with each other as they walked the short distance to the other offices.

Not long after they had arrived at Portcullis House, James Peveril arrived and escorted them into a fairly small office just off the reception area. He laughed when Juliet told him they had been to the Houses of

Parliament first. Looking at Sandy, he said, 'I am not surprised that you thought I was a Tory MP and not a Labour MP, with my father being Viscount William Harrison Peveril. However, I studied law at the London School of Economics and soon saw the light.' This comment brought smiles to all of their faces. James, although quite a tall man, was very slim in stature. He had on a smart blue suit and his round face had the appearance of being very welcoming.

Juliet said, 'Sandy studied law at Cambridge and I suspect he, unlike us, is a Tory voter!' She smiled knowingly.

'I am not going to reveal to either of you, and certainly not a labour MP, who I vote for,' Sandy said, as he tried to move the conversation on. He continued. 'Why are you so concerned about George? He is an adult, isn't he?'

At the mention of George's name, James Peveril's face changed, almost as if a switch had been flicked, and he immediately showed a look of extreme concern. Just as he was about to speak, the coffee that he had ordered for them all arrived.

Chapter Two

They took a mouthful of the lukewarm and, clearly from all of their facial expressions, very bitter tasting coffee. James was the first one to speak and said, 'Sorry, folks, not nice at all!' He put his coffee cup down after one sip; he'd had enough of it. He then said, 'DCI McFarlane, so you read law at Cambridge, did you? Are you by any chance related to Judge John McFarlane?'

'Yes, he is one of my grandfathers. Why?'

'I had a case before him when I was a practising solicitor in Sheffield. I thought he was an exceptionally hard and uncompromising judge.'

On hearing this, Sandy, who was unerringly loyal to his family, completely bristled by the comment and couldn't help himself, even though he was talking to an MP, replied, 'I presume it was a family law case and I am sure he was like that to protect the interests of the children involved.'

James realised straight away that he needed to apologise and said, 'I am sorry how that came across. Yes, I agree with you, both parents were the least of his concerns and the children were his prime focus. I just happened to be representing one of the parents in the case and we didn't get the result for which we were hoping.'

Juliet felt she needed to quickly soften the conversation and said, 'Please can you talk to us about George and why you are so concerned for him?'

'Of course, DS Ashton. I am sorry again, DCI McFarlane, that it seemed I put your grandfather in a bad light.'

'Please call me Sandy, which is the name most people call me by, and I am sure Juliet is quite happy for you to use her name as well.'

'Thank you. I probably need to put the family's concerns into context. George's mother and I split up when he was ten years old. I had been an MP for about eighteen months by then, living here in London for almost all of my time, and I had started a relationship with a lobbyist that worked around parliament. George took it badly, but he was away at school at the time, so I rarely saw him.'

'Which school did he go to?' Sandy asked.

'He was a boarder at Frobisher's school in Norfolk. My sister Arabella Montague lives at the Peveril Farm in Norfolk and she is very close to George. She and her husband have no children, so George is like a son to them both. They helped us to select the school for him.'

'I know Frobisher's well. I went to the King's School in Ely and we often played rugby against them. A lovely school in my opinion,' Sandy said.

'Not so wonderful when they found out when he was fourteen years old that he had drugs in his possession. They thought he was supplying to others in the school, but it was the other way round. I know I would say that as his parent. They have zero tolerance for drug dealing in the school and so they expelled him. It is a shame Arabella was away at the time in Canada, at the family estate in Manitoba, as I am sure she would have fought his cause. If she hadn't been able to keep him at Frobisher's, I am sure she at least would have got him into the school at Hunstanton, which is very near to where she lives.'

'What happened then?' Juliet asked.

'He came back to live with us in Derbyshire at our house in Hope. He could have gone to live with his mother Helen in Castleton, which is nearby, but unfortunately, they don't have a great relationship. I married Janice, the woman I was having a relationship with. We have two girls, five and seven years old, and we were all very happy for George to come and live with us.'

'So, he went to a local school then?'

'No, as soon as they heard about him being expelled for the drugs, they would not touch him. He went to a school closer to Chesterfield and that is where he came across the two yobs he has run away with.'

Sandy asked, 'How do you know that he has run away with others?'

'Because he stole his stepmother Janice's credit card and bought the three of them tickets for a BA flight to Toronto, then onto Winnipeg. That's how I know.'

∞

The tension in the room had somehow built up from nowhere. There was absolutely no doubt that James felt extremely worried about his son. Juliet asked, 'When was the last time you or any of the family heard from him then?'

'I haven't seen or spoken to him for over two weeks.' He paused and made a worried movement of rubbing his face with his hand, then James continued by saying, 'Sorry, you asked if anyone had heard from him. The last person who saw him was Arabella when he turned up at the farm on that Saturday morning. He grabbed a few clothes and a holdall from his room there, had a cup of tea and left. He didn't tell her he was going to Canada though. She also spoke to him in Canada when he was at the house there on the Peveril Estate. George said he was fine, just needed to get away from it all for a few weeks.'

Juliet asked, 'When was this conversation? If you know where he is, surely, he is not missing, is he?'

'Two brothers, Tim and Paul Williams, manage the estate and business for us in Manitoba. Arabella spoke to them last Wednesday and Tim said there had been some sort of problem in Portage la Prairie, the nearest

14

town to the estate. I suspect they had gone off to buy drugs and this had caused problems with the locals. As a result of this, George and the other two had taken one of the cars from the estate and gone off to our cottage on Lake Manitoba. We have all been trying to call the cottage, including Tim and Paul. However, no reply. George's mobile has been switched off since he left the UK. So, no one has heard from him since last Wednesday.'

'Have you reported him missing to the police in Derbyshire? And have you reported the theft of your wife's credit card and money for the flights to them as well?' Sandy asked.

'We have not reported the theft of money or the card. I am sorry, but I cannot do this to my son. Yes, I have reported him as missing and have spoken to the missing from home officer on a couple of occasions. His name is DC Wayne Dobson. A problem though is that he has been seconded to the PC Joseph Foster's murder enquiry. He is one of the family liaison officers.'

'What a tragic and awful murder,' Sandy and Juliet said almost in unison.

'Although Derby City is not part of my constituency, I wrote offering my condolences to PC Foster's wife – her name is Belinda – and also to the Chief Constable of Derbyshire. I am sure that you both, as police officers, also feel deeply about the death of a colleague, so I am really sorry for the loss of him.'

'Who are these two other boys then and what basis

do you have to call them yobs?'

'They are Ruben Cousins and Dean Kelly. I am not sure what it is about them I don't like. I am pretty certain they are into drug dealing. I know they have been arrested a few times. It is Dean Kelly that we feel unsettled with. We had to ask George not to bring them home. Janice and our two young daughters felt uncomfortable with them in the house. We had a big row with George about this, but he is a good boy and has not brought them to the house since.'

'Ruben Cousins rings a bell to me. Not really sure why,' Sandy said.

'I collected George's car from the Terminal Five short stay car park last Friday. DC Dobson rang me and said it had come up on the ANPR from the airport when he had asked them to search for it.'

'Where is the car now?' Juliet asked.

'Janice bought the spare set of keys down and we drove it back to our house in Hope. It is on the driveway,' James said. He looked at his watch and then told them that he needed to be in the House of Commons in ten minutes. They all exchanged mobile numbers, including the number he had for DC Wayne Dobson, and bid each other goodbye with a promise to speak to each other in the next couple of days.

∞

As they left Portcullis House and exited onto the

Embankment, Juliet asked, 'Do you think he is right to be as worried as he is about George?'

'Not sure. James and his family clearly are, so I think we should take it seriously. James might be oversensitive to his son, bearing in mind the divorce from his mother and no doubt the feeling of powerlessness to keep him at Frobisher's, and even as the local MP not to be able to get him into the local school. I will make a few calls later and see if we can have a trip to Derbyshire later in the week to speak to a few people. Are you okay to come with me?'

'Yes, as long as it is not on Friday as I have a school visit with my eldest son, that I don't want to miss.'

'Yes, no problems,' Sandy said as they parted for Juliet to get the train home and Sandy to head back to the office. Sandy looked across at the iconic London Eye. It had been installed for the millennium but had proved so popular that it had remained and was still a big draw for tourists to experience. Sandy had been on it himself several times and had once been in one of the observation pods when just as it reached the top, a person had gone on one knee and proposed to his girlfriend, who luckily for him had said yes!

On getting back into the office at the FCO building, Sandy rang the number for DC Wayne Dobson that James Peveril had given him. The phone was answered almost on the first ring. 'Hello, is that Wayne? This is DCI Alexander McFarlane from the FCO. I have been given your number by George Peveril's father.'

'Yes, sir, it is. What can I do for you?'

'George's family are really worried about him. Have you any updates for me? Have you spoken to anyone in Canada?'

'Unfortunately, I had already been seconded onto the Joseph Foster murder enquiry when the MFH report came in. I have done what I can to trace him, but this murder enquiry has overwhelmed all of us.'

'I am sure it has. I am so sorry to hear about the murder. Have you any time for us to come and meet you during the next couple of days at all?'

'I can do Wednesday morning, but you will need to come to the police headquarters to see me, is that okay?'

They agreed to meet at ten a.m. on Wednesday and Sandy sent a quick text message to Juliet letting her know the arrangement. Sandy then looked up the number and called the British High Commission in Ottawa, Canada. When Sandy eventually got through to someone to talk to, he noticed a strong French accent. The person was obviously a dual-speaking French/Canadian.

'Hello, this is Alexander McFarlane. I work in the FCO in London in the Consulate Investigation team. I would like to make a report of a missing person in Manitoba.'

'Do you know where in Manitoba? The RCMP cover most of it, but not the province capital Winnipeg.'

'It must be the RCMP, as he initially went missing from a farm in the southwest of the province, near a town called Portage la Prairie, and then north from there and Winnipeg to a cottage on Lake Manitoba.'

Sandy passed across the details of George, Ruben and Dean but was kicking himself as he had no idea of the dates of birth for Ruben or Dean. He was not sure why he hadn't asked Wayne Dobson.

'I have a record on our system now and I will pass across the men's details to the RCMP in Manitoba. I don't think they will do anything though without any further information. I will put you down as the contact, is that okay?'

After the call finished, Sandy felt excited that he might have the chance to be working with the RCMP. Even though he knew nothing about them, he assumed they probably only wore the uniform on ceremonial occasions, but it was the vision of an RCMP officer in their scarlet military-style tunic with a high-neck collar and wearing blue breeches with a yellow stripe down the sides that he couldn't put out of his mind whenever he thought of the RCMP.

Chapter Three

Early the next morning, the open-plan office floor in the FCO building already had several people at their desks. There was a high level of chatter and noise as Sandy walked by the desks and made his way to the section where the investigation team worked. The time was only seven thirty a.m. and it never ceased to amaze Sandy how early civil servants started work. The life of a commuter, he thought – get in early and go home early.

Sandy hoped to do the same by leaving early and heading back to Ely in the afternoon so that he was ready for his trip to Derbyshire the following morning. He switched on his laptop and looked at the list of outstanding cases to be reviewed. One of the tasks that the investigation team undertook was to review cases where a British citizen had died abroad in suspicious circumstances. A review was requested by regional police forces or families where they didn't agree with the findings from the police force in the country where their loved one had died.

The first case he looked at was a case sent to the team

from Durham Constabulary. Two of their young residents, John Groves and Tania Miles, both nineteen years old, whilst backpacking in Asia had been found dead in a hotel room in Singapore. The Singapore police had concluded that the deaths were from a drug overdose. This was not, in Sandy's view, an unreasonable conclusion, but the toxicology report's finding was of an unusual drug, not the usual cocaine or heroin. Both of their families had stated that as far as they were aware, neither of them were drug users. There were a couple of troubling aspects that he felt he needed to speak to the Durham investigating officer about. Sandy was just about to make the call when D/SUPT Jane Watson appeared beside him.

'How did it go with the Right Honourable James Peveril MP yesterday?' Jane asked, grinning whilst she did so, which was infectious and made Sandy grin too.

He replied, 'He is genuinely worried about George. He stole his step mum's credit card and has gone off to Canada with two thugs, as Mr Peveril described them.'

'What are the Derbyshire police doing about it? I hope you have notified the British High Commission in Canada. I presume it is in Toronto?' Jane was always very mindful that the correct protocol needed to be followed.

'The Derbyshire police are swamped with the shooting of the PC there, and yes, I have notified them. The High Commission is in Ottawa though, not Toronto.'

'It is awful, that murder of the PC. You had better stick with it Sandy and help them out. Please keep me informed in case one of our foreign office ministers gets to hear about it.'

Sandy was about to tell her what enquiries he and Juliet intended to do for the rest of the week, but as usual Jane's phone rang, and she waved at Sandy and off she went.

For a moment, forgetting what he had been working on and who he was about to call, Sandy got up and made himself a cup of tea. He didn't normally drink coffee; he preferred tea, especially as the one he had had a sip of yesterday at Portcullis House had almost put him off coffee for life!

Returning to his desk he made the call to Caroline Grant in Durham, who answered the phone almost immediately. 'This is DCI McFarlane from the FCO Consulate Investigation team. Please could I ask you a couple of questions about the deaths of Tania Miles and John Groves?'

'Yes of course, sir. I only had both families on the phone yesterday with queries about their belongings.'

'That is exactly what I am interested in. From what I can see, both of their passports, wallets, mobile phones and an iPad were missing when they were found dead, is that right?'

'Yes, the family are also quite distraught about the loss of their cameras as well. All of their pictures and memories from their trip are now missing. I thought it was just a mistake and the property hadn't been recorded properly, but when I rang Singapore, I was told no, they were missing, but no sign of a robbery or forced entry. They were insistent it was a drugs overdose and they had closed the case.'

'Thank you, Caroline. I will give the British Embassy in Singapore a call in the next few days and see if they can help at all, but I am not sure we can do anything more if the deaths are deemed to be self-drug related.'

There was something about the case that troubled Sandy. He thought that before he did anything else on it, he would talk to the much more experienced DCI Phil Harris when he returned from Brussels in the next couple of days.

∞

The train was almost ready to leave as Sandy jumped on it at the nearest door he could find. He was puffing quite hard and had loosened his tie and taken his jacket off. He looked extremely hot, not only because of the journey on the Tube, but also the effort he had made running to make the train in time. Sandy vowed to himself that he needed to start running again in order to get himself fit for the new rugby season, which was due to start in only a few weeks' time.

Finding a seat with a table quite easily, Sandy opened up the notebook that he had started writing in for the missing George Peveril enquiry. He thought he could make effective use of the time between London and Cambridge (he had decided to get off the train there to do a little bit of shopping) to record the actions that he felt he needed to complete.

Fast-track actions

- Interview James Peveril (father of George)
- Meet with DC Wayne Dobson (Derbyshire Police MFH officer)
- Inform British High Commission in Canada and for them to notify police in Manitoba
- Interview Mrs Janice Peveril (step mum)
- Interview Mrs Helen Peveril (mother)
- Interview Viscount William Harrison Peveril (grandfather)
- Interview Arabella Montague (aunty)
- Interview Tim and Paul Williams (brothers managing the Canadian Peveril Estate and last known people to have seen George)
- Check George's phone for activity, both cell site and call data
- Ensure an all-ports message had been circulated
- Place marker on George's passport record

Although Sandy had titled the page as "fast-track actions", this obviously wasn't the case here, and not strictly in keeping with what he understood as the definition of the term. The term "fast-track" he understood as any investigative activity that if done immediately, is likely to find out facts and could lead to early resolution of the investigation. In the case of George Peveril, this is confirming if he is alive and well. George though had been missing from his home in Derbyshire for just over ten days. So, what he was in the process of doing as investigative actions were, he accepted, hardly fast-track.

The enquiries he had written down were clearly ones that Sandy felt needed to be completed to try and find George. Other officers may decide on a less detailed enquiry; likewise, they may think of actions he hadn't thought of to try and locate George. He had already spoken to James and the High Commission in Canada, but the rest of the actions still needed doing and he planned to do these as fast as he could to finish his involvement with the case.

Sandy would have liked to have been meeting up with Hannah in Cambridge but knew from the text messages they had exchanged yesterday that she was busy prosecuting a rape case in Birmingham Crown Court. He had also sent a text message to meet up with his grandpa, John McFarlane, but had not received a reply, so no doubt he was busy, most probably playing golf, but he might be busy at the university or in chambers, all three activities of which kept the seventy-five-year-old very occupied.

The bus from Cambridge railway station dropped Sandy at Drummer Street bus station. Although Cambridge city centre was always busy, it seemed to be even more so this afternoon. There were several extremely smartly dressed people wandering about with men and women in suits, and some women wearing very bright and colourful summer dresses and the odd few wearing hats. Sandy's initial thought was that there must be a wedding taking place nearby. It then suddenly became clear what was happening in the city centre. What was taking place was a University of Cambridge graduation ceremony. The graduation ceremonies season had now commenced. There were also several extremely excited, happy and noisy students in gowns parading around the streets. This brought a huge smile to Sandy's face as he remembered very fondly his own graduation from St John's College in this very city, now almost nine years ago.

After buying a couple of shirts and a pair of shorts, Sandy went to stand on Kings Parade and looked across at the Senate House. The Senate House was an undoubtedly beautiful building that was almost three hundred years old and was a magnificent piece of neoclassical architecture, built of Portland stone. It was now mostly used for graduation ceremonies like the one that was happening this afternoon. The lovely late-June afternoon sunshine made the event happening in the Senate House even more special on that afternoon.

After thoroughly soaking in the atmosphere and watching the proceedings for an hour or so, Sandy headed back to the railway station. On a whim, he went into the wonderful Heffers bookstore and bought a

26

couple of guidebooks to Canada, in which Manitoba featured by having a chapter within them.

∞

When Sandy got to Ely, he had only a relatively short walk to his parents' house, which was situated overlooking the River Great Ouse. This was the home that he had known all of his life, and although he loved Cambridge and enjoyed working in London, there was no other place in the world that he ever wanted to be in more than Ely.

Sandy's mum, Katherine, worked three days a week at the local primary school and was busy working on her laptop as he walked through the door. Katherine had prepared a meal for them both and as Sandy was already aware, she was going out that evening as it was her book club night.

'Mum, what are you doing on your computer? Not cribbing reviews ready for your book club tonight, are you?' Sandy teased her.

'No, school report time I am afraid, Sandy, and thirty reports will take me and my poor IT skills a lot of time,' she said, laughing at her son. 'The book we are reading at the moment is "Where the Crawdads Sing" by Delia Owens. It is just fabulous and I don't need to read a review to know what I think about it!'

After Sandy had got changed, he exchanged a quick phone call to organise a meeting for a drink in the local pub that evening, with his maternal grandfather, Tom Fisher. He went downstairs and saw his mum looking through one of the guidebooks to Canada.

'Is it Manitoba that you said that boy had gone to? The town of Churchill looks like an incredible place to visit. Imagine seeing polar bears in the wild.'

'Churchill is in Northern Manitoba and is over one thousand kilometres from Winnipeg, so I won't be going there. In fact, I can't see any reason to go to Canada at all for this case. I have a much more interesting one I am looking at in Singapore at the moment, which I think from a pure investigative interest, I would rather be working on.'

After they had finished dinner, the walk along the river tow path to the Cutter Inn didn't take Sandy too long. Sandy bought his grandad a pint of beer and settled himself around a small table in the corner of the pub. This side of the pub was almost empty with it being Tuesday night, albeit the restaurant had several people in it. A number of his family, including his two sisters and their husbands, had had a wonderful time here on Saturday night celebrating his birthday.

'Hi, Grandad,' Sandy said, as his grandad arrived and made himself comfortable next to him. 'I am off to Derbyshire carrying out some missing person enquiries tomorrow for a couple of days.'

Tom Fisher was a retired detective inspector from the Cambridgeshire police force. He was the main reason that Sandy had joined the police. Sandy had always, from an incredibly young age, had a burning desire to become a detective. Tom's stories about the cases he had been involved in whilst Sandy was growing up had totally captivated his imagination. Tom was now seventy-five years old; funnily enough, all three of his surviving grandparents were seventy-five years old! Tom had put on quite a bit of weight over the last three or four years, which the whole family badgered him about, including Sandy.

Sandy outlined what the case was about whilst his grandad took a long sip of his pint of beer, smiling and licking his lips whilst he did so; in fact, Tom enjoyed nothing more in the world than being with his grandson talking about detective work.

'What I don't understand is why are they so worried about him? Has he gone missing before? Is this something that happens on a regular basis? If it is, I wouldn't be in the slightest bit worried.'

'I don't know if he has been missing before. I have a meeting with the MFH officer tomorrow morning. The worry is two-fold. Firstly, a little bit of guilt that George's mum and dad split up when he was young. Albeit that is not so unusual these days, but the real reason is the two friends he has gone off with are, in their opinion, pretty unsavoury characters.'

'Well, if they don't hear from him in the next few days you might need to do some proof of life enquiries.'

'What does that mean, Grandad?' Sandy asked.

'You have the start point from where they last had

contact, then do financial checks to see if there is any activity, and phone checks – what was the normal usage and is there any usage after your start point. This includes calls, messages, social media posts, etcetera. There is a policy somewhere you can refer to, either a College of Policing or National Crime Agency one.'

'I don't think it will come to this as I am sure he will turn up soon.'

Sandy was pleased that his grandad didn't question his level of experience as he sometimes did. He knew that becoming a DCI with less than nine years of police service was lightning fast, but he also knew he was capable of carrying out the role really well. Their conversation turned to cricket and football and George Peveril was soon forgotten.

Chapter Four

The red Morgan Roadster motor car was Sandy's pride and joy. He had received the car almost nine years ago as a graduation present from his Grandpa John McFarlane. As he drove down the road and past the magnificent sight of Ely Cathedral, he was smiling widely to himself. He headed out of Ely to travel to Derbyshire. It was extremely early in the morning as he lived quite some distance from Derby, where he was due to pick up Juliet at the railway station. Sandy had put the roof of the car down and although currently a bit chilly with the wind whistling about his head, Sandy knew that as soon as the sun rose a little bit higher, the journey would only be enhanced by driving an open-top sports car. His only challenge was to keep the speed of the car down; this was exceedingly difficult with the Morgan having a very sporty 3.7-litre engine.

In what seemed no time at all, no doubt due to how much he was enjoying the driving experience, Sandy got to the outskirts of Derby, whereupon he started to feel rather anxious that he was going to be late as the traffic had all of a sudden built up, but he managed to pull into the train station forecourt just as Juliet came walking out. Juliet, on seeing Sandy and his car, had a wide grin on her face.

'You really are a young Morse! You kept it quiet that you have the same classic car as he has,' Juliet said as she got into the car. DCI Morse was Colin Dexter's fictional book and a TV detective.

'Morse had a Jaguar car and went to Oxford; I went to Cambridge and this car is a Morgan motor car,' Sandy said, trying to be indignant about the comparison but failing to stop smiling back at Juliet. 'I thought as we have a little bit of time and are not far away, we could have a quick look at the scene where PC Joseph Foster was killed. Is that okay?'

They were soon outside the entrance to the market area in Derby city centre and walked through to look around Lock-Up-Yard. Both of them felt that they were investigative tourists, but as they were fascinated by the investigation of homicide, it was something that they couldn't resist. There were quite a few CCTV cameras jotted about, so it was quite possible that the offenders could have been noticed one or more of the cameras. Outside the spot where PC Foster had fallen were hundreds of bunches and bouquets of flowers, some of which had messages on. There was a police officer standing guard and several Derbyshire Constabulary notice boards dotted around asking if anyone had any information to contact the force switchboard. A few metres away from this area in a darkened corner was another line of police tape; this was the point that appeared to be probably where PC Foster had actually been shot, and Sandy and Juliet surmised to each other that he must have staggered to the place where all the flowers were – the place he had sadly died.

After Sandy and Juliet lowered their heads and took a moment to think about Joseph and his family, they got back into the car to head off to the police headquarters in Ripley, which, as it turned out, was quite a few miles away from Derby city centre and they only just made it in time, pulling into the car park at ten a.m. on the dot. They were lucky in the end to find a parking space as most of the car park was taken up with what Sandy could only describe as a media village. Every news broadcaster you could think of had a highly visible and marked-up large vehicle, some of which had massive communication discs attached to them. They could see as they walked towards the police reception area several news journalists whom they recognised from television carrying out interviews on camera.

Waiting in the reception area was DC Wayne Dobson. He was an extremely tall man, probably six foot six inches at least. After having introduced themselves to each other, Sandy asked him if he played rugby.

'I did, you will not be surprised to know, at position number eight. Too old now other than for the odd veteran's game,' Wayne said whilst he escorted them through reception and into an office block area. Sandy looked at Wayne, who was probably in his early to mid-forties and looked very fit. It didn't surprise him when Wayne said he was an extremely keen triathlete.

∞

Wayne took them along a corridor to stand outside an office that had on the door the nameplate "Detective Superintendent Joanne O'Connor". Just as he was about to knock on the door, it burst open and out came a relatively tall and very smartly dressed woman in her early forties, wearing a grey business suit with a bright pink blouse, and she had dyed blonde hair that really suited her. Wayne said to her, 'Ma'am, you said it would be all right for me to use your office this morning.'

'Yes, I am just about to do the morning press briefing. Looks like standing room only in there. Who are these two?' Joanne said, pointing at Sandy and Juliet. Not waiting for a reply, she said, 'I need you in an hour, Lofty, to go through what we want the family to know about our reconstruction on Friday.' Joanne then walked off down the corridor, carrying her laptop and a sheath of papers.

'Sorry about that. The boss is under incredible pressure as you can imagine.' Sandy and Juliet nodded at Wayne. They looked around the large office as they sat down around a table that had six seats. There was a poster on the wall that read "The ABC of an

34

investigation is Assume Nothing, Believe Nobody, Check Everything". Sandy wondered if this summed up D/SUPT Joanne O'Connor as a no-nonsense lady. When Sandy was in the Met police in London, they jokingly referred to the ABC as 'Arrest Everyone, Bail No One, Charge Everybody.' However, he knew it best from his SIO course as 'Ask questions, Be inquisitive, Clarify information.'

Wayne said, 'I have done little concerning looking into George being missing I am afraid. I was seconded to this murder enquiry on the Saturday as one of the family liaison officers to provide information from the family, and to the family from Mrs O'Connor and the investigation team. I am sure you both know what role a family liaison officer carries out.' On seeing them both nod, he continued. 'Although George was reported missing by his father on the Sunday, I didn't pick it up until the Tuesday. There is no backfill for me as an MFH officer, so I am juggling that job as well, but I am primarily focussing on the murder. Yesterday was the first day I had had off in eighteen days. I rang James Peveril on that first Tuesday and he told me that George left home in the night, came back before breakfast time, took a few belongings, including his stepmother's credit card, and has not been seen or heard from by them since. Gone off to Canada.'

'I think his aunty, Arabella, saw him later on the Saturday,' Sandy said.

'I didn't know that. He had bought petrol and then

booked flights for him and two of his friends to go to Canada on the stepmother's credit card. Mr Peveril didn't want to make a complaint about the theft of the card.'

'Did you check his phone? Is it still being used? If not, when was it last used? Any subscriber checks – who was he ringing, who was ringing him?' Juliet asked.

'I just rang the phone a few times but it was always switched off.'

'OK, what do you know about the other two?' Sandy said, checking his notes. 'Ruben Cousins and Dean Kelly, have you done any checks on them at all?'

'Dean Kelly is a nasty piece of work. Although he is only nineteen years old, he has been to prison for robbery, theft and assaults. Deals in drugs, as does Cousins, but he only has the odd arrest and conviction for drugs. Not done anything on them. They haven't been reported as missing.'

Sandy asked, 'Is it possible you could get a phone usage and subscriber check done for George's phone please?'

'Will do. I will get it done tomorrow. I do know that he has never gone missing before, but I see this as a case where he is missing but not lost, if you know what I mean. We know where he is. He is in Canada at a family home.'

Sandy thought that Wayne was right but in a separate way. This was a young man who was very much lost concerning the direction his young life was going.

Although they both wanted to ask lots of questions in relation to the shot PC murder enquiry, they knew it would have been something they were not entitled to find out about so they set off towards the Hope Valley.

The drive north into the Peak District from the Derbyshire police headquarters was through some of what, Sandy felt, was England's most beautiful countryside, which was made up of gentle uplands, moorland and valleys. Juliet, who almost always spent her holidays in Barbados, had never been here before and kept commenting to Sandy on how beautiful it all looked. It helped with it being such a glorious summer's day and to be travelling in an open-topped sports car.

As they drove into Castleton, Sandy and Juliet discussed whether to see Helen Peveril first or to stop and have some lunch. Seeing Helen seemed to be the most sensible idea. Finding her address wasn't too difficult and as they parked the car, they could see on the top of a steep hill behind them the ruins of a castle. The English Heritage notice board told them the castle was Peveril Castle and that it was almost a thousand years old. The keep was completed by King Henry II in 1176. The Peveril's seemed to be everywhere, and this castle must have once been built and owned by a very distant relative of George Peveril.

The house that Helen Peveril lived in was an old

stone terraced cottage and from the outside looked very pretty. On closer inspection, the front garden looked sadly neglected, without any gardening having taken place for a long time. As they approached the front door, it was clear that the woodwork of the doors and windows needed painting. Helen seemed to take a long time to come to the door. Sandy thought for a moment that she might have been drinking, as she was a little bit unsteady on her feet, but on being shown into the kitchen/diner at the rear of the cottage, he could see no signs that this was the case. Helen was a similar age to James, in her mid-forties, and was undoubtedly attractive, but her whole demeanour was of a sad and dower woman.

After they made the necessary introductions, Sandy asked, 'What sort of relationship do you have with George?'

'I am sad to say, in my view, almost non-existent. He only lives less than two miles away, but he calls and sees me about once every six weeks or so, sometimes even longer. He does phone, but for no more than two minutes every week.'

'When was the last time you saw or spoke to him then?'

'Saw him probably two months ago; spoke to him probably three weeks ago.'

'You did know though that he has been reported as missing by his father and has gone off to Canada?'

'Yes, James rang me over a week ago asking if I had

heard from George and told me that he had gone off to Canada. George loves Canada. I know when I was part of the family, when we visited, he loved the farm there and our trips to the cottage on Lake Manitoba. He is in a place where he is happy.'

'How long have you not been, as you describe it, part of the family?' Juliet asked.

'A long time. It was well before James and I separated and got divorced. George went off to school in Norfolk when he was seven or eight and that was really it for us as a family.'

There was nothing, it seemed, that Helen could help with, so they left her and headed off for lunch. They managed to get a seat outside at the Castle Inn, which was just around the corner from where Helen lived. The Castle Inn dated back almost two hundred years. There was no doubt that Castleton was definitely a very scenic and pretty village. As Sandy and Juliet sat eating their lunch, they thought about Helen's sad outlook on life. Sandy said he felt quite sorry for her, but Juliet, on the other hand, wanted to know why Helen hadn't, after all this time since her divorce, put in place some positive steps to get her life back on track. She did agree with Sandy though that everyone is different and it was maybe not fair to judge her by her own outlook to life.

∞

Before they got into Hope village, they took a turning to

their left and headed off the main road. It wasn't long before they pulled up on a long driveway to a house called Losehill Farmhouse. The views all around the house were stunning. Sandy had on several occasions walked or run along the ridgeway that was directly at the back of the Peveril's house. Sandy had always gone up onto the ridgeway near Castleton, where after making a short but steep climb to Mam Tor, which rose to five hundred and seventeen metres, the ridgeway went from there to Losehill.

When Janice answered the door, Sandy was surprised that she was of a similar age, if not slightly older than James. He had assumed that James had had an affair with a much younger woman. He thought back to the ABC poster in Joanne O'Connor's office: assume nothing. Maybe Joanne was right. Janice was attractive and had an extremely pleasant and welcoming personality. She made them cake and offered them tea or coffee, which, although they had just eaten, they gratefully accepted.

'How long do you think we are going to be DCI McFarlane as I will need to pick up the girls from school or sort someone else to do so?'

'I would have thought an hour at the most. DS Ashton needs to get a train back to London as well,' Sandy said, quickly finishing a mouthful of cake. 'I will cut straight to the point then. Tell us about what happened on the day that George went missing?'

Janice replied, 'I went up to bed at about eleven p.m.

on the Friday and as I went past, I heard him in his room on his Xbox. I hadn't seen him all evening as he had eaten in his room because I had eaten with the girls really early, which was too early for George. James was staying in London for the weekend. Then I heard him go out at about two in the morning. I got up out of bed worried something was wrong and saw his car heading down the driveway.'

'Was there anything worrying George that you know of?' Juliet asked.

'No, he seemed to be doing okay. Since he came to live with us, he had been very up and down. He seemed to do well in his exams at sixteen years old, but then dropped out this last year. He had got in with the wrong sort and was still smoking cannabis.'

'The wrong sort. Do you mean Ruben Cousins and Dean Kelly?'

'They were his two main friends but there were others. I asked James to tell George not to bring them home. Dean Kelly must have ADHD or something similar; he seemed to love scaring George's sisters.' Janice was clearly not a fan of Kelly or Cousins.

'How did George take this? Did it cause any tensions at home or with you?'

'George and I...' Janice sighed and seemed to have tears form in her eyes. 'After a very rocky start, as he blamed me for his parents' marriage breaking up, our relationship improved, in particular when he moved back home to live here permanently. He was very cross when we banned his friends from the house, but he loves his sisters so accepted it.'

Sandy asked, 'George came back the next day, on the Saturday morning, didn't he?'

'I didn't hear him at first, but I heard the front door slam and then the car drive off. I looked in his room and although it is never tidy, it looked as if all his drawers were open. He must have been searching for his passport. I went downstairs and my purse had been taken out of my handbag and I thought twenty pounds was missing.' Janice said, picking up her purse as if to show them the one she was talking about. 'I rang James, who tried to get hold of George, but his phone was switched off.'

'George then went to Norfolk to see Arabella and he flew later that evening to Canada, is that right? Having stolen your credit card and bought three flights on it, and neither you nor James have heard from him since?'

'He had also bought petrol and two hundred pounds in Canadian dollars. He knew my pin number as he had got money out for me in the past. We have not heard a thing from him. James is really worried.'

'You're not then?' Sandy asked, surprised by her comment.

'I am not sure what to think. He is almost nineteen years old, he is not on his own and he loves Canada, so probably a lot less worried than James. George is no doubt, well hopefully, embarrassed about stealing from us.'

The time had come for the girls to be collected from their school and for Juliet to catch the train from Hope to Sheffield and then on to London. They said their goodbyes and went their separate ways as Sandy was staying overnight in Hope and then going to see Viscount Peveril later the next morning.

Chapter Five

The previous evening in the Old Hall Hotel in Hope had been excellent. Sandy had met up with a friend, who was an ex-colleague from the Met police, along with his wife; they had both been marvellous company. The evening had possibly been a little too good as Sandy could feel the faintest touch of a headache. He stood outside his friends' cottage door early the next morning ready to run and walk to the top of Win Hill and back. The sun was already beaming down as he set off at an easy jog, along which, at the moment, was a fairly gentle upward slope heading out of the village of Hope.

The run, with a walk at the steepest stages, was going to be a round trip of just over ten kilometres. Sandy needed to cover it all in a maximum of one and half hours in order to have a shower and breakfast and be able to get to Peveril Hall in time for his appointment with Viscount Peveril. He raised his pace a bit and as he started to climb to the summit, which was four hundred and sixty-two metres high, the views were spectacular. After needing to walk a few steep parts of the route,

Sandy reached the summit, where he was quite pleased to say he wasn't unduly out of breath. At that time of the morning, he was quite alone, albeit he had seen the odd dog walker, a number of cows and quite a few sheep on his trip up to the summit.

From the summit he could see Castleton Ridge, which included Losehill. He could also see across to Edale and the moors around Kinder Scout, the highest peak in Derbyshire. He then looked further round to Ladybower Reservoir.

Whenever he had looked at the dam walls in the past, he always thought of the Second World War film *The Dam Busters*. This was a re-creation of the period when the area between Ladybower Reservoir and Howden Dam was used by the Lancaster bomber pilots to practice the bombing runs and for target practice. The dam was used because of its close resemblance to the German dams. The bombs used at the time were an innovative design called bouncing bombs.

The trip down was much quicker. Sandy was well ahead of time. After finishing breakfast in his friend's cottage, which was called Bobbin Cottage, he packed up the car and sent a message to Hannah asking how her court case was going and whether they could meet up at the weekend when he got home to Ely after seeing Arabella in Norfolk. Sandy had a few emails to deal with, including sending D/SUPT Jane Watson an update, just in case she was wondering why he hadn't been in the office the last couple of days. He wasn't surprised to get an instant response saying that she knew what he was doing and needed him in the office on Monday to chair the team meeting and attend a couple of other meetings on her behalf.

The trip to Peveril Hall was very pleasant and Sandy enjoyed driving around the countryside. He was a member of National Heritage, who now owned the hall, so rather than show his warrant card he showed his membership card. Sandy had a bit of time, so he wandered around the outside of the hall, which was an Elizabethan masterpiece of architecture. It was still in wonderful condition over four hundred years later. Sandy was directed by one of the National Heritage staff around to the entrance of the private apartment that the Peveril family still had there. Just before he was going to knock on the door, Sandy saw that he had received a message from Hannah telling him that her court case had closed that morning and she was not required in Birmingham until the next Monday morning. She could come with him to Norfolk if he wanted her company.

∞

Sandy had a wide grin on his face after having read the message from Hannah – of course he would love Hannah to go with him to Norfolk. The door opened whilst he was still grinning and standing there in front of him was someone that Sandy had no doubt was not Lady Peveril.

46

'What can I do for you?' the woman who was aged in her late sixties or early seventies asked. She was wearing a dark coloured woollen dress and had an apron on.

'I am DCI Alexander McFarlane and I have an appointment with Viscount Peveril.'

'Well, I am sorry, he is not here. He has gone off to his house in London. I have not been feeling too well so haven't been at work this week. Her Ladyship wouldn't want to be doing anything like looking after the apartment or His Lordship unfortunately. That is why they have gone.'

It was quite clear that the woman Sandy was talking to was the housekeeper, who, without a doubt, had a very low opinion of Lady Peveril.

'Do you know when he will be back here or how long he will be staying in London?'

'He only very occasionally comes here now, so I doubt he will be back for some weeks. He normally visits the chateau in France every July so he might be heading off there soon, seeing it is the start of July now.'

'How long have you worked here?'

'I have been here since William's first wife became ill. William asked me to stay on after she died, and I have been here and coped with both the second, and now the third, Lady Peveril. I am not sure why he marries them!' the indignant sounding housekeeper said.

'Is James and Arabella's mother the first Lady Peveril?'

47

'Yes, she is. Arabella is lovely.'

'James is not, then?' Sandy said smiling.

'Yes, of course he is,' the housekeeper said, smiling back at Sandy widely. 'It is just that Arabella is such a special person.'

'I am looking for George, who is missing in Canada. Do you know him well?'

'Yes, of course, I have known him all of his life. He doesn't come here very often and only if His Lordship is at home, although he came once when he wasn't here during the last few months.'

Sandy felt that there was nothing else that the housekeeper could help with and felt frustrated that he hadn't been told that Viscount Peveril wasn't going to be there. As he left, he immediately rang James Peveril.

'Hello,' a voice said, which Sandy didn't think belonged to James Peveril.

'This is DCI McFarlane. I would like to speak to Mr Peveril please.'

'He is in the Chamber in the House of Commons at the moment but should be free in ten minutes or so. I will tell him that you called. Hang on, he is here now.' After a few moments, James came on the phone.

'Sandy, have you found George?' a clearly out-of-breath James said.

'No, sorry. I was only calling to say I am at Peveril Hall, but your father is not here as apparently, he is in London,' Sandy said, trying not to sound too cross or frustrated, which he really was.

'I am so sorry, I forgot to let you know he turned up at our London house late Tuesday evening. Can you come here tomorrow?'

'I am seeing Arabella tomorrow. Will he still be there on Monday or Tuesday next week?' Sandy said. He was starting to feel even more frustrated that he was being expected to fit in with the whim of Viscount Peveril, or more to the point, his wife, Lady Monica.

'I will ring him and tell him to be in London on Monday or Tuesday and that it is concerning George; that will convince him.'

Sandy wasn't convinced he would end up seeing William Peveril at all. He then suddenly had a thought about the weekend and sent a message to Hannah asking her if she wanted to make a weekend of it in Norfolk. His hand was shaking as he pressed the send button.

The phone made a beeping sound almost immediately and Sandy pulled it quickly out of his pocket, hoping that Hannah had said yes, only to find it was a message from James Peveril telling him his father would be at Peveril House in Eaton Square, nine a.m. on Tuesday, definitely and without fail. Although he was pleased to see the message, it was not the one he really wanted to see.

Sandy thought he would now head off and drive back to Ely. Just as he was about to leave the car park at the hall, his phone beeped again. When he looked at the message, he was extremely pleased to see that Hannah had replied and said yes, that would be lovely, and did

49

he need her to do anything like find them a hotel.

Sandy reversed back into a parking spot and after a Google search, booked a room in the Lodge Hotel in Old Hunstanton for two nights.

∞

Thursday evening seemed to drag by slowly even though Sandy was filling his time with a lot of the work from the FCO that he had to catch up on. His mother Katherine asked him what was troubling him. In fact, he was feeling quite the opposite of troubled; he was not in the slightest bit troubled about anything. He was trying to contain himself so as not to show how excited he was about his weekend. Sandy had decided not to tell her that he was going away with Hannah for the weekend as he didn't want his mother, and then no doubt his two sisters, getting involved and all three of them getting ahead of themselves about his relationship.

The next morning, Sandy arrived early in Cambridge to meet Hannah, so he drove around aimlessly for a while until it was time to pick her up. Hannah came straight out of her flat wearing a lovely pink summer dress and a red straw hat, which Sandy was worried might blow out of the car with the top down. He asked if Hannah wanted him to put the roof up, but she was quite happy to take the hat off and let her, in Sandy's opinion, lovely dark brown hair blow in the wind as they drove back the way Sandy had come that morning, past

Ely, firstly to King's Lynn and then to head on past Sandringham to Hunstanton.

Hannah was keen to offload about what had happened during her week and said, 'The defence barrister in my court case is driving me crazy! He is not letting me introduce bad character evidence about the accused, which, let me tell you, is quite extensive! He has been arrested three times and charged once with rape, although not convicted; they are all of a remarkably similar type of offence to the case I am prosecuting.' Hannah sounded as though she was still really cross about losing the legal argument. 'The judge said it was unduly prejudicial. They then wanted to introduce WhatsApp messages between my victim and an old boyfriend of hers!'

Sandy laughed and said, 'If you were the one defending this case, isn't that exactly what you would do?' Hannah couldn't argue with this, and she laughed as she nodded in agreement and said, 'You know that it is the prosecutor's job in the court system we have in England to build the case and then the defence's job is to dismantle it. Don't blame me and other barristers for just doing the job we are meant to do!'

As they drove past the roads that led to Sandringham, they saw the wild rhododendrons that seemed to be growing everywhere. Sandy wasn't too disappointed that the flowers were now finishing as they were still an incredible sight to see. Hannah had booked them a visit to Sandringham House and the gardens and a tour of the

51

walled garden for Saturday afternoon, which they were both looking forward to. As they drove a bit further along, in a field to the left there was a beautiful display of bright red poppies, which Hannah thought were wild, but Sandy thought must have been cultivated. Almost directly to their right after this was a lavender farm and the road up to where Peveril Farm was situated.

After reaching the very quaint Victorian seaside town of Hunstanton, Sandy made sure they drove along the seafront towards their hotel. Although the sea looked a murky brown, there were a number of children and families quite happily paddling and swimming in the sea. They went on further to Old Hunstanton and checked into the Lodge Hotel. Sandy left Hannah to unpack for them both and headed back to see Arabella Montague. Hannah had told him that after unpacking she planned to firstly take a walk, then to sit outside in the sunshine and review some witness statements for another forthcoming case, so he could take as long as he needed.

Chapter Six

As he drove up to the farmhouse, Sandy wondered what the crop was that they were growing at Peveril Farm as he didn't recognise the plants, which had dark green foliage and striking blue flowers. He parked outside the back of a large, sprawling old brick- and flint-built farmhouse, next to a large new black Range Rover. As soon as he got out of his car, Sandy was met by two big golden retriever dogs, who, although very friendly, were both continuously jumping up onto him. A woman came out of the back door and, after shouting to the dogs to calm down, invited Sandy into a large farmhouse kitchen with a table that the woman gestured for Sandy to sit at.

'I presume you are DCI McFarlane. I, as you have no doubt already guessed, am Arabella Montague. Have you found George yet?' Arabella was probably in her early forties, had highlighted blonde hair and was wearing cream-coloured chinos and a mustard-coloured top. There was a tweed checked jacket hanging over the chair next to the one Sandy was sitting at. 'Tea or coffee? I have cake as well. Sorry, didn't have time to make it myself, but I bought it fresh this morning, only from the Lidl supermarket along the road though.' Arabella was a bundle of activity, and Sandy could only agree with the housekeeper from Peveril Hall that she oozed loveliness.

'No to finding George, and yes please to tea. What is the crop you grow here?'

'We grow linseed. I have two hundred acres of it here and we have almost two thousand acres in Manitoba, although it is more often referred to as flax there in Canada. I took over as CEO about ten years ago and repositioned our focus to the use of it purely for organic health purposes. The last few years have been an enormous success for us and will be, I am sure, more so in the future. Plant-based products are the future, DCI McFarlane!'

'How did you come to have the land in Canada?'

'A great, great grandfather who wasn't due to inherit the family title went there to seek his fortune, but then had to come back when his brother died. We also have a chateau in France with a large vineyard and winery. We only make the Chateau Peveril, a red wine, there.'

'I have heard about that wine but never tasted it.'

Arabella placed the tea and a slice of cake for them both on the table and then picked up a bottle of the Chateau Peveril from the wine rack. 'For you to take away or have a taste of it now if you want. That is if you are allowed to drink on duty, DCI.' They both laughed as it was far too early on Friday morning for wine, rather than not wanting to drink on duty.

'Please tell me about George and call me Sandy.'

'I have been awfully close to George all his life. He never bonded with his mother for whatever reason, so he increasingly spent time here and we got him into a fairly local school to us. We haven't got a mother–son relationship, but it's one of those close, special family bonds that you get sometimes. George and I have it, not because I can't have children; our bond started before that ever came to be a reality for Monty and me.' Arabella looked very melancholy for a moment. 'That is why I am so worried about him. He does love Canada; he has been there many times with me and also his father when he was young.'

'When was the last time you saw him?'

'He came here almost two weeks ago on Saturday morning. He seemed more troubled than I have ever seen him before. He went straight up to his room and was there for only a short while, then he came down with some clothes. When he arrived, he came in with a plastic bag, but he didn't have it anymore when he came back down but had one of his holdalls. He didn't tell me he was going to Canada. He asked to use the computer. I now realise it must have been to book the flights or book his Canadian visa. I was making him tea so was not sure what he was up to on the computer. I checked the search history afterwards though and it was the Canadian visa waiver site he was on.'

'When was the last time you spoke to him?'

'The brothers, Tim and Paul Williams, who manage the estate and all of our commercial operations in Canada and the USA, rang to say that the three of them had turned up and were staying in the guest house. I rang George there and he told me he was fine and had brought his friends with him to get a break from things in England. Not sure what that means. He told me he would be back in two to three weeks or so.' Arabella paused whilst she refilled both of their mugs with more tea. 'I asked Tim to give him a couple of hundred dollars and I would pay him back. The brothers have been with us all of their lives; they are part of the family as their father was the manager before them. I knew they would look out for George.'

'You haven't seen or heard from George since then?'

'None of us have. They went up to our cottage on Lake Manitoba. I have telephoned the cottage and have got no reply. Tim went up there last weekend and he presumed the boys had gone out on the boat as there was no sign of them or the boat. I am very worried.'

'Did you see the two boys with him when he arrived on that Saturday?'

'No, he didn't even mention them.'

∞

The two dogs were excited to see Sandy again when he went out to his car to put the wine away and to get a pair of latex gloves, ready for when he had a look through George's room. The dogs kept jumping up on him, pushing each other out of the way vying for Sandy's attention.

George's room on the first floor was large and looked fairly tidy except for the open drawers where clothing might have been taken out, and the clothes rejected and not to be taken either hung out of the drawers or were on the floor.

Sandy looked in an old but not quite antique wardrobe, which he presumed was made out of oak but he just wasn't sure. He looked around the bottom of the wardrobe and there were a couple of shopping bags. As he picked up and opened the first bag, he stood back in shock by what he saw inside. It was a gun. Either a handgun or revolver; he didn't know the difference between the two or if there actually was a difference. He also didn't know if it was a real gun or a replica.

Sandy went downstairs having put the gun back in the shopping carrier bag. 'Arabella, do you recognise or know anything about this gun?' Sandy asked as he put the bag on the table and opened it up for Arabella to see inside.

Arabella was clearly shocked to see a gun in her house. 'I've no idea, but that is the bag that George was carrying when he arrived the other Saturday. Is George in trouble?'

'I think he will be if it is a real gun, I am afraid. I am going to have to call the Norfolk police to attend and collect the gun.' Arabella knew the local number for the officers in Hunstanton, so she phoned them whilst Sandy took a few pictures of the gun and bag on his phone camera. He also sent a message to Hannah letting her know he might be quite delayed and was pleased when she replied not to worry.

When the officer arrived, he walked straight over to where the gun was and was about to pick it up when Sandy said, 'Stop, you haven't got gloves on. What about if there are any fingerprints on it?'

The officer looked him up and down and aggressively said in response, 'Who are you, and please don't presume to tell me what to do?' He did however swiftly remove his hand from being about to touch the gun.

'Frank, he is DCI McFarlane from the police in London,' Arabella said, who clearly knew the officer.

He instantly said, 'Sorry, sir, I had no idea. I will get officers from an armed response vehicle to examine the gun and get the CID down here.'

Sandy was shocked when within ten minutes, an armed response vehicle flew into the driveway and two burly and well-armed officers wearing body armour and endless equipment on overflowing belts walked through the open door of the kitchen. One of the officers got a pair of latex gloves straight out of his pocket, put them on and picked up the gun to examine it.

'How did you get here so quickly?' Sandy asked, having thought he was in for a long wait as he was sure

Hunstanton had no need for an armed response unit.

'We are protection for the royal family at Sandringham,' the officer said.

The one examining the gun said, 'This is a real gun; it is a Smith & Wesson service revolver. They made many millions of them. Our armed service men and women got them as personal issue. I would be surprised if this isn't one from the Second World War or not long afterwards. Excellent job you called us as there are still two bullets in the chamber.' As he said this, a CID officer arrived.

∞

Sandy informed the CID officer that he was making enquiries into George Peveril who was missing from home, and he told the CID officer where he had found the gun. The other three uniformed officers left the farmhouse kitchen, which although was large, was getting pretty crowded, only though after each of them had had a piece of the cake that Arabella wanted to tell them that she had made but admitted to them that she had bought it. They also told Sandy that they loved his Morgan sports car.

'I will book the gun into the property store at Hunstanton, and I will have to raise a crime against George Peveril for illegal possession of a firearm,' the detective said to Sandy, as he put the gun into one evidence bag and the shopping carrier bag into another.

'Is it possible to send it off straight away for checking with NABIS, the National Ballistics Intelligence Service? I would be keen to know if it has been used criminally at all.'

'I am sorry, sir, I am not authorised to spend any money on submissions, but I can speak to someone next week to see how we could submit it then. We have no firearms crimes in Norfolk that would make it urgent.'

'George is not from round here so it could have been used anywhere. Give me a few moments whilst I ring one of my team's CSIs, please.'

Sandy rang Clare Symonds, who was a CSI on the FCO Consulate Investigation team with him and had twice been part of the investigation in India with him. After he explained to her what he was doing and what he had found, he asked if some of their budget could be used for sending the revolver off for examination. He had a nagging feeling that the gun might have been used in one of England's big cities like London, Birmingham or Liverpool.

Clare told him she would authorise it and would ring him back after speaking to the scientific support manager for Norfolk. Clare, who was always very efficient, rang Sandy back after only ten minutes.

'Sandy, the NABIS London hub is coming to collect it on Monday morning, but the officer needs to get it to King's Lynn Police Station, where a CSI will package it up in the proper boxes for him,' Clare said.

Sandy was hopeful that the detective wouldn't find

60

this too onerous a task as he had visions of losing another two hours of his time with Hannah by having to go to King's Lynn. Luckily, the detective, whose name was DC David Masters, thought it was all quite exciting and he would happily do it for him.

After quickly saying goodbye to a quite shell-shocked Arabella, he leapt into his car and headed off to the Lodge Hotel to meet up with Hannah. He was sure that even before he had left the driveway, Arabella would be on the phone to her brother James, telling him what had just happened, and the already worried James would undoubtedly be even more concerned for his son.

Chapter Seven

The Lodge Hotel, or certainly parts of it, had been built three hundred years ago, and it had actually only been a hotel for just over one hundred years. Although Sandy had found the hotel by a chance internet search, it was a lovely hotel in a terrific location in Old Hunstanton. When Sandy got back to the hotel, he realised that he had missed lunch and was pleased to find that Hannah had booked them in for an early meal in the restaurant at six p.m.

When he got upstairs and into their room, Sandy found that Hannah was in the bath. He didn't know what to do as he felt embarrassed about going into the bathroom. They were not at that stage, just at the moment, in their relationship. Instead, he grabbed the complimentary biscuits and made a call to the number Arabella had given him for the Peveril Estate office in Winnipeg. Tim Williams answered the phone.

'Hello, Mr Williams, it is DCI Alexander McFarlane from the police in England. I have been asked by the Peveril family to see if I can find George. I wonder if you could help me with some questions I have. When was the last time that you or your brother saw him?'

'It is well over a week now. I had a drive up to the cottage on Lake Manitoba last Sunday and although they were not there, I am sure they were about, due to how messy the cottage looked.'

'How did you find George when he was with you on the farm at the Peveril Estate?'

'I have known George almost all his life and I am extremely fond of him, but this version of George was not very nice and one I had not seen before. He was rude and arrogant. I am sure he was playing up to his two friends, who were equally as rude. We were all pleased when they went off.'

'What do you mean by rude?'

'I am not sure which one of the friends it was, because for some reason George didn't tell me their names, but this friend's language was absolutely vile. He also spoke like this in front of our children. I pulled him up about it and the look he gave me was as if he could kill me for telling him off. He would have, I am sure, if given a chance. I was ready for him to launch a vicious attack on me, but fortunately George led him away. If any of us hear anything, we will let Arabella know straight away.'

Sandy lay back on the bed and switched on the television and was watching it when he saw that Hannah was out of the bath and had come into the room wearing only a bath robe. They started kissing very intently and passionately, then Sandy's ears picked up on hearing the name PC Joseph Foster on the television. They both looked up and could see D/SUPT Joanne O'Connor about to deliver a briefing. Standing next to her was Joseph's young widow, Belinda Foster, who they both recognised from seeing her photograph in the newspapers.

'Nearly two weeks ago, PC Joseph Foster lost his life. People harmed him for the job that he was doing to protect members of the public. Sadly, Joseph paid the price with his life through no fault of his own, by doing what he loved, and doing it well. PC Foster was not a big risk-taker, but he wasn't afraid to challenge people who were committing crime or wrongdoing. We know he was really proud to be a police officer. This evening and overnight we are carrying out a reconstruction in the hope that something jogs someone's memory. Please, if you remember anything, give the incident room a call.'

Sandy and Hannah were waiting for Belinda Foster to say something, but she didn't, and the press appeal was finished.

'I am not a hundred percent sure those two women get on,' Hannah said. 'The superintendent came across well, but ruthlessly efficient. I just think the human touch of the grieving widow might have helped get the message across even better.'

Sandy felt that Hannah was mostly right, but Joanne O'Connor had given, in his view, a powerful message. The moment of passion for both of them had now waned, so Sandy went to take a shower and they decided to go down for an early drink before their meal.

∞

The next morning as they were having breakfast, Sandy and Hannah noticed that whenever the waitress or waiter served them, they were smiling at them. Was it because they were holding hands whenever they could and exchanging smiles at each other? They had had a wonderful night and morning together.

As they were finishing breakfast, Sandy's phone beeped telling him he had a message. He presumed it was either his mum or one of his sisters asking how he was. On looking at it, he saw it was a message from Arabella asking him to phone her. He assumed she was struggling to process what had happened yesterday. As they left the table, Sandy made the call.

'Good morning, Arabella. What can I do for you?'

'Sorry to trouble you at the weekend, but I think you said you were staying somewhere in Hunstanton. Can Monty and I come and see you as he might have some information to add to what I told you yesterday?'

'We are going to Sandringham today. We could meet there if you want. It must only be ten minutes from you,' Sandy offered her, as he could feel the urgency in Arabella's voice. He hoped, but really knew, that Hannah would be okay with this.

When Sandy and Hannah had parked the car in the

car park at Sandringham and walked to the café, he saw Arabella with a man he presumed was her husband, Charles Montague. They already had a table, so they went and joined them. After introductions, Hannah went off to look around the shop.

'Your girlfriend is incredibly beautiful, Sandy. Sorry to disturb your time together but Monty saw the two boys that were with George. They were smoking by a barn, just at the side of the house, when he got home. Sorry for talking for you, sweetheart.' She looked across at her husband and said, 'You tell Sandy.'

'Let me make a call and then see if you can confirm to me who you saw,' Sandy said. He then rang DC Wayne Dobson in Derbyshire, assuming and hoping he was at work that day. He was. 'Wayne, is it possible to send me a picture of Dean Kelly and Ruben Cousins, please? I am with George's aunty and uncle, who might be able to recognise them.'

'Have you made progress finding George then? I will send the photographs to you now via email.'

'No, not found him. You told me that although he is missing, he is not lost.'

Sandy turned back to face Arabella and Monty. Arabella was holding two cigarette butts in separate kitchen plastic bags. Monty laughingly said, 'I know! Arabella is a right Miss Marple isn't she!' Sandy couldn't help but laugh as well as he placed the bags with the cigarette butts in his pocket. He knew if it ever came to it, by showing Monty the pictures of Cousins and Kelly, it might prejudice any identification process that could take place. The boys' identification through DNA from the cigarette buts would negate this as a problem, so well done to Arabella.

'I might also know where that revolver may have come from,' Monty said. 'Arabella told me you took some photographs on your phone. If I could see the photographs of the gun, I might be able to help.'

Sandy showed him the photographs. 'I am almost a hundred per cent sure this belonged to one of Arabella's grandfathers. It is his revolver from the Second World War. It should be in a cabinet titled "Family at war" at Peveril Hall.'

Arabella then said, 'I rang the National Heritage manager for the hall this morning and the lock on the cabinet has been tampered with and the gun is missing.'

'I told you she is a proper Miss Marple, didn't I?'

Even though the family were not making a complaint about the theft and use of the credit card, the crimes that George had committed were starting to rise. The photographs came through from DC Dobson just as Hannah came out of the shop clutching a couple of purchases that she had made. Sandy indicated to her he would only be five minutes.

As Sandy knew he would, Monty positively identified Kelly and Cousins as the two boys who were with George outside Peveril Farm, now two weeks earlier. As he waved goodbye to them and re-joined Hannah, he thought what a delightful couple Arabella and Monty were.

∞

They went to the car and dropped off the gifts that Hannah had bought, which were for her father, and to drop off the cigarette butts that Arabella had brought for him. The walk that Hannah had planned for them took them through two and half miles of beautiful woodland. The Queen's Sandringham Estate, which is her countryside retreat, covered thousands of acres.

As they walked along, Hannah asked, 'Is this case of the missing MP's son troubling you?' Sandy had shared with her only the briefest details, including that the boy had run away to Canada.

'No, not really, and it does not fit our threshold in the FCO at all, which makes it a bit annoying as it has taken a lot of my time this week and I still have one more interview next week, but then my work on it will be finished.'

They had finished the walk, which they had extended and had continued on a bit further, but they were still early for the timed visit into the house and gardens, in particular for the guided tour of the walled garden, so Sandy's thoughts strayed to thinking about food. Hannah felt that she didn't need any lunch as she still felt full of the large, cooked breakfast that she had eaten. Sandy, on the other hand, got in the queue at the café to get a sandwich. Whilst there, he had a thought and rang

Arabella.

'Hi, it's Sandy. If you do ever get hold of George, please can you ensure you don't mention that we have found the gun.'

'I did wonder about what to say. Monty told me definitely not to mention it and let the police deal with all of the issues in relation to the gun.'

'Yes, good advice. I am worried that if he gets to hear about us now knowing about the gun he will go further underground. We know where he is, so he might be missing, but he is not lost.'

'Speak for yourself. I feel he is a very lost young man.' That view fitted with what Sandy's initial thoughts were about George Peveril.

Sandringham House was well worth them visiting. The house had been completed in 1870 by the then future king, Edward VII and his queen. Sandringham House had been passed down as a private home through four generations of British monarchs. It is now the country retreat of the Queen and the Duke of Edinburgh, who lived much of the time in a farmhouse on the estate. The main ground floor rooms are extensively used by the Queen when she is there. The rooms are open to the public when the Queen, or other members of the royal family, are not in residence. Hannah and Sandy were enjoying the opportunity to look around the rooms.

After the visit to Sandringham and a stroll around Hunstanton with an ice cream, they headed back to the hotel, where they both planned to get caught up with a bit of work before dinner. Sandy felt he needed to make sure his notes on the George Peveril case were fully up to date whilst all of the information was fresh in his mind.

Sandy and Hannah had planned the next day to have a walk on the beach after breakfast to Thornham and back before they needed to head home to Cambridge and Ely. They both had to make sure they had everything in place ready for their busy weeks, for Hannah in Birmingham and Sandy in London.

They had both during the weekend made a commitment to each other, but they knew, due to how their working lives operated, they would both need to make a considerable effort to ensure they saw each other on a regular and consistent basis. Sandy had offered to give up rugby, but Hannah thought it better if he still played whilst he could, and she would go to watch and support him.

Chapter Eight

Monday was extremely busy for Sandy. When he had been chairing the team meeting in the morning, there had been lots of comments by the team about him being Morse. Juliet had obviously told the whole team that Sandy owned a classic sports car; even if it was a modern Morgan motor car, it was built in a classic style. It was all very light-hearted, and if he was honest, Sandy enjoyed the gentle teasing.

After he had updated Juliet on what had happened in the George Peveril case, she said to him, 'You seem to have a warm glow today, Sandy, why is that?' He presumed it was women's intuition as even Detective Superintendent Jane Watson had commented, 'You clearly had a good weekend!' when she had passed him in the corridor earlier in the day.

Sandy told Juliet that he had spent the weekend in Norfolk with his girlfriend, so that might be why he seemed so happy. Juliet said, 'I thought there was something going on!' She smiled at Sandy then continued saying, 'Poor George Peveril has got himself into a lot of trouble, hasn't he. He's not only missing but now wanted by two police forces for offences of theft and illegal possession of a firearm.'

'Obviously, I don't know George at all, but his family, in particular his father and aunty, are such nice people they do not need this added information to add to their worries about him being missing.'

They planned to meet outside Peveril House in Eaton Square the next morning. Sandy had to chair and attend meetings within the FCO building for the rest of the day and was pleased to get to the flat that evening. He immediately went out for a run as he had had little, if any, fresh air all day. Even the train in from Ely and the underground had been stifling in the warm July weather. Sandy's dad, Gregor, was away working for two weeks in Hamilton, Bermuda, which had a head office for the international investment bank that he worked for. Sandy had the flat all to himself and he had floated the idea to Hannah of staying in London for the weekend and her joining him. No decision had been made as yet.

The next morning, Sandy walked to Belgravia and into Eaton Square. The square was beautiful, but as Sandy looked around, he saw it wasn't in fact a square but a large rectangle. Sandy was not surprised that it was said to be the largest square in London. It had been built by the immensely wealthy landowning Duke of Grosvenor and built in the nineteenth century. Sandy could see that the houses were all exceptionally large and joined in regular terraces with the architecture in a

72

classical style. Most houses looked at least four storeys in height with attic rooms on top. Sandy thought though that the smaller garden squares in places like Kensington, Chelsea and Notting Hill were more to his liking with the private gardens in the centre of the square.

As he met up with Juliet, who was already waiting outside the house, which was in the same classical style as the other houses, they saw Vivienne Jones and Adam Scott coming down the steps and onto the pavement. They were an extremely high-profile celebrity couple. Both were A list actors and Vivienne had, within the last two years, won both an Oscar and an Academy Award for best actress in a film. Vivienne was wearing a polka-dot red sundress and had sunglasses placed on her head, where her long, very dark brunette hair was luxuriously lying loosely over her shoulders. Sandy could not deny he was starstruck and his knees nearly melted when Vivienne looked directly at him with her smouldering brown eyes. She looked straight into his eyes and smiled at him. He had to admit that Adam was stunningly handsome too.

Juliet, who was also equally pleased to see the two movie stars, said, 'I know it would have been a bit crass, but we should have asked for an autograph and a selfie!'

They were now at the door to the house and before they knocked, Juliet asked, 'What do we call a viscount? His Lordship?'

'We start with my Lord and then call him sir. Not,

my old mate Bill, or love!' They were both still laughing when the door opened.

∞

They were surprised to see James was the person who opened the door. Sandy started to feel cross; he was just about to say something about surely Lord Peveril had not stood him up again, when James said, 'Please can you not mention the gun to my father. I don't want him to think badly about George, or to get involved in trying to sort it out or try to smooth it over with the National Heritage, who probably, technically, own the gun.' Arabella had, as Sandy had imagined she would, told her brother all about it.

'No problems. Could you, likewise, not mention it to George if he ever gets in touch?'

James nodded and led them into a beautiful large hall, which had a grand staircase in the middle that looked as though it was made of marble. James said, 'The house has been in the Peveril family since it was built as the family townhouse. We still use it much the same. The ground floor is communal for the family. Janice and I have the top floor, Arabella and Monty the middle one, and my father and his wife, Monica, the first floor.'

When they walked into a large reception/lounge area, they saw Viscount Peveril sitting in a soft lounge chair reading the Telegraph newspaper. Monica, who Sandy was pleased to say was the age he'd assumed, being a similar age to James and Arabella, was reading Vogue magazine. She was very glamorous, not in the same league as her next-door neighbour Vivienne, but yes, she was very glamorous. James went off and left them with his father.

'DCI McFarlane, would you and the sergeant like a drink of tea or coffee? Our housekeeper will sort it out for you.' They both nodded and mouthed tea. 'I must apologise for not being there at the hall last week; it had just skipped my mind. I would not want you though, for one second, to read into this that I am not extremely worried about my grandson.'

Sandy looked at Viscount Peveril. He was probably slightly younger than his grandparents, but definitely at least seventy, and Monica must only be in her early forties. He wondered how they had got together. The Viscount was a man immaculately dressed in a blue linen suit and was oozing charisma and confidence.

'Sir, could you let us know when the last time was that you saw or spoke to George?'

'Saw him? I cannot be sure about that. I would say probably two months ago. I did however speak to him during the week he went missing. We have a conversation every couple of weeks. I was trying to see if I could get him some work in London, in finance, but he wasn't too keen. He wanted to get involved in the farm business, which Arabella was keen to help with, once he sorted himself out and stopped any drug taking.'

'You knew he took drugs then?' Juliet asked.

'Yes, it was a bit of a problem with his father as I give George a four-hundred-pound allowance each month. James felt this helped to facilitate his cannabis smoking. I have planned to save it for him rather than giving the allowance to him, but hadn't done this yet, so he will have this money available to him in Canada.'

'Why do you think he went to Canada?'

'He just loves it there. I have never been there with him, but he has been dozens of times and is happy, and I believe safe there.'

'So, you don't believe he has come to harm then?' Juliet asked.

'I don't know anything about his two friends, but if they are his friends why would they hurt him, and the three of them would protect each other.'

Sandy felt this summed up the situation well but wondered why no one had heard anything from George. There was nothing else they needed to discuss. Although Monica had remained present throughout, she hadn't said a word, which Sandy couldn't decide was strange or not. She had been George's step grandmother for over three years so must have a view about him. Juliet said, as they walked down the road, that Monica probably only had views that concerned herself, and although that sounded catty, it was probably a correct assumption.

∞

The next day, Sandy was terribly busy all morning so didn't have a chance to think about the George Peveril case. It wasn't until the afternoon when he had a few moments to himself that he pulled out of his briefcase the notebook he was using for the missing person investigations. He was pretty happy that he had now completed all of his enquiries on the case. He thought of what his grandad, Tom Fisher, had mentioned to him about proof of life enquiries in long-term missing persons. He started to write in the book the following information.

Missing person investigations

- What was the reason he went missing? – George told Arabella Montague (Aunty) he needed to get away for a few days.
- Was George going missing unusual? – Yes, not known to go missing before.
- Did he prepare to go missing? – No, it was all very last-minute and with haste. He stole to facilitate it.
- When was the last sighting, or when did someone last have contact? – Exactly two weeks ago. Both the Williams brothers at Peveril Estate saw him and Arabella spoke to him.
- Was George Peveril at risk? – The family seemed to think so, but the police seem less concerned.

- Had George made use of a phone, in particular his mobile phone? – Not believed used and switched off since leaving England. Used the phone in the house on the Peveril Estate two weeks ago. Not answering the phone in the cottage.
- Any use of credit card or debit card? – Only the stolen one used for flights and cash. Not known if any use on another card.
- Any other financial enquiry needed? – Not known.
- Any use of computers? – Only time known at Arabella's.
- Any use of other cards, e.g., loyalty cards? – Not known.

Sandy could have gone on writing more questions but as he knew he wouldn't know the answers to these further questions, such as, had George needed to be seen by health professionals, he didn't bother. Looking at what he had written, he was feeling more than slightly uneasy that something may have happened to George, he just didn't know what. And the key question: was George Peveril still alive? He could only say he presumed so, as there was nothing to suggest otherwise.

Sandy emailed all of George's details to the UK Missing Persons Unit so they could log him on their database. He then called DC Wayne Dobson, who he thought would be getting tired of him, especially as he was so busy on the PC Foster murder enquiry. When Wayne answered his phone, Sandy said, 'Hi, Wayne, sorry, it is me again. Have you got the phone call data check back as yet?'

'Yes, I have. Sorry, I have not looked at it yet. I have it on my computer, if you give me one minute… OK, nothing at all on the phone since the 20th of June when calls were made to British Airways, I presume to book his and the other two's flights. I also presume that after this was when the phone was switched off, or the battery ran out of power. On the 20th of June, there was an incoming call at two in the morning, then another outgoing call at three fifteen a.m., both to the same unknown number with the SIM card not registered. There are four or five calls to and from this number during the previous three or four days. Lots of calls to the home address and his father's mobile. So that is it really.'

'Am I safe to assume that the number in the early hours of the morning is from either Kelly or Cousins?'

'I would say so, but the number is not linked to them on our intelligence system. It is a simple pay as you go phone that is disposed of after a brief time.'

Sandy rang off as he had an incoming call from Hannah. 'Sandy, my victim gave great evidence in court today. We applied for special measures and had screens so she couldn't see the defendant and he couldn't see her. I don't think I can come to London this weekend as the way the trial is going, I will need to prepare my closing statement over the weekend. I hope you don't mind. It would have been lovely. I am sorry.'

'Don't worry, Hannah, I fully understand. I am going back to Ely tonight. My father is away, so I am going with my mum to a garden party at the Bishop's Palace in Ely tomorrow. I could stay there, then maybe on Saturday give you a guided tour of Ely then drop you back in good time in Cambridge?'

'Yes, that would be absolutely great.'

Chapter Nine

On the train back to Ely, Sandy suddenly realised that the one thing he should probably have done first, in the George Peveril missing person investigation, was to ask a police officer in Canada to visit George and make sure he was alive and well.

When he worked as a young police officer walking the beat in the West End of London, he would often conduct these enquiries on behalf of police forces around the country who had people missing from home. He would check the rough sleepers or hostels and the night shelters. He must admit though, that only once was this successful.

He had to admit to himself that he had been seduced, probably because he enjoyed investigating so much, to make all of the enquiries that he had done so far. After leaving the train, he walked straight back to his parents' house, which was in a beautiful location overlooking the River Great Ouse. His mum was still busy, now amending school reports ready for the end of the school year, and she hardly looked up when he walked in. This suited Sandy and after shouting a quick hello he went straight up to his room.

After a brief search, he found the number he needed for the Royal Canadian Mounted Police detachment in Portage la Prairie. The time there was five hours behind, so only early afternoon. The phone was answered straight away.

'RCMP Portage la Prairie. This is Staff Sergeant John Hopkins; how can I help you?'

'Hello, I am DCI Alexander McFarlane from the British police. I am making enquiries into a missing person: George Peveril.'

'Has he been visiting here then?'

Sandy felt a bit frustrated that the British High Commission in Ottawa hadn't notified them as they had said they would. 'You should have been told by the British High Commission. However, he has been visiting the family Peveril Estate, which I think is only a little southwest from you. If you give me your email address, I will send you pictures of him and the two people who are there with him.'

'I know the Peveril Estate well. My brother, when he was a student, used to help out on the harvest there. I will go and visit it myself for you.'

'They have left there and gone to a cottage on Lake Manitoba. The place is called Laurentia Beach.'

'I also know that area. It is only thirty miles or so from Portage la Prairie. We don't police it from here, but I can get an officer based out of the municipality of

St Laurent to visit. It is a really old cottage area, which would fit with it being owned probably for a hundred years by the Peveril family.'

'Thank you. Could you just check if you had a disturbance in your town just over two weeks ago? I understand they fell out with some locals over drugs, which was the reason they headed off to the cottage.' Sandy could hear the keyboard banging. John Hopkins wasn't a gentle user and Sandy presumed he was an older officer that found computers more of a challenge than an asset. 'No, nothing that I can see, but I am not particularly good at searching on our system.'

Sandy thanked him and when he sent the sergeant an email, he said he would be quite happy for an email response when they had seen George. He also decided not to send a stinging email to his contact in the High Commission Office in Ottawa as it was quite probable that there might be a record on the RCMP system, but John Hopkins just didn't know where to look.

After getting changed and before going downstairs to meet up with his mother, he saw that Sergeant Hopkins was in fact really efficient and had already sent him an email. He had already tasked someone to visit the cottage and was going to the Peveril Estate himself to see what he could find out.

∞

The run that Sandy took that morning was his usual one

along the bank of the river that ran in front of his parents' house. It was very pleasant, albeit he felt quite warm in the early morning summer sunshine. Whilst running, Sandy had no thoughts about George Peveril or, in fact, his work at the FCO. His thoughts were entirely about the route he was going to take on Saturday to show Ely off to Hannah. He absolutely loved Ely and he wanted Hannah to as well. It was without doubt the place he called home.

He thought he would meet her at the train station and then join an established walk called the Ely Eel Trail. This had been created to show off the heritage of Ely and was waymarked by seventy-way markers. The trail started at the Oliver Cromwell House, which had some parts of the building from the thirteenth century and had been home to the Roundhead Oliver Cromwell during the sixteenth century. The house was also Ely's tourist information centre. The trail went around the town, obviously taking in all aspects and views of the magnificent cathedral. It passed his parents' house then back around and up into the marketplace, which would be buzzing with activity on a Saturday. Sandy wanted to make sure he included some of the King's School buildings where, whilst at school, he had spent a lot of his time.

When he reached home, Sandy's mum was just heading out to do her stint of volunteering at the cathedral. She gave Sandy instructions to be ready shortly after lunch for them to walk to the garden party.

Sandy settled into a chair, got out his laptop and started to work through the files that some of the officers for the consulate investigation team had sent through to him for signing off. It was pretty straightforward work as they were an experienced team. They knew that if there were no investigative leads or opportunities on the deaths abroad, no further work would be needed. He appreciated that this was not good news for the families, but the right thing to do in these circumstances was to recommend closure of the cases.

After a couple of hours of completing the tasks, he had cleared the folder so thought he might look at some of the cases he had himself, including the troubling backpacker case from Singapore. He had found out from enquiries that they had only been in Singapore for two days, having arrived from the island of Penang. He first looked at his emails and saw that the RCMP staff sergeant had sent a reply to him at midnight. Sandy felt excited with anticipation that his enquiries looking for George Peveril might hopefully be over.

The email said the sergeant had found out little at the Peveril Estate and had spoken to the Williams brothers and their wives. The sergeant's brother had actually worked for their father, who was the estate manager before them. The family seemed glad George and his friends had gone. Sandy knew this already though after having spoken to Tim Williams himself.

An officer had visited the cottage and John Hopkins had efficiently cut and pasted in the reply that Constable

Gary Hughes had no doubt sent him. It said that there was no one at the cottage when he visited (Sandy now felt disappointed again), the car was on the drive, but the boat was missing from the garden. There was no one at either of the adjacent houses, but there probably would be in a couple of days when the weekend came around. He had called at a nearby shop, and they had seen all three of the boys about a week ago (Sandy felt happier now as his timeline for George being seen had moved forward at least a week from when they left the Peveril Estate). However, since then, the owner of the shop had only seen one of the boys, who was not George (whom he knew), but he had identified it was Ruben Cousins by looking at the photographs that Sandy had sent across.

Sandy felt his enquiries had moved forward. The constable would no doubt revisit and see them within the next couple of days and then the matter for him would hopefully be resolved. Sandy decided to transfer across the information into his notebook, so all of the enquiries were meticulously kept in one place.

∞

Sandy looked at one of the guidebooks that he had bought at Heffers in Cambridge and saw the map that showed Portage la Prairie, which was on the Trans-Canada Highway heading out west from Winnipeg. Sandy thought that that would be an incredible journey to go on, to travel from East to West Canada on this highway, or what he probably would rather do would be to take the train. He was sure that would be fabulous, and he must add it to his overflowing bucket list of trips he wanted to take. He was not sure where exactly the Peveril Flax Estate was, but presumed it was not that many miles southwest of the town that looked on the map, and in the information, larger than the size of Ely. He could see Lake Manitoba to the north and now fully understood why if you had the money, you would buy a cottage there as it looked a short distance for the weekenders heading there from the town.

The morning seemed to have flown past, so Sandy quickly took a shower and was changed and waiting for his mother when she arrived home to get changed herself. They walked together through Jubilee Gardens and then into what Sandy always called Cherry Hill Park to the Gallery. The view of the cathedral from here was just stunning. They joined the queue to enter the Bishop's House and the garden. Sandy for some reason thought the party was in the Bishop's Palace but it was in fact nearby. Ely was blessed with all of these historical buildings. He saw his Grandma Margaret ahead in the queue, who also volunteered in the cathedral, and with her was his Grandad Tom. They were waiting for them as they went into the garden.

After a short while, it seemed as if the garden was quite full of people. Sandy moved himself closer to the table where a lovely finger buffet had been laid out. He also had his eye on the glasses of wine that were poured out ready. He felt his phone vibrating in his pocket and because it kept vibrating, he knew it was a call rather than a message. He thought he had better answer it to see who it was, but just before he did, the Bishop of Ely, Andrew, started to talk. Bishop Andrew, Sandy thought, was a delightful man. No, not thought, he knew he was a delightful man. Bishop Andrew talked about the cathedral, its history and how much upkeep the many-centuries-old building needed. He then went on to stress it was the people gathered within the garden and the church community in the Ely area who were the key, as much as if not more than a building.

Sandy's phone had rung twice more whilst Bishop Andrew was talking. As soon as the bishop finished, Sandy pulled his phone out of his pocket, but he didn't recognise the number that he had missed calls from, then the person whose number it was rang again. 'Hello, is that DCI McFarlane?'

'Yes, who is this?' Sandy asked, as he didn't recognise the voice.

'It is DC David Masters from Hunstanton CID. I didn't know what to do, I didn't know who to ring first.' Get on with it, Sandy thought, as I am keen to get a plate full of the buffet. 'I didn't know whether to phone one of my bosses first. I was just so shocked when I got the call.' Please, please get on with it quickly, Sandy almost said to David, but held his tongue. 'I firstly thought after I took the call I should phone my boss, but they wouldn't know anything about it, so I thought I should call you,

88

then I couldn't find the number you gave me – it was in another notebook in my car that I had to go and fetch.'

Sandy could stand it no longer. 'Who called you that made you think you should call me?' He had no idea what David was on about and felt he needed to take control of the rambling conversation.

'NABIS have called with information.' David now had Sandy's full attention. 'The gun that you seized from Peveril Farm is, they are almost 100% sure, the one that fired the bullet that shot and killed PC Joseph Foster!'

Chapter Ten

The nearby chair almost toppled over as Sandy crashed down onto it. The shock of what he had just heard was reverberating throughout his whole body. He didn't know for a moment what to say to David Masters about what he had just been told. At the same time, David kept saying, 'Sir, sir, did you hear what I just said? George Peveril must have murdered PC Foster.'

After a few seconds, which must have felt like minutes, the professional in Sandy kicked in and he said, 'David, please don't say that. We don't know that George was the person who murdered PC Foster.'

'He must surely now be the prime suspect though. Surely, he must be, mustn't he?'

'Absolutely, I agree he must be,' Sandy said, at the same time thinking to himself, poor George, what have you gone and done? You are a sad, lost boy. His family, in a short while when they found out, were going to be devastated. 'Have you still got the shopping carrier bag in the crime property store in King's Lynn?' he asked David.

'Yes, I was going to collect it and take it to the Scientific Support Department offices at police headquarters in Norwich.'

'Don't do anything else until you hear directly from someone who is working on Operation Primrose. That is the name for the Derbyshire police murder enquiry. I will ring them now.'

Sandy sat there for a few moments contemplating what he had just heard. He felt he needed time to process what to do next. He absentmindedly, whilst sitting there, answered his phone, which had been buzzing again in his hand. The female voice on the other end of the phone was shouting at him very loudly. 'Who do you think you are? Coming into Derbyshire, the big London detective swanning around the county, in fact the country. Not telling one person what you have been up here doing.'

The person was shouting so loudly that Sandy could almost feel her spittle coming out of the phone and drenching him. He had no idea who it was that was shouting at him with such venom. He tried to speak but wasn't able to as the voice continued aggressively. 'Send me immediately all the statements that you have taken. You recovered the gun that killed Joseph Foster and didn't think for one moment to share that with us in Operation Primrose. We have been looking for a Smith & Wesson revolver for days now and you had possession of it almost a week ago. Unbelievable! You are unbelievable!'

It all suddenly clicked into place. The person doing

the shouting was Detective Superintendent Joanne O'Connor. Sandy responded rather sheepishly. 'I didn't know you were looking for a Smith & Wesson revolver and I am sorry, but I haven't taken any statements.' Sandy wanted to go on and defend himself by saying, if you hadn't walked off the other day without hearing my reply when I saw you at Derbyshire Police headquarters, you would have known I was looking into George Peveril being missing from home, but he wasn't able to as Joanne started another machine gun-type tirade at him again.

'What!' Sandy was sure that everyone in the Bishop's garden must have heard the explosion that erupted out of his phone. Sandy could only whisper as he thought everyone must now be overhearing the drama going on in his conversation. He quickly said, 'My notes though are excellent.'

'They better had be, young man! Send them to me now. We urgently need the information. I presume you have done something right and know where Kelly, Peveril and Cousins are?'

'Yes, they are in Canada.'

'What! Oh, for goodness sake! Is nothing ever going to get any easier on this investigation?' Joanne O'Connor sighed in a much more even tone. Her explosive, emotive and high-octane verbal eruption was clearly now beginning to subside.

'I have an RCMP officer in Manitoba tracking them. They are in a cottage on Lake Manitoba.'

'That is at least something. OK, send the notes to Lofty Dobson. He will bring them to me, and he will also place another copy in the incident room.'

As abruptly as the conversation had started, Joanne O'Connor had ended the call. Sandy saw that he had missed calls and a text message from DC Dobson saying, 'Sorry, Ma'am O'Connor insisted on me passing to her your mobile phone number.'

Sandy sat in the chair in shock. It took a few seconds for him to realise that his Grandad Tom was sitting next to him. Grandad Tom put his arm round his grandson. Sandy prodded his grandad's stomach, which was growing large, and said, 'Grandad, we are going to have to do something about you losing this stomach!'

They both laughed together. 'Don't you worry about me, Sandy. What is going on? That conversation didn't sound like it seemed much fun for you?' Sandy explained to his grandad what had just occurred in the conversation.

'I know that is not how you or I would speak to any of our staff, or in fact anyone. However, imagine just for one second the pressure Detective Superintendent O'Connor must be under. She is the SIO of a murder enquiry into the death of one of her police officers. You saw the newspaper headlines earlier in the week: "Almost three weeks and police have no idea!" "No Clues!" I know I am making excuses for her but the stress she is under must be so immense that she must be almost at breaking point.'

93

'I know, Grandad, but without me they may still have no clue! I have found them the gun and provided them with three suspects. My current problem is our printer and scanner at home is broken and I need to urgently send them my notes. I could photograph them and send them that way, but I am not sure that would look very professional. I will though send them the pictures of the gun and bag I took.'

'I must say, Sandy, well done for what you have found out. It is actually great investigative work. I am not sure our printer at home would be much use to you either I am afraid. I do think the first person you should ring is your boss, Detective Superintendent Watson, and whilst you are doing that, I can ring the front desk at Ely police station to see if you could use their scanner. Failing that, you could go across the road from the police station to the East Cambs District Council offices. They would let you use their scanner or a fax machine.'

Sandy felt much more settled now having spoken to his grandad, who was already on his phone to the police station where he had worked for most of his thirty-four years in the force. Sandy rang Jane Watson, praying she wasn't tied up in a meeting. Jane answered the phone after a couple of rings. 'Sandy, I can't talk now. The director general here in the FCO and I are on the phone to the Chief Constable of Derbyshire. I will ring you back within the hour.' She abruptly ended the call.

The feeling he had of being settled had gone as

quickly as it had arrived. He must be in horrendous trouble now!

His grandad told him to ask for Rose at the front desk of the police station. He then went off to find Sandy's mum and grandma to tell them Sandy had had to leave for an urgent work issue. Sandy decided to grab a sandwich to eat as he was about to leave, but he turned back and went and found Bishop Andrew – he just couldn't leave without saying thank you to the kind and lovely bishop.

At the police station in Nutholt Lane, Rose, the enquiry office clerk, spent all of her time gushing on about what a great man Sandy's Grandad Tom was. Sandy already knew what a great man his grandad was. All he wanted was to be left in peace as he had lost quite a bit of time at home looking through his notes and making sure they were as full and up to date as they could be.

When he was more than halfway through scanning his notes and sending them through to DC Dobson's email address, his phone buzzed. It was Jane Watson. 'Sandy, great work on the George Peveril enquiry.' Maybe he wasn't in trouble after all, and not really great work as he hadn't found him quite yet. The next thing Jane said absolutely shocked him. 'We have agreed to transfer you to be the deputy SIO on the Operation Primrose team as of now. They want you first thing tomorrow for a forensic meeting. I can't let Juliet go with you as I am going to give her temporary promotion to inspector to cover for you, but Clare Symonds will be with you tomorrow.

'Surely, Detective Superintendent O'Connor hasn't agreed to this? She absolutely hates me.'

'Yes, she has, and don't worry, Joanne will absolutely love you very soon, like we all do. I am sorry to lose you for a few weeks.'

∞

There was a lovely plate of pasta waiting for Sandy when he got home from the police station. His mother, Katherine, had known he would be hungry so had quickly prepared the food ready for him on his return. Sandy explained to her that he would need to pack that evening as he had an early start to head for Derby the next morning.

Sandy also sent text messages to his grandad explaining what had happened since they had last spoken and that he was now the deputy SIO on a huge murder enquiry. He also sent a text message to Hannah letting her know that he was now working full time on the PC Foster murder case, and he needed to cancel their date on Saturday. He told her he would call tomorrow when he knew what was happening and promised her that on his first day off, he would travel to whatever court she was in so that they could spend time together.

The MFH enquiries that Sandy had been carrying out were pretty straightforward investigative actions that most detective constables would happily complete on a daily basis. To suddenly go from this level of investigative activity to become a deputy SIO was, Sandy realised, a huge difference in role and responsibility. He needed to get his mindset changed pretty quickly.

Whilst he was on his SIO course, Sandy remembered the words he thought came from America and were something known there as the homicide investigator's creed. The words he could still recite, and although thinking about them made him nervous, they did in fact inspire him.

The creed said: 'No greater honour will ever be bestowed on you as a police officer, or a more profound duty imposed on you than when you are entrusted with the investigation of the death of a human being. It is your moral duty, and, as an officer entrusted with such a duty, it is incumbent upon you to follow the course of events and the facts as they develop to their ultimate conclusion. It is a heavy responsibility. As such, let no person deter you from the truth or your personal conviction to see that justice is done.'

Sandy's phone buzzed. He was pleased to see it was DC Dobson calling. 'Hi, boss. Really pleased that we are going to be working together. Thank you for your comprehensive notes. I received them safely and I have already submitted them. I am sorry I gave your number to Ma'am O'Connor. I had no idea she was going to shout at you like she did.'

'Has she calmed down yet? I think she hates me!'

'Oh yes, fully calmed down. I apologised and told her I did know what enquiries you have done, and that your notes are excellent, so she has seen exactly what has been done.'

'So, I don't need to avoid her tomorrow and keep my head down?'

'No, you don't. I have just come out of a briefing with her. You are going to lead on forensics, family liaison and overseas enquiries. You will be supported by DI Rich Singh, and I am also on your team. Mrs O'Connor was talking very highly to the group about you having developed the breakthrough.'

'Wow, that is good news,' Sandy said, feeling quite proud from these comments. To be fair, all of it had happened unintentionally but came about by just doing basic detective work. After finishing his pasta, Sandy struggled to pack, with clothes going into his case and just as quickly going out of his case. The problem was, he just didn't know how long he would be staying in Derbyshire before he had an opportunity to return home.

A text message from Joanne O'Connor unsettled him even more as it instructed him to be in her office at seven thirty a.m. the next morning. The sleepless night that he was expecting just became much shorter. He didn't think his mum was helping either as she was keen for him to drive to Ripley that evening rather than first thing in the morning. She thought that that was the safest thing to do, rather than leave at four thirty in the morning as he was planning to. However, for Sandy, as much as he was very content to stay in the Premier Inn at Ripley, which he had already booked for the next few days, the lure of one more night in his own bed was, in his view, the better option.

Chapter Eleven

There was a flask of coffee, freshly made jam sandwiches and a bunch of grapes waiting on the kitchen top for Sandy as he left home the next morning. His mother was without a doubt an absolute sweetheart. 'Thanks, Mum. Speak to you soon,' he shouted up to her, as he went out to his car and set off for Derbyshire.

It had turned out that he had slept pretty well and the trip to Derbyshire was uneventful. When he pulled into the visitor's car park at the police headquarters, he found that the media village he had seen there before was now greatly reduced and there were relatively fewer large media vehicles left in the car park. As he walked to the reception area, which was in darkness, Sandy realised that he had no idea how to get into the building or how to find Joanne O'Connor's office. This was not going to be a good start.

He stood for a moment outside the entrance door, a bit lost, debating whether to call Joanne directly or maybe try Wayne Dobson. It was at that moment that he was relieved to see the extremely tall figure of Wayne

Dobson saunter over from the staff car park. 'Sorry I am late, boss. Let us go in and see Ma'am O'Connor.' Sandy was pretty sure they hadn't arranged to meet that morning but was extremely glad that Wayne thought so.

Joanne O'Connor hardly looked up as they went into her office. She seemed to have on the same grey trouser suit but with a purple blouse instead of the pink one that she was wearing the last time he had seen her in person.

'DCI McFarlane, welcome to the team. I understand you are already aware of the areas that I want you to look after for me. Is that right?' Although Sandy thought, no apology for shouting at me, no thanks for what I have done so far, he just said, 'Yes, Ma'am.'

'OK, please call me Joanne when it is just the two of us and Mrs O'Connor in front of the team. Is that clear?'

'Absolutely, and I am called Sandy.' It was most certainly all business with Joanne O'Connor.

'There is a forensic meeting starting in thirty minutes that I want you to lead on with Rich, then I want you to go with Lofty to see Belinda Foster. Her and my relationship is pretty strained at the moment, not sure why. I am sure she would appreciate you visiting to explain that you will be the lead senior detective for her to have contact with and not me.'

Sandy wanted to ask why her relationship was strained with the widow of their murder victim, but before he could, Joanne said, 'I have a number of teams ready to carry out a strike at four addresses, which is happening in thirty minutes: the home addresses of all three of the suspects and Peveril Farm in Norfolk where you found the gun. I am coordinating this and if you gain any information from your meeting, convey it to me first and then I can send it out to the teams. OK, see you later, and not a word to the media please. Let me deal with that. I am not sure I am going to tell them any names until we have hands on the suspects, so you can't tell Belinda names either.'

The meeting had ended as abruptly as it started. Sandy picked up on the feeling of the immense stress Joanne was under as she was continually pushing her hands through her long, dyed blonde hair. He left her office feeling this was an SIO who was showing positive leadership and clear – maybe, in his view, too clear – direction for the investigation. You probably couldn't argue with any SIO who led like this and to be fair to Joanne, very exciting things were happening with the investigation that very morning, which Sandy found was quite exhilarating.

Outside the office, DC Dobson and a young, handsome Asian man were waiting for him. They all set off together to the room that the forensic meeting was going to be held in. Sandy introduced himself to the Asian man, who had on a modern fashioned electric, blue-coloured suit and who replied, 'I am DI Rich Singh, pleased to meet you.'

Sandy stopped walking and looked directly at him. 'When I heard the name Rich, I presumed it was short for Richard. My mistake, I should know by now not to presume anything!'

Rich laughed and said, 'Didn't Singh give it away?' They were all laughing now. 'Rich is short for Rishabh, but I was born here, and I am quite western in my outlook, so Rich it is!'

'And Lofty it is for me,' DC Dobson said.

∞

The room they went into was full of people. Clare Symonds was there having arrived the previous night. It appeared there were a number of crime scene investigators, forensic scientists, crime analysts, including digital media investigators, and detectives in the room. Also present was Dr Nicholas Stroud, a Home Office forensic pathologist. He was very pleased to see that Sandy was now involved in the case as they had worked together very recently on the Robert Smythe death.

The room was called to be quiet and after introducing himself, Sandy opened the meeting up by saying he wanted to go through a number of categories to see how best they should try and find forensic evidence in the case. 'I would like us to look at PC Joseph Foster, the victim, first. What was on his body-worn video footage?'

Rich answered this question. 'Sorry, boss, his body-worn camera hadn't been switched on all night. Some officers tend to only switch them on when they go to an incident, and they feel its use is appropriate. We have completed a review of Joseph's past use and he only switches his on when a violent incident is already happening. This leads us to hypothesise that he was shot very soon after coming across the youths when he arrived in Lock-Up-Yard.'

'Dr Stroud, are you able to tell us about the shooting please and what you found out during your post-mortem examination?'

'I will leave it for others to tell you the details of the gun and ammunition used. What I can tell you is that the bullet entered him at an upper angle through a gap in his body armour, not that, on my examination of the armour, which I believe is better described as a stab proof vest, feel that it would have stopped a bullet. I don't think so anyway. I have an entry wound at that point, with the bullet slicing through his liver and just nicking his heart, and an exit wound through his side. The bullet was probably fired from a distance away. So, there was no personal physical contact with the offenders that I found, I am afraid.'

'Any questions for Dr Stroud?' Sandy asked. Looking around the room, he could see that the detectives in the room were visibly shaken by the information on how their colleague had actually died, so said, 'I am happy if any of you need a few moments to process this information and to pause for a moment.'

No one did and someone asked, 'He didn't die where he was shot though did, he, Dr Stroud?'

'No, a bullet would normally stop someone in their tracks, but due to the distance it was probably fired from, and I believe he was probably moving at speed, his momentum would have carried him slightly forward and he then probably crawled the ten yards before bleeding out and dying. The police search team found the bullet in the corner here,' he replied, pointing to a large street map of the area on the wall.

'Thank you,' Sandy said to Dr Stroud.

Sandy didn't know if there was a ballistics or firearms expert at the meeting, or if there was, who they were. It was at that moment he knew he had made a mistake by only introducing himself and not asking others to introduce themselves, so he just asked a question to the whole room. 'Does anyone know what gun and bullet was used?'

'I am from NABIS and have a ballistics expert with me,' the voice of a woman who was sitting only three people away from Sandy said.

'Please tell us what you know then.'

'The gun used is a Smith & Wesson service revolver .38. As you know DCI McFarlane, you have recovered the weapon that we are pretty certain fired the bullet. This weapon and bullet were part of the standard service issue, probably during the Second World War. PC Foster was possibly shot from as far away as thirty feet.'

'Any CCTV to help us with that?'

'Yes and no,' someone said, who was either an analyst or from the digital forensics team. 'No because we haven't got an image of anyone firing the gun or of Joseph being shot. We do have it of him at the site where he is collapsing and dying though.'

'Anything else to help us with who the offenders might be?'

'We have managed to put together a slide pack of the images of these two hooded individuals.' At that moment, a projector came to life and displayed on a screen on the back wall a number of different shots of two males together, wearing hoodies, with their hoods up so that they pretty much covered their faces. The images were all of varying quality so you could not make out who it was in them. One wore a blue Fat Face hoodie and the other an orange one.

'We can see them around the city area for about an hour beforehand, sometimes in conversation with people and handing over what we presume are drugs. We also see them in the market area and Lock-Up-Yard very shortly before the murder, so we are presuming it must be them. We have them running at speed just down the road, probably shortly after the shooting would have taken place.'

Sandy didn't like the number of times the term "probably" was being used and asked someone who he hoped was a digital media investigations officer, 'Any phone intelligence to help tie things down?'

'Yes,' came the reply. 'We have completed a grab of phone numbers used in the area at the time of the murder, and one number, a pay as you go phone, had been in the area at the exact time. We know that, to use non-technical terms, the phone was shaking hands with a couple of phone masts that pinpoint it in this area.'

Sandy didn't need them to tell him the number, as he had, as it turned out, guessed rightly that it was the number that had called George Peveril on that particular night. The meeting continued for another couple of hours, also covering information on a stolen car, which had later been found burnt out some distance north of the city.

∞

After the meeting finished, Sandy spent a few minutes catching up with Dr Nicholas Stroud, and they made a firm agreement to meet up for a meal in the near future, either in Cambridge or London. On looking at his phone, he found he had two missed calls from James Peveril and three missed calls from Arabella, as well as a message from her asking: 'Sandy, what is going on? What has George done?'

He went outside and saw that Lofty Dobson had pulled up in a car in front of the reception area ready to take them to see Belinda Foster. 'Why is there a strained relationship between Joanne and Belinda?' Sandy asked him after getting into the car.

'Apparently, Joseph applied to become a detective a few weeks ago and Ma'am O'Connor failed him. Belinda feels he wouldn't have been on the beat and therefore not in a position to be killed if she hadn't done that.'

'Although technically correct, Joanne was probably only doing what she thought was right, and she wasn't the one who fired the bullet that killed him.'

Sandy needed to make an urgent phone call to get some advice from his colleague, DCI Phil Harris. When Phil answered the phone, he asked, 'Phil, what do I do about talking to a suspect's family?' Sandy didn't know what to do about all of his missed calls from James and Arabella.

'Two options, my friend. One, hand them over to someone else to liaise with them. Second, if you have as good a rapport as it seems that you have, I would be honest with them. Say to them that there are things you can't tell them, but you will tell them what you can, when you can. And make sure you record everything.'

Sandy didn't have time to make any more calls as they had already pulled up outside the Foster's address, which was a nice-looking three-bedroom, semi-detached house in a pleasant suburb of Derby. On getting out of the car, Sandy noticed a suitcase and backpack on the back seat of the car.

'Lofty, are you staying in the same place as me in the Premier Inn?'

Lofty looked at him with an extremely confused expression. 'We are flying to Toronto tonight on the ten p.m. BA flight, then on to Winnipeg, arriving first thing tomorrow morning.'

'When you say "we", I presume you mean me as part of the we, do you?'

Before Lofty could respond and Sandy had time to process what he had just heard and try and work out how he could put his hands on his passport, which was in his bedroom in Ely, and even more importantly to him how to get his beautiful Morgan motor car home, the door opened.

The person at the door, Lofty quickly told him, was Belinda's dad. They were shown into a lounge, which was absolutely overflowing with cards and flowers, and the room had taken on what could be described as being a chapel of rest. In the room, they saw the incredibly young Belinda Foster. It was clear she was pleased to see DC Dobson, and he introduced Sandy to her.

'I can see you looking, DCI McFarlane, but these are not all of the cards or the flowers. Amazingly, I have received them from all over the country, in fact, all over the world. People are truly kind. I was going to leave them out until after the memorial service, which we hope to hold in about ten days to two weeks' time. Lofty is attending, will you be able to attend as well please, DCI McFarlane?'

'Yes, I will if I am able to, thank you.' Sandy at that very moment didn't know if and when he would be back from Canada. His mind sadly slipped to his passport, car and letting Hannah know what was happening. He snapped himself back into the room by saying to Belinda, who was holding her emotions surprisingly in check, 'I have come to tell you that we have three good suspects now in our sights. I am not able to tell you about their names at the moment as we haven't fully located them.'

'I presume you believe that Joe wasn't targeted but came across a crime or something?'

'Absolutely, we believe the crime was drug dealing in Derby city centre.' Sandy could see the look of disgust in Belinda's face. He did notice, despite the reasonable amount of makeup that Belinda had applied, that her face showed signs of immense tiredness, sadness and grief. 'I know so many other people must have said this to you, but I am genuinely sorry for your loss of Joseph. I know I never knew him, but really do feel for you, and between Lofty and myself we will keep you updated on any news as and when we are able to.'

The two young girls, Joseph's daughters, had come back into the lounge and Sandy looked at them wondering how their future life would now be without their father. After finishing their tea and coffee, Sandy and DC Dobson left the house, their mood now very sombre.

Chapter Twelve

Grandad Tom was the answer that Sandy came up with for getting his passport to him and for getting his car back home. He was terrified of his car getting damaged, but his father was in Hamilton, Bermuda, and his other grandpa only drove an automatic car. Tom was the only answer that Sandy had to get his beloved Morgan Roadster home so that it would not have to be left for an unknown period of time in the police headquarters car park, or at an airport car park. When Sandy rang his grandad, he was happy to help. They planned a rendezvous for in just over two hours' time. This would allow Sandy and Lofty time to get to Heathrow for their flight and for his grandad to go to his parents' house, collect his passport and get a train to Peterborough to meet them on route to London.

'Lofty, why wasn't I told we are off to Canada almost immediately?'

'I thought you were! I am not sure if it was Rich, me or Ma'am O'Connor who should have told you. Obviously, we need to get our hands on these three as soon as possible, don't you agree?'

'Absolutely. As you have just overheard, we need to be in Peterborough at the railway station in a couple of hours to meet my grandad. If you follow me there, that will be great.'

He firstly visited the Operation Primrose major incident room to ensure that the agreed decisions from the forensic meeting had been actioned. Whilst there, Sandy also made sure he submitted the cigarette butts found by Arabella. He then headed back in his car along a similar route that he had driven only a few hours ago that morning, but in the opposite direction. Hannah had called on her way back to Cambridge as her court case had concluded for the week and it was all set, as she had presumed, for closing speeches on the Monday.

Sandy rang both Arabella and James. To be fair, they both understood what he was saying, but were quite distraught as to what they presumed George had got himself involved in. Sandy promised to update them as soon as he could, even though he wasn't sure when that would be. Sandy had wondered whether or not to tell Arabella he was just about to fly to Canada to try and find George. He knew that she would find out anyway from one of the Williams brothers almost as soon as he arrived in Winnipeg, so he told her where he was heading to and was surprised by her reaction, which was one of great appreciation.

The train from Ely, carrying Grandad Tom, had arrived at Peterborough before Sandy got there. Sandy

112

was pleased to see him waiting in the car park for him. He had Sandy's passport and two clean short-sleeved shirts, as well as the Canadian guidebooks that Sandy had bought the previous week.

'Right, Grandad, let me go through where each of the controls for the car are positioned,' Sandy said, as he worriedly talked to his grandad, whilst he was sitting in the driver's seat. 'Make sure you keep your speed down as this engine is very powerful.'

'I will keep it in the third gear then.'

'No, don't do that,' Sandy said in horror. 'It will race the engine. Just drive as you would normally, Grandad, but keep your speed down.'

Much to Sandy's despair, the Morgan car sped out of the car park. His grandad then stopped and lowered the roof of the car. Sandy looked at Lofty, who couldn't stop laughing at how worried and uncomfortable Sandy was looking and behaving. 'Neither he nor my mother will be able to put that roof back up. I have made an awful mistake,' Sandy said, shaking his head in mock despair.

As it turned out, Tom got back to Ely safely, long before they pulled into Terminal Five at Heathrow for their flight. There were in fact six of them heading to Canada. Sandy, Rich, Clare Symonds and another CSI from Operation Primrose, plus Lofty and one other Derbyshire DC. Lofty had been given an exit seat, due to the endlessly long legs that he had. There was no spare seat next to him, so Sandy positioned himself next to Rich, who was going to update him on the results of the searches that had taken place that morning.

∞

The aircraft didn't take very long at all to reach its cruising height and speed. The drinks trolley had completed its first pass when Sandy got out his notebook. He had started a second notebook, which went from the time he officially started as a member of the Operation Primrose team.

'Joanne O'Connor is pretty sure that the car that was stolen not long after the shooting, which is a Volkswagen Golf, is connected and is probably the getaway car,' Rich said.

'Shame that it has been found burnt out then. Locard's principle will not be of much use here as the fire will have burnt away all contact material.'

'You mean Dr Edmond Locard's theory that every object that comes into contact with each other will leave some trace of that contact? Don't be so sure that we will not find out something. We have footage of the car going through three speed cameras and the photos of the front seat occupants. We will hopefully be able to identify the petrol used to burn the car out as some spilt on the soil nearby. We also have tyre tracks where the car was abandoned. That will hopefully lead us to another vehicle.'

Sandy looked across at Rich. He was probably only two or three years older than himself, and as well as

114

being a very sharp dresser, there was no doubt he was extremely bright and destined for the higher echelons of the police service, if that was what he intended as his ambition. He also thought that Locard's principle equally applied to people. He thought about the times he had come into contact with Detective Superintendent O'Connor and her lasting contact on him. He was not sure how favourable an impression each of them had made on the other. Something to work on, he decided.

'How did we get on at Peveril Farm?'

'Norfolk police took over this search and helped us there, though it revealed nothing extra from what you had found out. You did a good job there, Sandy!'

'What about Losehill Farmhouse then?'

'Yes, another good job by you Sandy. Same there, nothing extra, but we took George's car away with a full lift. I am sure we will find lots of traces of the three of them together in the car. The question we will not be able to answer is when that contact would have taken place.'

'They have been friends for three or four years or so. I am sure they have all been in and out of that car during that time.'

'The home of Ruben Cousins was also not very fruitful. His mum says she hadn't seen him for weeks. She is a single mum, and we could get nothing more out of her. One of the siblings though said Ruben came home early one morning and woke him up as he shares a bedroom with him; he was looking through drawers.

Unfortunately, he has no idea when that visit took place.'

'What happened at Dean Kelly's home then?' Sandy could see the dinner trolley making progress towards them and was keen to get settled before it arrived. It had been an incredibly long and unexpected day for him. He had had no idea when he woke up so early that morning that he would end the day being on a plane to Canada. His brain had almost had enough now, and sleep was what was needed.

'Both the mum and dad are very anti-police, as is the whole neighbourhood. Apparently, he was at home all night and they are providing an alibi for him. A neighbour, Eleanor Danvers, across the street heard a noise on the morning we are interested in at five thirty a.m. She saw Dean go into the home having got out of a Ford Fiesta car. She heard a big row going on in the house and then Dean came out and got in the car, which then drove off at speed. She recognised Ruben Cousins who was sitting in the rear of the car but not the driver. She had never seen him before.'

'How can she be so sure what day it was?' Sandy asked.

'She says it was her grandad's birthday, which is why she remembers.'

The food had arrived, and Sandy planned that he would try and sleep as quickly as possible after he had finished his meal and it had been cleared away.

Whoever had made the hotel booking in Winnipeg had probably, unknowingly, put them in a wonderful location right in the centre of The Forks. This location was beside the Red River and also alongside the Assinibone River, right up to where this river meets the Red River. Alongside this riverside location was shopping, eating and parks. Great, thought Sandy, as Lofty pulled their hire car into the hotel car park.

Their flights had kept to time, and it was still very early in the morning. They all planned to grab a couple more hours sleep before their working day started. Rich, who was driving the other hire car, had Clare and the others with him. This team were going to head off to the Peveril Estate later that morning. Lofty was going back to the airport to view and seize as an exhibit any CCTV of the three suspects he could find, whilst Sandy was going to interview the two Williams brothers, who were working that day from the Peveril office in the centre of Winnipeg.

Lofty though was one person who had no intention of sleeping. He planned to head out almost immediately for a run. He had a big triathlon race coming up next month and felt he needed to keep his training schedule going. This schedule had taken a backward step due to the hours he was working on Operation Primrose. Sandy reluctantly agreed to run with him. As they set off, he realised what a strong runner Lofty was. He would undoubtedly beat Lofty in a short sprint, but that was as far as it went. They ran over the wonderful looking Esplanade Riel pedestrian bridge. Sandy loved pedestrian bridges, with the Millennium Bridge over the Thames to or from St Paul's Cathedral in London his favourite. The church this bridge went across to was also a cathedral – the stunning St Boniface Cathedral.

They ran alongside the Red River and through Whittler Park. It was already a hot day and Sandy was starting to fall away from the pace Lofty was setting. He had not been surprised to hear that Lofty had played for the British Police Rugby first team for a number of years. He was relieved when they turned back over a bridge and started to head towards the hotel through Fort Douglas Park and down into The Forks. There were lots of people out exercising and Sandy could see Lofty well on the way ahead of him. Manitoba, in fact all of Canada, was a country where everyone seemed to enjoy being outdoors. This was regardless of the huge difference in the range of temperature, varying between minus twenty-three Celsius and up into the late twenties Celsius in the summer months. In fact, that was how today was already feeling.

Whilst in the shower, Sandy was surprised that he seemed to have the odd mosquito bite. He had come unprepared so vowed to buy some bite spray later in the day. Breakfast in the hotel was excellent and he couldn't resist the bacon smothered in maple syrup. Sitting next to Clare, he was impressed with her plans for the forensic recovery of any relevant items in the room the boys had been staying at the Peveril Estate. Clare, a vegan, was visibly not impressed with what he was eating, but made no comment.

The run, shower and breakfast had put Sandy in a great frame of mind for the day. He had seen he had a number of emails to answer but decided to avoid them until later in the day.

Chapter Thirteen

The Exchange District in downtown Winnipeg was designated as a National Historic site. Some of the warehouses were well over one hundred years old. Sandy was enjoying walking around and looking at the architecture when just off Main Street, he found the Peveril Estate office building.

Waiting for him inside was both Tim and Paul Williams. Tim said, 'Good to see you in person, DCI McFarlane. Sorry we couldn't meet up at the farm. I understand from my wife that your team has already arrived there.'

'Not a problem to me, but I must admit I was keen to see the farm. Maybe I'll get a chance to visit later on during this trip. What is the big deal that you are both working on that is keeping you in Winnipeg over the weekend?'

'It is not us really. This is all down to Arabella. In fact, all of our current success is down to Arabella's vision.'

Paul joined in the conversation, saying, 'Since we

changed our focus to being totally organic and totally for nutritional purposes, the business has gone stratospheric. We have been looking both here and in Norfolk to buy more land to grow the flax, or as you call it, linseed, but what Arabella has us doing now is buying whole crops from other farms, then we process them. We already have a market who will take all that we can send to them.'

'Sounds like a good idea, with obviously lower profit but I presume still with profit,' Sandy said.

'The challenge is making sure the farms are totally organic. We are meeting prospective farm owners this afternoon from here in Manitoba, other areas of Canada and across the border in the United States. Then Arabella is turning up on Tuesday or Wednesday to finalise the deals.'

'Over to my business now please,' Sandy said, taking a sip from the coffee Paul had poured for him. The offices were impressive but at the same time, for a reason he couldn't put his finger on, it had a family friendly feel to it, no doubt Arabella Montague's influence again. 'Is there anything either of you can add to your involvement with the three boys when they were staying on the estate?'

Both the Williams brothers looked at each other and shook their heads.

'Did you see them wearing hoodies at all?'

Paul said, 'Only when I picked them up at the airport. Too hot here to wear them after arrival in Winnipeg.'

'Do you remember who was wearing what?'

'Now you are asking. I am pretty sure George had on an orange hoodie; the other two had on blue ones. They all had the brand Fat Face on the front of them.'

Sandy was a bit shocked that George was wearing the orange hoodie but maybe they swapped clothes at times. He then asked, 'Did you see any signs that any of them were showing symptoms of withdrawal from drugs?'

'They all seemed anxious, until they had gone into town and clearly bought some dope. That relaxed them.'

'Town, is that Portage la Prairie? Dope, is that cannabis or something stronger?'

'Yes, and yes to cannabis.'

'The cottage on Lake Manitoba, how easy is it to gain access to it without them knowing we are coming?'

'Not at all. I am afraid that even from the lake you would soon be seen.'

'Any firearms in the cottage?'

'You don't think they are dangerous, do you? That Dean was a nasty character, but not like that, I wouldn't have thought,' Tim added.

Sandy didn't answer this but instead asked again, 'Is there a firearm in the cottage then?'

'There is only the one rifle. You can get black bears in the area once in a while. We have a firearms licence for the rifle that allows us to have possession of it.'

The access to the gun worried Sandy but he didn't let on why. He spent the next couple of hours taking the brothers' statements, finishing just in time as the Peveril business customers started arriving. He could see how excited the brothers were with this aspect of the business. Arabella had converted them from being fairly large-scale farmers into business leaders in their field.

∞

As Sandy walked away from the building that the Peveril's offices were in, he had an overriding thought that they needed to hurry up with finding the suspects before Arabella arrived. He was worried that she would end up getting herself into trouble by trying to intervene for George and doing things that she shouldn't get involved in.

As Sandy walked through the Exchange District, he had to admit that he was enjoying being in Canada. He felt rather guilty about this as today was the day on which he was meant to be taking Hannah on a guided tour of Ely, so he decided to make a call to her. 'Hi, how is your Saturday going?' he asked, when she answered the phone.

'Wonderful. I have been out to lunch with a charming man. How is your trip going?'

'Great,' Sandy said, and then quickly asked, 'Who have you been out for lunch with?'

'Wouldn't you love to know?' Hannah teased him, then after waiting a few seconds, she said, 'If you must know, it was your grandfather, Judge McFarlane.'

Sandy was sure Hannah must have heard his sigh as

he relaxed on hearing this news. 'I have a serious rival with him, haven't I?' It was in fact Sandy's grandfather who had helped with the matchmaking for the pair of them. 'I hope you didn't call him Judge all the time during lunch?'

'No, I call him John now. He has been helping me with some pointers for my closing speech for the trial on Monday.' Sandy's grandfather helped mentor a few of the younger barristers in the chambers that he belonged to and Hannah was one of them.

'I will try to talk to you before Monday if I can, Hannah, but I have another call coming in on this phone, I must go.' He ended the call to Hannah and then answered the other call that had been making his phone flash, and said, 'Hello, this is Alexander McFarlane.'

'DCI McFarlane, this is the fingerprint department at Derbyshire Police headquarters. Just thought we would update you on the shopping bag you seized from Peveril Farm in Norfolk.'

'Great, what have you found out?'

'Lots of fingerprints on the outside of the bag; they all match George Peveril. Three partial prints on the inside of the bag. One partial is George's and the other two belong to Dean Kelly.'

'Are the partials good enough to present as evidence in court?'

'You may be aware that what we used to have in England was a very high bar of needing sixteen points to match the two fingerprints, but this was scrapped a number of years ago now. Did you know that DCI McFarlane?'

'Yes, I did, so please tell me as we now use your judgement as a fingerprint expert, do we have enough on the partial prints for you to say that both George Peveril and Dean Kelly had their hands on the bag that contained the gun that killed PC Joseph Foster?'

The delay in answering the question Sandy had posed was quite considerable, so much so that Sandy was desperate to fill the silence but waited. 'Obviously for George, it is an easy yes, but for Dean Kelly, I am not so sure… yes, probably. I will have another look and think some more.'

The fingerprint news, although not the perfect answer that he had hoped for, as he already knew there were no fingerprints or DNA on the gun, was, in reality, positive news and Sandy was sure that Joanne O'Connor would have no problem persuading the fingerprint expert on which way to jump. As he walked past the very concrete looking City Hall, Sandy, spontaneously, knowing he had time before the others returned, turned around and went under the tunnel and into the Manitoba museum to have a quick look around.

∞

Lofty Dobson was already waiting in the conference room at the hotel, which they had managed to book for a team meeting, when Sandy entered it. Lofty had obtained the CCTV footage and the three boys were seen laughing and joking as they went through the Arrivals terminal. The other members of the team had returned from the farm and were just changing ready for dinner, which they were going to have straight after the meeting was finished.

When they had all assembled, Sandy, who was pleased to see RCMP Staff Sergeant John Hopkins also in attendance, asked Rich to let them know what they had found out. 'Two of us interviewed the other family members of the two brothers you saw, Sandy. Nothing of any note, I am afraid, other than to say none of them were too keen on any of the boys, including George on this occasion, and they were happy to see them leave. The children are unhappy as they should be going to the cottage next weekend for a week to play on and in the lake, but unfortunately this is currently not happening due to the boys being in residence there at the cottage.'

There were no questions asked, so Sandy asked Clare to outline what she had found from the searches of the room the boys had been staying in. 'We have found a few items that may be key.' Clare had taken photographs and was sharing them on the screen in the room. 'Firstly, three hoodies. These two blue ones and the orange one, I think, match the ones seen on CCTV in Derby city centre on the night Joseph Foster was shot.'

Sandy interjected and said, 'George was wearing the orange one on arrival in Manitoba.'

'We will check when we get back to England for DNA to see who wore it the most.'

'We can do that here for you,' interjected John Hopkins, who seemed desperate to be a part of the Operation Primrose team.

'Sergeant Hopkins, if it is okay with you, we really need to take them back to the UK, so everything is looked at together,' Sandy said. 'We will need you tomorrow though in Portage la Prairie to help us find out what the disturbance the boys engaged in was about.'

This satisfied John, so Clare continued. 'Another key find was this mobile, or cell phone as it is called here. I have sent the serial numbers off to the incident room, but I am sure that it will be the phone whose number was captured in the area at the time of the murder, and the number will be the one that called George Peveril in the middle of the night. We will check it for DNA and fingerprints, including on the SIM card, when we get back to the UK.'

Lofty asked, 'Any thoughts on checking for gunshot residue on any of the clothing?'

'Absolutely. I have put the clothing in exhibit bags for that purpose. Although it does fall off fairly quickly, I am pretty sure the hoodies will show traces if they were in the vicinity of the Smith & Wesson revolver when it was fired.'

There was nothing else to discuss and all of the team from England were feeling the effects of jet lag, so they headed into the restaurant for food, with those of them

who ate meat keen to sample the bison burger
highlighted on the menu.

Chapter Fourteen

When Sandy woke up extremely early the next morning, he found that he was worrying about the investigation. He didn't think he had been during the night, but he must have been as this was the first thing on his mind that morning. The investigation into the murder of Joseph Foster was in reality no longer a whodunnit but a manhunt; in fact, a three-person-suspect manhunt.

Keeping an investigative mindset meant ensuring that the SIO kept an open mind as to what had happened, which must be based on the information they have at that time. As Sandy thought about it more, he was happy that the way the investigation was going at the moment was in the right direction, as it was based on the information they had to date. There was no doubt that George Peveril, Ruben Cousins and Dean Kelly had some serious questions to answer about what had happened to PC Joseph Foster.

After breakfast, where Sandy managed to avoid eating the bacon in maple syrup, Lofty and Sandy took the direct route west, travelling on the Trans-Canada

Highway to Portage la Prairie. Sandy had to admit that this was a boring drive. The Prairie lands were flatlands, a bit like Fenland from his home area, but different as the fields seemed to go on endlessly, not interspersed with dykes, drains and rivers as they were around Ely. Sandy felt that they should have taken time to drive a more scenic route. He had to also keep reminding himself that he was there to work and not as a tourist, so the direct route was, unfortunately, appropriate. He enjoyed talking to Lofty about his sporting achievements. There was no doubt that DC Wayne Dobson was a very talented man.

As they neared the town, they passed Fort la Reine, which was a museum dedicated to collecting, preserving and exhibiting the history of frontier living through the ages in and around Portage la Prairie. Lofty and Sandy both commented on how pretty it was being situated alongside the meandering Assinibone River. They did, however, notice how quiet the small town of Portage la Prairie seemed to be that Sunday morning.

Waiting for them at the RCMP detachment building was Staff Sergeant John Hopkins, whom they had met the previous night, along with two other constables. John was a slightly overweight man, probably the same age as Sandy's parents, so in his early to mid-fifties. He had clearly lost some of his hair through premature balding, but he looked very smart having shaved his whole head to compensate and his uniform looked extremely sharply pressed.

'Why is it so quiet this morning?' Sandy asked.

'A lot of people will have gone to church, but they will soon be coming out, then they will either be going for breakfast or heading home. We are actually getting ready for our annual strawberry festival when the town will be full of tourists,' John said, who it was clear to see was very proud of his town.

'I presume you have a lot of commuters who live here as it only took us just over an hour to get here from Winnipeg?'

'Oh yes! The complexion of the town has changed but it is good to have the investment. We still though have virtually no crime here.'

Sandy was impressed with this statistic, but wondered how the boys had managed to buy drugs, so asked, 'I presume you can still buy drugs here though? Have you managed to find the report of the incident George and the others were involved in?'

'No record at all. I got one of the other officers here in the detachment to check for me as well. Yes, you can buy drugs here, as you can anywhere in the world, DCI McFarlane.'

Sandy realised that he needed to be careful not to upset Portage la Prairie's number one fan. They were waiting for Rich and the rest of the team to arrive and Sandy presumed that they had taken a more scenic route. The plan was to split up into three teams with each having an RCMP officer with them, then they would just ask around to find out if anyone knew anything about the boys' visit to the town.

When Rich arrived, he had clearly taken a different route to Sandy as he mentioned having seen the world's largest Coca Cola can, a statue, on the way into the town, but this was on the north-west side of the town rather than the northeast, which was the direction they should have travelled in from.

∞

Rich told Sandy that he had received an email that morning from the incident room telling him that the cigarette stubs he had brought in had the DNA on each stub respectively of Dean Kelly and Ruben Cousins. Good work, Arabella, Sandy thought.

Clare, Sandy and John Hopkins visited a number of the restaurants and diners, asking around to see if anyone had come across the three English boys when they had been into town a few days earlier. They were having no luck and hoped the others were finding out more than they were. They were probably talking to the wrong group of people anyway. Sandy enjoyed the feel of the town and thought it must be a pleasant place to live.

Everyone seemed to know John Hopkins and he was clearly popular with everyone they met. Sandy asked him about the First Nations people they were coming across. 'What are the main First Nations tribes you have in and around this town?'

'The most populous is the Dakota Ojibway. They used to have their own police service, but they have now transitioned to become part of the Manitoba First Nations Police. I did contact them, but they had no information that was any help.'

'How many RCMP officers do you have in Portage la Prairie?'

'We have access to over a thousand police officers,' John said, who was clearly not going to answer this question directly. 'Our headquarters is in Winnipeg and I can call for help and support from them and the whole western district detachment.' As well as being a proud Portage la Prairie man, he was also a very proud RCMP officer. In this respect, Sandy felt John reminded him of his own Grandad Tom, who still spoke like this when talking about the Cambridgeshire Constabulary.

'How long have you been a police officer for, John?' Clare asked.

'Thirty-four years, man and boy and all stationed here in this detachment.' One of his officers called up and asked to meet up with them in a side street just off Saskatchewan Avenue.

On arriving there, they found Lofty and one of the RCMP constables talking to a group of four young men. John Hopkins went up to the group and spoke to one of them, who was probably the leader. 'Right, Tony, tell us what happened with the English boys?'

The youth, wearing black jeans and a white t-shirt, didn't want to talk, but seemed to respect John.

'Sergeant Hopkins, there was no trouble and not sure why your officer and this very tall, loud Englishman is making it seem like there was.' As he said this, Lofty went as if to square up to the youth. Lofty was definitely not used to being talked badly about. Sandy quickly put his hand on his arm and nodded at him that it was all in hand.

John Hopkins said, 'You are not in any trouble, but if they threatened you, we need you to make a statement so that we can detain them and then send them out of the country with these nice officers.'

'We are not making any statements. We are not grasses!'

'Tell us what happened then, without giving us a statement at the moment,' Sandy asked, trying to get something that would assist them.

'No statements. They thought we had drugs for sale.' Tony grinned as if to say we did, but we are not telling you, the police, about it. 'Of course, we hadn't and a fight was about to start when one of them pulled them away and said they would try somewhere else to buy them.'

'Did they threaten you?'

One of the other boys said, 'One of them threatened to blow our heads off if we didn't sell them any drugs. We are not making statements.' The boys then walked off. Although Lofty was keen to grab all of them by the scruff of the neck and pull them back, there was no point in stopping them from walking away as they could see

134

they would get nothing else from them.

Although they had now found the underlying cause of what had happened in the town, this didn't help them with having an offence in Canada to arrest them for. The small amount of cannabis found in their room in the Peveril Estate was negligible and not worth the bother.

∞

There was no point in the others staying in the town, so they headed off back to Winnipeg. The plan was to leave early the next morning for the cottage on Lake Manitoba. Lofty, Rich and Sandy had remained behind, sitting in an office drinking coffee with John Hopkins, who said, 'I am sorry, guys. I had hoped to have something to detain them all for you, but we have nothing.'

The need to help was huge in John and they were all so grateful for him being so supportive. Sandy said, 'Have you had any more updates from Constable Gary Hughes on his enquiries at Laurentia Beach?'

'No luck, I am afraid. He has visited twice this weekend. He is sure they are in the house but because he has no right of entry, he left. One of the neighbours is there this weekend and told Gary that he has seen all three boys outside on the grass that leads to the beach and the lake from the cottage. The neighbours thought that they didn't look very well at all.'

'Do you think it might be that they are showing the

effects of not being able to have drugs?' Rich asked.

'I don't think so as they were all only taking cannabis on a regular basis, which doesn't normally cause this sort of reaction,' Lofty answered.

'Anyway, Constable Hughes is going to go back in the morning to see if he can catch them out. What I want to know is, what we are going to use to detain them for you so you can extradite them back to the UK, as at the moment I have no local offence that I can detain them for to buy us some time.'

'Let me make some enquiries in relation to how we can detain them and I will hopefully have an answer in the morning for when we head up to the cottage. I believe you are going to meet us there, aren't you, Sergeant Hopkins?' Sandy asked.

'Yes, let's talk in the morning and meet together in St Laurent and we can go together from there.'

Lofty drove the three of them back to Winnipeg, taking a different route this time away from the Trans-Canada Highway. Sandy was busy sending an email to DCI Phil Harris asking for help and advice in relation to extradition and international arrest warrants. He also copied in Detective Superintendent Jane Watson to ensure she was kept in the loop. Rich, at the same time, was sending a similar message to Joanne O'Connor asking for a decision and direction on the next course of action. They were busy looking down at their phones and were missing the beautiful countryside until Lofty shouted for them to look at some whitetail deer as they went past a wooded area. This made Sandy put his phone back in his pocket and focus on the scenery for the rest of the journey.

Later that evening, Lofty, Clare and Sandy headed out walking together to see a bit more of Winnipeg. Sandy had seen that he had already received a reply from Jane and also Phil, which on the face of it was a complicated description of what was required in relation to getting the three suspects detained. However, in essence, the bit that Sandy understood was that Canada was one of the countries that had a mutual agreement with the UK. Phil had to get Interpol involved and he needed to speak to Detective Superintendent O'Connor, but the most important point in all of the message, in Sandy's view, was that Phil said he would get it sorted tomorrow. Phil Harris was, in Sandy's eyes, a top detective.

They walked in a different direction from the way that Lofty and Sandy had run the previous morning. They followed the route that Sandy had taken to the Peveril Estate office in the Exchange District, then strolled along the Assiniboine Riverwalk and into the gardens, where they could see the very impressive Manitoba Legislative Building, which had been finished in 1920 and was built in a neoclassical style. The gold-covered bronze statue on the top of the building's cupola was extremely impressive and was called Golden Boy.

Eating food, by this time, was what the three of them really wanted to do. They went into a nearby restaurant, only to find just about everything on the menu was something that involved bison, which was not suitable for Clare. However, another restaurant nearby had a good selection of plant-based food as well as the bison burgers, which Lofty and Sandy ordered for the second night in a row.

Chapter Fifteen

At last, he was beginning to sleep a little bit later, Sandy thought, as he looked at his travel alarm clock that was showing five a.m. He picked his phone up, realising straight away what a bad habit he had got into, as looking at his phone was the first thing he did each morning, even before he seemed to be fully awake. This is a habit I must break, he thought to himself. He did though have a good reason this morning as he wanted to send Hannah a good luck message, which he promptly did.

After he had made himself a cup of tea, he saw she had already replied: "I was just about to put my phone off and go into court, so pleased I hadn't. Thank you. I am really nervous xxx." Sandy liked the look of those kisses and he genuinely felt nervous for Hannah as well. He knew though that she would be excellent. His Grandpa John had told him that Hannah had the potential to be an outstanding barrister.

Rich had forwarded him a message during the night from Joanne O'Connor. What was he doing not sleeping and looking at his phone in the night? This was an epidemic that was not healthy. The message from Joanne though had made Sandy smile: "Now you listen to me, Rishabh Singh. If you and Alexander McFarlane do not get your hands on the suspects and take them into custody, do not for one second, either of you, imagine you will be working one minute longer on Operation Primrose. In fact, I may hunt you both down myself and do you both a serious injury. Have I made myself quite clear!"

Although he was smiling, Sandy knew that Joanne O'Connor meant every word of it. This had the potential of him setting a world record for the least amount of time for being a deputy SIO on a murder enquiry. Sandy's phone rang and he saw it was Phil Harris calling. It was only just five thirty a.m. in Winnipeg, but it was now past eleven a.m. in London.

'Good morning, Sandy, how is life in Canada? Just to keep you updated, my friend, I have spoken to Detective Superintendent O'Connor this morning. She has a meeting organised with senior members of her local CPS at two p.m. this afternoon to get their agreement in relation to any proposed charges.'

'I thought she had already discussed this with them on Friday afternoon?' Sandy said.

'The CPS want a file with all of the evidence in it that Operation Primrose currently has. Joanne was moaning that she had made a mistake by sending both her deputy SIOs to Canada as she would have got one of them to put the evidence file together!' Both Sandy and Phil laughed at the thought of the poor boss of the enquiry having to put a file together. 'The National Crime Agency have no problem if that file is shared with them. They will be able to put out through Interpol a red notice for them being wanted, or, if CPS decide a charge is appropriate, to go for an arrest warrant and work with the Canadian law enforcement agencies directly to apprehend and extradite back to the UK. This is such exciting work, don't you think, Sandy?'

'I absolutely agree, but only if we can get hold of the three suspects. They were seen at the cottage only a day or so ago, so we know where they are. I will call you later, Phil, after I have got the team to send you a copy of the evidence file and have got to the cottage.'

He sent Rich and Lofty a message asking them to meet him as soon as possible in the restaurant for breakfast. They needed to go through the evidence they thought they would send to Joanne O'Connor to assist her file preparation. He got dressed quickly and put together a few things in his backpack, so he was ready to head off with the other two straight after they had finished breakfast. Today had the potential to be an incredible day for progress in the investigation into the murder of Joseph Foster.

∞

When Sandy walked into the restaurant, he saw that

Rich and Lofty were already there. They both had their plates piled high with the contents of the breakfast buffet. As Sandy walked by to get his own food, Rich said, 'Did you see that we have upset the headmistress?'

They all laughed, and Sandy said, 'That was nothing compared to the tongue-lashing Mrs O'Connor gave me last Thursday. I can tell you! My knees still wobble thinking about it!'

Lofty interjected after finishing a mouthful of his food. 'She is though, without doubt, the best SIO we have got and if it were one of my loved ones who had been murdered, I would want her leading the investigation.' Rich nodded in agreement; his mouth too full of food to talk.

Sandy said, 'She is also right that if we are not able to detain our three suspects, that would be a monumental failure on our part.'

With a similar loaded plateful of food and large cup of coffee, Sandy returned to the table to join them both. Rich had got out his laptop and had already begun an email to Joanne O'Connor.

'Let's help Joanne out then by giving her some facts as we know them. Do either of you know the 5WH principle to use in investigations?' Sandy asked them. Rich nodded and Lofty shook his head, neither wanting to speak with their mouths full again.

'My Grandad Tom calls them Kipling's friends. Basically, they are used to help with decision-making by answering or asking questions based on five headings: what, why, when, where, who and how, hence 5WH – five Ws and one H. Shall we just concentrate on the what we know bit of it?'

'Okay, you talk, and I will type,' Rich said.

'What we know is that Joseph Foster was murdered using a Smith & Wesson revolver. What we know is that a Smith & Wesson revolver has been recovered from Peveril Farm in Norfolk and NABIS say this is almost certainly the weapon used. What we know is that this revolver was placed there at the farm by George Peveril as his aunty saw him carrying the bag that the revolver was in. What we know is that it was most probably stolen by George from Peveril Hall.'

'That is a probably, not what we definitely know. I am not sure we should say that yet,' Rich said.

'OK, but hopefully that might have been firmed up by now with National Heritage who manage Peveril Hall. What we do know is that on the bag the gun was found in are the fingerprints of George Peveril and Dean Kelly. What we do know is that there are numerous sightings of two youths matching the description of Kelly and Cousins in the area at the time. What we do know is that as well as Joseph's phone, there was only one other number in the area at the time of his murder. Lofty, could you call one of the DMIs working on Operation Primrose to see if they have been able to identify the number of the phone that was recovered from Peveril Estate?'

'Leave it with me, Sandy. I will do it now,' Lofty

said, as he moved away to make his phone call. Clare arrived and took her place joining them at the breakfast table.

'What we know is that we have recovered hoodies similar to the ones seen on the two youths in Derby city centre. Anything else you can think of at the moment, Rich?'

'I would say we can confirm the association linking the three of them together.'

Before he could finish speaking, Lofty shouted 'Yes!' They all looked around at him as did the other couple of diners in the restaurant. 'The number for that phone is confirmed as the one that was in the area at the time of the murder.'

'Excellent,' Sandy said, who was as equally excited as Lofty. 'Clare, I think we could do with getting the phone and the other exhibits, like the hoodies, back to England as soon as possible. Can I get you to fly back this afternoon?'

Clare was not too keen on this idea and said, 'I see your point, and it is the right decision to get them all forensically examined straight away, but I would like to see this through and be able to examine the cottage where the boys are staying. Wouldn't it be better if the Operation Primrose CSI who is with us did this?'

Rich interjected before Sandy could answer. 'Yes, I agree with Clare. I will send back the Derbyshire CSI as that makes good sense. I have added into the email to Joanne the phone information and will send this email now before time runs out for her meeting with CPS.'

'Rich, please can you also copy into the email DCI Phil Harris? Clare, we are going to head off to the cottage soon. Can you stay here and organise all of the exhibits we have so far for sending back to England. I will call you later once we have gained control of the boys and access to the cottage, they are staying in.' Sandy could see that Clare was thrilled that her Canadian adventure was continuing. The phone evidence that they now had had the potential to be pretty compelling. The next challenge was for the analysts and team back in England to see if they could connect the suspects to that phone.

Chapter Sixteen

As they drove out of Winnipeg, they could see streams of traffic coming in the opposite direction heading back towards the city. It appeared clear to them that this was not only the usual commuter traffic but must also be weekenders heading home to the city from their cottages that they owned on one of the numerous lakes that there are in Manitoba. The weekenders' cars were jam packed with stuff, including bikes and kayaks secured to car racks. They had eked out every last moment of their weekends, getting home at the last-minute ready for the working week ahead.

Lofty was driving with Rich in the front seat and Sandy in the rear. Sandy had received a text message from Hannah. Her closing speech had gone well and the defence closing speech had made her want to jump up several times and tell them they were painting the wrong impression to the jury. The defence had said there were no witnesses, but the victim was an eyewitness, Hannah said. Welcome to the police world, Sandy thought, but was so pleased at how passionate Hannah was for getting justice for her victim.

Rich said, 'I have just seen an email saying that the tyre tracks found at the scene where the stolen car was burnt out match George's Fiesta. In particular, one of the tyres is an excellent match as it has a lot of wear and tear with a distinctive cut to the rubber on it. The burner phone hasn't been picked up though at the location where the car was burnt out, probably due to it either being switched off or the lack of phone masts in the area as it is quite rural.'

'Which phone are they calling the burner phone? I presume it is the one we have recovered here in Canada which is the phone whose signal is being picked up in Lock-Up-Yard at the key time of the murder. Is that right?' Sandy asked.

'Yes, absolutely.'

The journey to the lake only took about an hour and as they passed into a lakeside town, they saw a large, impressive statue of what looked like a Viking. A number of signs told them the town they were in was called Gimli. None of them had a map with them and the hire car didn't have a sat nav, so it was safe to say that they were lost. They went down to the lakeshore and saw a pretty harbour and marina. They had also passed some beautiful beaches on the lakeshore itself. The lake looked like a massive expanse of water that was lying out before them. This was more like a huge inland sea than the lakes that Sandy knew from home in England.

'Lofty, I am not sure where we are or how we can get to St Laurent from here. It can't be too far away though. Can you please pull over and we can ask that couple?' Sandy said, pointing to an elderly couple on the kerbside only a few metres ahead of them.

Lofty pressed the button for his electric window to go down and said to the couple, 'Excuse me, could you tell me how to get to St Laurent, please?' The couple looked at each other, giving the impression they were quite bemused by this question. 'Why do you want to go there? Far better here. This is a great place for fishing and Gimli is the Icelandic heritage centre of Manitoba.'

'As much as we would love to sample the delights of your town, we urgently need to get to St Laurent,' Lofty said a little bit more loudly.

'It is now our adopted town and yes, it is a lovely place to live. We retired here three years ago from Winnipeg and don't regret it for one moment, do we?' The woman said to both Lofty but also to her husband.

Sandy, who was getting impatient as he knew by now, they needed to be in St Laurent, where they had arranged to meet Sergeant Hopkins, said, 'I am sorry to hurry you, but you see we are in a bit of a rush. Do you know how we can get there, please?'

The woman continued. 'You are English, aren't you? You have such a lovely accent. We have been to London a couple of times. What an incredibly beautiful city it is, with all that history.'

'Lofty, we had better ask someone else. Thank you,'

Sandy said to both Lofty and the couple. The man then said, 'We know where it is. I am sorry you are in such a hurry. However, you are totally in the wrong place as St Laurent is on Lake Manitoba and we are here on the southern shore of Lake Winnipeg.'

The three men in the car all looked at each other. More to the point, Lofty and Rich looked straight at Sandy, who said, 'I know St Laurent is on Lake Manitoba.'

'You didn't tell me though, did you? I just presumed it was Lake Winnipeg and whilst we have been driving here, all of the signposts that we passed mentioned Lake Winnipeg, so why didn't you say we were going in the wrong direction?' Lofty huffed very loudly. He then asked and received from the man some detailed instruction on how to get to St Laurent from where they were. It looked like it was a trip across country on much smaller side roads and the elderly couple estimated it could take up to two hours to get there.

The tension that had built up as a result of this mistake in the car was quickly dissolved by Rich, who started laughing. 'Whatever happens, don't say anything to Mrs O'Connor about this or we will be eaten alive by her. I can imagine the telling off now!' They all laughed at this and the friendly equilibrium they had together returned as quickly as it had left them. Sandy, however, was mortified with himself that he had failed to brief Lofty appropriately, and because he had been too busy looking down at his phone, he had also failed to notice the signs. Even worse, here he was in a beautiful country and he was focussed on a tiny screen in his hands. He promptly put his phone away into his pocket.

∞

Lofty drove the car very quickly with great skill and dexterity. Sandy said, 'Were you a traffic officer before you became a detective by any chance?'

'Yes, for almost fifteen years. I am a class one driver,' he proudly said.

Sandy, who had spent a lot of his police service to date stationed in the West End of London, had hardly ever driven a police car and was marvelling at the skill of Lofty as he overtook any cars that were getting in their way and were slowing them down.

'A traffic officer until we saved him and he saw the light. Don't you think, Lofty?' Rich said, laughing in the front of the car.

'I am surprised you weren't a traffic patrol officer, Sandy, with you owning a Morgan sports car. You must like a bit of speed,' Lofty said, trying to deflect the conversation from himself.

'Impressive, what colour is your car then?' Rich asked.

Before Sandy could reply, Lofty said, 'Red. You should have seen his face when his grandad drove off in it the other day.'

'I knew it, and I bet you went to Oxford, didn't you? You really are the new Morse,' Rich said, laughing.

Sandy muttered under his breath, 'It was St John's College, Cambridge, actually.' But he had found the whole conversation very pleasant and thoroughly enjoyed the friendly banter.

Sandy's vow to not look at his phone lasted no longer than ten minutes as he had an incoming call. It was from Staff Sergeant John Hopkins. Sandy didn't quite know what to say to him as he didn't want to be thought of as having made a mistake. Sandy need not have worried though because as soon as he answered the phone, John said, 'We have got them, DCI McFarlane. We have got the critters.'

Sandy's heart rose as a result of hearing this news. Unfortunately, the phone signal was appalling and he lost John before he could reply, or John could say anything else. 'They have got them!' Sandy shouted to the other two. They both cheered and Lofty banged his hand hard down on the steering wheel. Sandy kept looking at his phone, waiting for a signal to call John back, but it wasn't happening.

Suddenly, the phone signal must have connected and the phone rang again. 'What is happening, son? I must have tried twenty times to get you.'

'Bad phone signal out here. Where are they detained and did they come quietly?'

'We haven't detained them. I didn't say that, did I? Surely, I didn't say that! But we now have an offence to detain them and hold them for you.'

'But I thought you had them in custody,' a bitterly disappointed Sandy said. Lofty and Rich had picked up on the conversation and Sandy could see their disappointment as well, with both of their shoulders dropping down dejectedly.

'Sorry about that. However, when Constable Hughes approached the front door this morning, he was met with the barrel of a rifle pointing at him and one of the youths told him to get off of the property, if not he would blow his brains out.'

'I presume he got off of the property quickly. Did he recognise who it was that said this and was pointing the gun at him?'

'No, it was pointing out of the window at him. He thinks it was a rifle-type weapon. He then took up position to see if anyone came out of the rear of the house.'

'Not sure how long before we are with you, but we will get to you as soon as possible.' Lofty was driving at extreme speed and at this rate, they would be in St Laurent in no time. 'What is happening now, Sergeant?'

'I am in St Laurent with the staff sergeant who is in charge of the RCMP detachment for this area and his inspector is on route to us. They now have two constables at the rear of next door's cottage, one of which is Constable Hughes, and two near the front on Laurentia Beach Road. They have set up a cordon either side and the same on the beach side, so no one can go by the cottage, front or back. We have specialist firearms teams with their inspector coming from Winnipeg and two negotiators also coming from Winnipeg.'

Sandy whistled as a full-scale major police operation was now in progress to arrest their three suspects. He sincerely hoped there would be no casualties and a gun fight could be avoided.

The signal had now gone again, which was a good thing as Sandy could concentrate on Lofty, who was driving the car like it was a bullet. Sandy held onto the handle by his door but that didn't stop him from being thrown about in the back of the car. There were times on the bumpy, uneven road when he thought that they might take off. Rich was not enjoying the ride and kept telling Lofty that it was better to arrive in one piece rather than not at all. This appeal fell on deaf ears as the car seemed to be getting faster and faster. Sandy could almost see the whites of Lofty's knuckles because he was gripping the steering wheel so tightly.

Then, ahead of them, from almost nowhere, a large black Ford truck turned off from a side road onto the road in front of them. The truck driver was oblivious to their presence on the road; he was probably so used to not seeing too many other road users. Lofty slammed on his brakes, causing the car to swerve violently and start to zig-zag across the road. Sandy was convinced that at any moment they were about to roll over. Lofty realised he wasn't going to be able to stop in time before hitting the Ford truck in front. He pulled down hard on the steering wheel whilst also applying the handbrake at the same time, and the car completed a three-hundred-and-sixty-degree turn before coming abruptly to a halt.

They all got out of the car as it seemed the most sensible thing to do. Unbelievably, they had survived without injury and there was no damage to the car. Lofty had performed an incredible manoeuvre, which now, having survived the experience, decided the whole thing had been a lot of fun and he told Sandy and Rich, he had enjoyed it.

This was definitely not what Rich thought and he insisted that the rest of the journey was a lot more sedate. When they arrived in St Laurent, Lofty proudly told them the journey had taken them only one hour and five minutes, a feat of which he was extremely proud.

Chapter Seventeen

On arrival in St Laurent, they were surprised to see that there was no centre to the town as such, but the RCMP police vehicles were easy to spot, as they were parked all along the main road. When the Peveril family had told Sandy their cottage was on Lake Manitoba, he had not imagined that the lake would be so huge, but then again it was the third largest in the province. Lofty, Rich and Sandy had been greatly impressed with both of the lakes that they had seen that morning.

They went with John Hopkins and got themselves a coffee. They reflected that the scenery they had seen earlier that morning had been well worth getting lost for. The Interlake region between Lakes Winnipeg and Manitoba was also known as part of the Manitoba lowlands. It was definitely something they were glad they hadn't missed, although it would have been better to experience it at a much slower speed than they had.

Rich, who found he had a signal for his phone, felt he needed to update Detective Superintendent O'Connor on the situation they now found themselves in at Laurentia Beach. Sandy said, 'Don't mention us getting lost by going to the wrong lake or that we nearly got ourselves killed in a car crash.'

'Speak for yourself. I didn't get us lost, that was you, and I didn't almost crash the car, that was Lofty, so I am in the clear!' Rich said, laughing.

The staff sergeant that covered the local detachment looked the exact opposite to John Hopkins. He had on a t-shirt, not a smartly pressed shirt like John; he had scruffy, long brown, greying hair; and his whole manner gave the impression of someone very laissez-faire. John, on the other hand, was as sharp as he looked. As a result of this, the local sergeant let John lead the briefing to the English team. An inspector was on route to take charge anyway, so why worry, was the impression he was giving to all of them.

'The plan, I have been told by the inspector, is that we are going to try and negotiate with the boys to surrender. We will use this location, where we are now in St Laurent, as our main control point, and we have commandeered the next-door cottage's bunkie, which is on the lakeshore as our forward point. If the negotiation fails, we will try and carry out a rapid assault firearms operation at first light tomorrow morning. In order to help us plan the operation, we could do with a description of what the inside of the cottage looks like. The municipal headquarters here have no plans of the old cottages like this one.'

'I should be able to get a description,' Sandy said,

thinking he could make a call to either the Williams brothers or Arabella. 'Leave it with me. I will make a couple of calls now.'

The first-person Sandy called was Tim Williams. 'Hi, Tim, are you able to describe for me the layout of the floor plan for the cottage?'

'Of course, I have been there hundreds of times. On entering from Laurentia Beach Road, you go into a hallway. To your right is a kitchen, which is open plan. That goes down into a large living area that faces the grass, which goes down to the beach and the lake itself. There is a bedroom off this large open-plan living space. There are two further bedrooms in the basement.'

'Have you got any photos to help us see it better?'

'I have, but not here with me in Winnipeg, but my wife is very good at drawing, so I will get her to draw you a plan now and will email it to you. Paul has just gone to the airport to collect Arabella, so you might get to meet up with her later.'

'Whatever happens, please make sure Arabella does not come up to the cottage. It would be very unhelpful to what we are trying to do here.' Sandy was worried for Arabella's safety as he knew she would not sit quietly if she came up to Laurentia Beach. 'Thank your wife in advance from me for the plan. I will talk to you later.'

The firearms inspector, Alan Wise, had arrived. He was the embodiment of a military commander without being in the military, because he was a police officer. He was dressed totally in black and he had so much kit on that Sandy was shocked he could stand up. He was also carrying a semi-automatic rifle and had a handgun in a holster on his belt. He told Sandy he had dispatched two snipers to the front and rear of the cottage. His team would start rehearsing their rapid entry later that afternoon and evening. He thanked Sandy for the plan he was getting as that would help greatly. The negotiators had still not arrived, but Alan Wise was very dismissive of any success that they might have. Sandy, on the other hand, had seen good results by negotiators in his police career.

Rich returned to the group. 'CPS want a day to think about the next steps. They kept asking Joanne who had shot the PC. Unless we get confessions, I am not sure that we will ever know. Joanne had a message for us: we must make sure that one of the boys survives and does not get shot as she wants a trial and justice to take place,' Rich said.

Sandy gestured towards Inspector Alan Wise and shook his head, not convinced that if the rapid assault firearms operation took place, anyone would survive.

∞

The RCMP and the chief executive for the municipality of St Laurent, who they found out was called the reeve, for the area, were incredibly organised and refreshments had arrived, which the three detectives hungrily took their share of. John Hopkins said, 'I am sorry but there is only space for two of you at the bunkie down at the cottage.'

'I will stay here and wait for Clare,' Sandy said. He had rung Clare and she was on her way to them, with the other Operation Primrose detective. 'What is a bunkie?'

'It is really a small lodge, but in this instance, it is a boat house and not so small. OK, I will take the other two of you down there now. The two negotiators have arrived. They are called Milly and Simon so we can head down there with them.'

Rich said, 'Sandy, you should go. Lofty and I will take it in turns.' He looked straight at Sandy and said, 'After all of your hard work, you shouldn't miss out on the excitement of seeing the three of them being taken into custody.'

Rich, John and Sandy set off down to the cottage and the forward point of the next-door neighbour's bunkie. The cottages were, in reality, large houses, and anybody would be more than happy with these as first homes, let alone second and in some cases hardly used homes. The bunkie was as described – really quite large and actually sat on the grass just off the beach at the edge of the lake. The excitement and anticipation of everyone there was incredible, so much so that Sandy felt as though he could cut it with a knife.

The negotiators were both in their mid- to late thirties, dressed in matching black t-shirts that had the words "negotiator" printed across the back of them.

'That is so the firearms people know not to shoot them,' Rich said, laughing.

The negotiators were apparently very experienced; both of them had been negotiating for over five years. Sandy and Rich briefed them on what they knew about each of the three boys and that George was definitely the weak link. Constable Gary Hughes told them he thought they were now probably low on food as they hadn't been to the shop for over three days. Gary was showing no signs of any trauma from having a gun pointed at him, and it turned out there was probably no chance of him being shot due to the position of the gun and his distance from it.

The negotiators went forward into the next-door garden to talk to the boys. Sandy looked at Peveril Cottage. It was large, but maybe not as large as one or two of the others they had seen on the way. It had an incredible outlook down to the lake, with glass doors all along its frontage, giving some beautiful views. What a wonderful place, thought Sandy. Looking down onto the lake itself, there was a small motorboat pulled up on the grass before the sand that had fishing rods laying inside. The boys might have caught some fish, so maybe they did have something to eat, he thought.

Rich said, as they both watched the negotiators slowly move forward, 'I didn't mention earlier that Joanne told me she has had a facial recognition expert look at the pictures of the two men in their hoodies in Derby city centre. He is unable to say who it is, although he thinks it is highly likely the images are of Cousins and Kelly. The speed camera photos though of the stolen car heading out of Derby are, in his opinion, conclusively of Cousins and Kelly.' In Sandy's mind the investigation was inching forward nicely and a real picture of what happened that fatal night was emerging.

'My name is Milly, and my friend's name is Simon,' the negotiator shouted out towards the house. This shout would have been clearly heard in the cottage. 'We are here to help you and see if there is anything you need. Do you want us to get you any food?'

'Get off the property now,' a loud voice shouted out from inside the cottage.

Due to the shutters being closed across the whole of the front of the cottage, it was impossible to see inside, but then a different voice shouted out from the cottage, 'Yes please, and something to drink.' Was that George? Sandy wondered.

'OK, we will organise that now,' Milly said. 'What we do want you to do is talk to us about how we can resolve this situation and get you all to somewhere safe.'

'Get us the food first. We are starving,' another voice added. 'And get us some medicine; we have the flu.'

'I can get a doctor to come in and examine you, that will be better.'

'No one is coming in here. I warn you I have a gun if anyone tries.'

The negotiators returned to the bunkie. Food was being brought from St Laurent for the three boys with

161

some sodas. There was a technical officer at the main control point in St Laurent who was apparently fitting a microscopic listening device to the bottom of the food packaging, so this might take a little bit longer than expected. Milly and Simon thought this early engagement was extremely positive. They didn't know about any medicine, so asked for some non-prescription medication. 'It might be withdrawal from drugs,' Rich suggested to the negotiators, who decided to see if someone could get them advice on this.

A shout came from the cottage: 'Get us some cigarettes as well.'

This seemed positive engagement, but Sandy thought when you negotiated, you gave something and received something in return, which wasn't happening here as they seemed to be doing all of the giving. The negotiators were happy that a rapport had already started and once the boys had their physical needs satisfied with food, drink, medication and a smoke, it would be straightforward. Sandy did not think so, although he hoped he was wrong, but these boys had gone as far as to murder a policeman, so they were not going to just come quietly.

Chapter Eighteen

The food seemed to be taking a long time to organise, but because there were no voices from the cottage asking where it was, this didn't seem to be a problem. Sandy felt his initial excited anticipation had abated greatly due to the delay and inactivity. As he had no phone signal, he was unable to make any calls, send messages or deal with emails, which he was getting frustrated about.

The beautiful scenery he was looking at down by the lakeside helped to pass the time, as did talking to Rich, who told him that his father had spent thirty-five years as an engineer at the large Rolls Royce factory in Derby and was just about to retire. Rich was rightly ambitious and he couldn't understand why Sandy, who was a DCI with only nine years' police service, didn't equally want, like he did, to reach the higher echelons of the police service. Sandy was happy to be the detective he currently was.

The time had already moved round to the early evening before the food arrived. Simon took it forward to the cottage. The firearm officers carrying out the role of snipers went up to a state of hyper alert and Simon, slowly and carefully, walked up and placed the food in bags outside one of the large, glazed patio doors. He walked backwards, shouting, 'Your food, medication and cigarettes are here.'

The doors opened and out stepped one of the boys, who Sandy recognised from his photograph as Ruben Cousins. He had on grey-coloured baggy bottoms and a long-sleeved t-shirt. He looked straight at Simon and made a small nodding motion then disappeared with the food back inside. The listening device was working as one of them, presumably Ruben, was heard on it. 'Food is here! We have burgers, fries and coke. Excellent.' All they then heard on the listening device for the next ten minutes or so was the boys chomping on the food, all of them clearly enjoying and relishing the long-awaited meal.

Maybe the negotiators were right, that by providing one of life's necessities such as food, you get a chance to intervene. Sandy remembered this from one of his psychology courses at school. If he remembered rightly, it was called Maslow's hierarchy of needs. The more he thought about it, he realised that to be a good negotiator you needed to understand human psychology.

One of the boys said, 'What are we going to do? Shouldn't we just give ourselves up?'

One of the others said, 'Absolutely no way, they will just throw us in jail here.'

Another one, or maybe the first one who had been talking, then said, 'Aren't we better going back to England and just facing the music? My lawyer will get me off.'

The door opened slightly, and a voice shouted, 'You, the woman who spoke to us earlier. Where are you? We want a private jet to take us back to England. We are not coming out until that happens.' The door shut again.

Milly said to them, 'We will see what we can do. A private jet is probably not going to happen, but a plane to England from Winnipeg could be something on which we could work.'

The listening device didn't seem to pick up anything after this. It had clearly been left in the kitchen, most probably in the bottom of a bin, and the boys were now far away from it right at the front of the cottage facing out to the lake.

Rich said, 'The person making a note of the conversation on the log at the main control point might have more success than us as they can turn up the sound; our repeater speaker here does not have that facility. A big problem we have is we don't know which one of them is talking, as none of us can recognise the voices.'

Sandy thought that someone from the Williams family could possibly do this for them, but they hadn't had that much contact with Cousins or Kelly to clearly tell them apart. Arabella would obviously know George's voice but had not met the others. This might end up being a problem if any one of them admitted anything.

Sandy's phone must have had a signal for a short while as he had received a message from Arabella asking: 'What is going on? Paul is telling me to keep clear of the cottage.' Sandy sent a response telling her to keep away as they hoped to detain all three of the boys and needed her to not get involved as this would complicate things. He was not sure the message had been sent as he didn't know if he had a signal at the time or after pressing the send button.

∞

The listening device was now clearly in the wrong place and discussions were being held by the RCMP officers about placing a bigger and more sensitive one right by the glass doors, where the boys clearly were spending almost all of their time. Molly had tried to get them to accept a mobile phone to stop them having to shout to each other, but they were not accepting this, which was a shame as the phone had a camera within it to see what was going on and another listening device fitted to it.

The glass doors opened and out stepped George Peveril. He was lighting up a cigarette. Sandy was mesmerised looking at him; he was now seeing George, at last, in person. He was actually looking at George Peveril the person who had consumed Sandy's thoughts, conversations and actions for over two weeks now. George looked much younger than his eighteen years and was of a slighter build than Sandy had envisaged from having just seen him in photographs. George was wearing blue sports shorts and a yellow Norwich City football club top. It took every ounce of Sandy's will power to not run over and grab George and bring him back to the bunkie and to safety.

George shouted, 'Can someone get me some cannabis, or do you call it marijuana, hash, dope or something like that. Whatever you call it, I desperately need it now?'

Milly shouted back, 'Not sure we can do that, as it would be us supplying drugs. I will see what I can sort out for some sort of substitute though.' George laughed and then went back inside. Sandy had now seen George alive. He had completed the key action that he had set for himself at the very start of his missing from home investigation. So, George could no longer be classified as a missing person.

There was a change in the firearms tactics planned after seeing two of the boys now freely coming out of the premises. The new order from the firearms inspector was that as soon as all three of them were outside together, and had no weapon with them, the officers were all to use non-lethal force, which Sandy presumed was using something like a taser, to incapacitate them.

Rich and Lofty had exchanged places. Lofty had told him that the firearms assault intervention team had been rehearsing and practising manoeuvres. They now had the plan that the Williams family had supplied, and they were practising so much that he was surprised they weren't now exhausted. The plan still stood that at first light, they would enter the premises. They looked out over the lake and agreed how beautiful it was. Lofty said he would have loved to swim in the lake – what great practice that would be as part of his triathlon training. The water was probably cold, and he would need to wear a dry suit. They had though seen bathers, both in this lake and Lake Winnipeg, without suits on. The lake did freeze over in winter. Manitoba was a place, depending on what time of year you visited, where you could get frostbite in the winter and sunburn in the summer.

The listening device was not picking up any talking, but there was the sound of faint snoring. A covert surveillance man took advantage of this and was seen to crawl from the opposite side garden and place quietly, and carefully, what was undoubtedly a new listening device adjacent to the glass doors. Everybody held their breath. They could clearly hear the noise of this being put into place. The snoring paused. This is it, thought the firearms officers, as there was a man exposed, lying on the ground just by the lake front glass doors. The sigh of relief when the snoring started again was equally loud enough to stir them in the cottage, but at least the device was in place, and the covert surveillance man as quickly and silently as he arrived made his exit.

'Have you got a wi-fi signal at all back at the main control point?' Sandy asked Lofty, 'I was pretty sure I had earlier, but hardly anything down here I am afraid.'

'Good for you because Ma'am O'Connor couldn't get hold of DI Singh or you. I have been constantly bugged by her asking for updates. The fact that there has been very little activity has sent her blood pressure sky high. At least she has gone to bed now, but she expects updates throughout her night ready for her when she wakes in the morning.'

'I have seen George in the flesh. He is alive. So, DC Dobson, we have found our MFH. Well done to us.'

They both laughed together and Lofty said, 'I heard an interesting story back at the main control point. Apparently, Lake Manitoba has a similar creature to our Loch Ness Monster within its waters.'

'What is this one called and is there any photographic proof?' Sandy asked.

'I probably got this name totally wrong, but it is called something like Manipogo. I am sure that was what they called it. Might be out there in the semi-dark like it is now.' This caused Sandy to look even more intently across the lake. He thought he spied some eyes in a tree beside the lake and went off to investigate. Lofty headed off to the bunkie to see what was happening in there.

As Sandy approached the tree, a bird took off. It turned out that it was a large owl and was a wonderful sight as it soared along the lakeside. Sandy felt he was getting terribly bitten by mosquitos; he had been happy to have on a short-sleeved shirt due to the heat earlier, but at this time he was regretting it.

On getting back to the bunkie, Sandy saw that John Hopkins was there with a large coffee for him. He looked at Sandy and said, 'Didn't you bring any mosquito repellent with you, son?'

'I did mean to get some yesterday but didn't get round to it. Gosh, these are small but pretty annoying bites.'

John went out to his car and reappeared with one of his own long-sleeved shirts, a tube of bite cream and some insect spray. 'Here, put this cream on, it will soon calm things down. Put the shirt on afterwards and spray yourself the next time you go outside, especially at this time of night or first thing in the morning.'

'Thank you so much. Not sure why they are biting me so much – Lofty has not been touched! I saw a lovely owl earlier, not sure what it was, but we have barn owls at home, and it wasn't one of those.'

'I saw an Eastern screech owl on the way here. Might have been one of those.'

'What a lovely name for an owl. Not a lot happening here and the boys have been fast asleep for hours now.'

Staff Sergeant Hopkins headed off back to the main control point. What a lovely man John Hopkins is, Sandy and Lofty commented to each other.

The listening device suddenly burst into life: 'What

are we going to do? Shall we make a run for it? The car wouldn't be any use, but we could take the boat.'

'Then what will we do, you stupid fool? Not got anything on us to steal a car once we get the boat to the other shore, have we?'

'If you hadn't have shot that policeman, we wouldn't be in this awful position. It is you who is the idiot.'

'It is that brainless idiot's fault for giving me a loaded weapon. No one cares about a dead copper anyway. I did the world a good thing by shooting him. Not sure how I hit him from that distance though.'

'We knew it had bullets in it; both of us were playing with it.'

'I didn't know it was loaded. You pulled the trigger – why do that? You are the idiot.'

'Don't you call me that, I will pummel you into the ground. You said no one would find us in Canada. We would be safe here, but here we are, no doubt surrounded by trigger-happy cops. We could try to shoot our way out.'

No one, including Sandy and Lofty, knew who was saying what. They could only presume which of the boys was saying what, but they couldn't be at all sure. The firearms inspector decided to call up his men to come down as close as they could to be ready to act. He definitely didn't like the sound of "shoot our way out" at all. The plan to go in at first light might have to be brought forward by a couple of hours or so.

'Why do I feel so ill?'

'I think you have both got the flu after being bitten by so many mosquitos when we were in the boat on the lake. I told you to put the insect repellent on. Look, I have no bites.'

So, it wasn't withdrawal from drugs but excessive mosquito bites, thought Sandy.

'How come you are so clever always. You and your high and mighty family. It's as I have always thought. You always look down on us. I really am going to do you in before I am finished here.'

'Let's go and give ourselves up, get ourselves back to England and let our lawyers fight it out for us.'

'Good idea let's do that. I am going to go outside now with my hands up. You two come as well.'

'If you take one step outside, it's you who is going to be the one I shoot next.'

There was no need for the listening device as the sound of the shot that rang out was heard outside by all of them. Even louder than the sound of the shot was someone crying out in excruciating pain.

Sandy, without thinking for his own safety, ran forward as he was sure it was George Peveril who had been shot and his first instinct was to save his life.

Chapter Nineteen

As Sandy went to run out of the bunkie, a hand grabbed him and propelled him backwards. He tried to turn around just as Lofty, who had placed his hand on him, placed him in a vice-like grip. Gosh, Lofty was incredibly strong, and he almost picked Sandy up in the air and slammed him into a sitting position on a chair. Lofty said, 'No, Sandy, you are not going anywhere. It is not safe for you.'

He was right, Sandy knew he was, but he still wanted to do all that he could to save the person who they could still hear groaning in immense pain. There was, surprisingly, no sound from the other two in the cottage. They saw Ruben Cousins pull back one of the shutters and look outside. He clearly couldn't see anything or anybody, as he disappeared quickly from the glass doors.

Alan Wise, the RCMP firearms inspector, was briefing his team, who he had already summoned forwards immediately after he had heard one of the boys say they would shoot their way out. Good job and very inciteful, Sandy thought, as he sat in the chair feeling totally helpless, but understanding it was all in Alan Wise's hands now.

The rapid-entry firearms teams were all dressed completely in black clothing and wore full helmets with visors. The helmets had lights fitted on the top of them. The firearms officers, two of whom were women, were all carrying semi-automatic weapons and handguns in holsters on their belts. There were six of them in total. The snipers were still in position at the front and rear of the cottage. They looked extremely professional and were in no doubt what the plan was that they were shortly going to be carrying out.

Alan said to Sandy, Lofty and the two negotiators, 'Right, you lot. Move back to the main control point in St Laurent.'

Before Sandy could speak, Lofty said, 'I am sorry, sir, but we have got to be here. We will not move out of this room until you give us an all-clear command.' This satisfied the inspector but the two negotiators, Milly and Simon, didn't need telling twice. It had been a long day and they headed off out of the way, back to St Laurent.

The team moved forwards and Sandy was surprised to see four of them went round to Laurentia Beach roadside. One of them was carrying a large and heavy-looking black, handheld battering ram door opener.

The action happened extremely quickly. The lights to the cottage went off, plunging it into darkness, no doubt cut off by one of the technical officers who also must be around the front of the cottage. One of the two firearms officers still on the lakeside walked up to the doors whilst her colleague raised their semi-automatic rifle and covered her. Almost simultaneously, she slightly opened one of the glass doors and threw in a cannister; the bangs, which clearly came from this canister, went off.

The bangs were extremely loud and sounded just like a series of loud firecrackers. The sound was, of course, amplified, as they could hear it on the speaker to the listening device in the bunkie. The sound of bangs must have muffled the noise of the front door being smashed open, as the next thing they heard were loud and commanding shouts of, 'Don't move, armed police!' They heard lots of shouts of, 'Armed police! Armed police!'

Sandy held his breath, waiting for the noise of the inevitable shots being fired. He didn't hear anything. He saw that the two firearms officers on the lakeside entrance to the house had now entered. There was a lot of smoke in the air within the cottage. The cannister, as well as emitting noise in the form of bangs, also emitted smoke, hence the firearms officers' helmets having lights on the top of them. Sandy then heard, 'Three in custody, two cuffed and one not in a fit state to cuff.' He could also hear several shouts of, 'Clear!' He presumed that the other firearms officers were going through each room, one by one, making sure it was safe.

The firearms operation had been a total success as

not one shot had been fired and the three suspects were in custody. Great job, Inspector Alan Wise and your firearms team. Breathtakingly and professionally executed.

∞

Using his best ever rugby sidestep on hearing the word "clear", Sandy didn't care that it wasn't Alan Wise telling them all clear. He burst out of the bunkie away from Lofty and ran across the grass at an adrenaline-filled speed. He went through the now open lakeside glass doors, shouting, 'Police! Don't shoot, don't shoot, I am a police officer.' Although he couldn't clearly see, due to the smoke that was now dispersing, he saw two males lying on their fronts on the floor and handcuffed behind their backs. Each had a single firearms officer with them. An officer was with the third male, who was lying flat on his back, and his right leg just above the knee had blood oozing out of it. The person was barely conscious.

Sandy fell to his knees by the man on the floor and he saw that the person was, as he presumed, George Peveril, who had been injured. The firearms officer said, 'He doesn't look at all well. I'm not sure he is going to make it.' Sandy ripped off the shirt that John Hopkins had given him and tied it swiftly round George's upper right thigh, using the shirt as a type of tourniquet. He took off his short-sleeved shirt and applied it as hard as

176

he could into the wound, pressing down as firmly as he could. When he did this, George in his semi-conscious state screamed out in intense pain.

'Where are the paramedics and the ambulance?' shouted Sandy to the firearms officer guarding George. Alan Wise, who was somewhere in the room, said, 'On their way from St Laurent. I gave the call for them to move forward the minute we entered the cottage, so they won't be too long.' Looking at the state of George, he added, 'I hope.'

Sandy started to pray quietly to himself, equally for George to survive and for the ambulance to hurry up. He could feel his own heart beating rapidly in his chest. He said to George, 'Come on, George, hold on.'

He could see that George was unconscious now, so whilst still applying the pressure to the wound with one hand, he used his other hand, which he had to work hard to control as it was shaking, no doubt due to how nervous he was feeling, to feel to see if there was a pulse, as he didn't know whether to start CPR and get the firearms officer to apply the wound pressure. There was a definite pulse, so he said, 'Come on, George, your aunty Arabella has arrived in Canada and is desperate to see you. She will be with you soon. You just need to fight.'

Sandy could feel something wet under his knee. He knew it wasn't the wound leaking as the blood oozing from that had stopped. Then he realised it might be an exit wound at the back of George's leg. He was relieved when Lofty, whom he hadn't realised was standing behind him, dropped to his knees and took his own shirt off and applied it hard under the leg, which did the trick. Sandy looked at him gratefully and they just nodded together, in unison, focussed on George Peveril.

'Where is that ambulance?' Sandy shouted, but as he was saying this, he could hear the sound of the sirens.

'Two minutes or less.' A firearms officer shouted.

Then someone else in the room near the front door said, 'They are pulling up now.'

The paramedics rushed into the room and came straight over to George. They put an oxygen mask on him and asked Sandy and Lofty to step aside. Their speed of working and professionalism was amazing. They applied a new tourniquet, dressings to the two wounds and inserted a drip. Sandy overheard them say that George urgently needed a blood transfusion of several litres of blood. He also needed surgery if they could ever stabilise him.

They began to leave, having placed George on a stretcher. He was showing no signs of life other than he was still breathing; the one comforting sight that could be seen was the steady rise and fall of his chest. One of the paramedics looked at Sandy and said, 'We have shelved the plan to take him by air ambulance but are going to take him by road. I am afraid that I am not sure if he will make it, but if he does, you will have saved his life. Well done for trying.'

Without any further talk or hesitation, they went with

George out into the Manitoba morning and almost in seconds, an ambulance siren could be heard, as could other sirens, with no doubt a police escort leading the way. They had made the decision to go directly to St Boniface Hospital in Winnipeg.

Chapter Twenty

When Sandy looked back into the room, he saw that everyone had now vacated the cottage. He had been aware of something going on around him, but because he was concentrating so hard on George, he was oblivious to what had occurred in the room.

He saw that just outside the glass doors was Clare, already fully dressed in her all-in-one white CSI boiler suit. She also had on the blue paper shoes, but she hadn't yet applied a mask or put the hood on over her head. Also standing there were Rich and two others; they too were wearing white CSI suits.

John Hopkins stood on the grass slightly further back from Clare. Sandy went straight across to him and said, 'I am so sorry, John, but I have ruined the shirt that you lent me. I couldn't think what else to use.'

'Don't worry, son, you did a good thing. Let's hope your efforts work out.'

'Where have Cousins and Kelly gone to? I didn't notice them leaving. I presume they went quietly and without a fight?'

'They have gone to the main police headquarters in Winnipeg. All three have been arrested for threatening a police officer with a firearm. Kelly and Cousins also for the attempted murder, which might end up being murder later today, of George Peveril. No problems from them. It helps having the firepower that the arresting officers had.'

Clare said, 'We need you and Lofty to get out of those trousers so we can take them as exhibits. You probably need to somehow have a wash, as you are both covered in blood.'

Sandy hadn't even thought about this, and on looking at his hands, body and trousers, he saw that he was covered in George Peveril's blood. Lofty needed no prompting. He had only one place in mind to have a wash. He marched purposely across the grass, taking off his trousers, and walked over the sand and went straight into the lake. Sandy now had no other choice but to follow him. There were people starting to move about. Clearly the police cordons had now been removed. These people looked quizzically at the extremely tall Lofty in only his boxer shorts. Sandy also walked across the sand and was surprised that the lake was quite shallow at the place where they entered it.

As he walked a bit further out into the lake, he found the water was really cold, especially as he was only wearing his boxer shorts. Suddenly, from nowhere, he felt the shove of a rugby tackle and he went completely under. Lofty was having fun and as well as shoving him down into the water, was busy splashing him. This moment of fun was, in a strange way, a good antidote to relieve the stress of the last day or so. Sandy looked back across the beach and the grass to the cottage with the tree line behind it. He thought what an incredible holiday destination this must have been for the Peveril family over many decades. Whether they will think the same again now, in particular if George dies, he was not so sure.

As they got out of the water and walked across the sand back onto the grass, they saw Clare was waiting there for them. She had a white suit for both of them to put on. Looking Lofty up and down, she laughingly said, 'I have brought you both an extra-large suit, but you Lofty clearly need extra, extra, extra-large!'

They all, including John Hopkins, laughed extremely loudly to see Lofty in his suit with his arms and legs sticking out of the cuffs of the suit. The arm cuffs were probably a foot short and the leg cuffs even shorter, only just reaching the top of his calf. Lofty really did look a picture, but he took it all in good heart and was laughing equally as loudly as the others. Sandy wished he had his phone with him so that he could take a photo of Lofty in the white suit, but his phone was in his backpack in the bunkie.

John said, 'Right, guys. I will drive you back to Winnipeg and get you back to your hotel. One of my colleagues will follow in my police car and get me back home to Portage la Prairie.'

'John, we will get ourselves back. We have been on duty for twenty-six hours now and you must be as tired as we are,' Sandy said, thinking, but not saying it, and you are twenty-five years older than me.

John was having none of their protestations and after both Lofty and Sandy had collected all of their belongings out of the bunkie, headed back to Winnipeg. Guiltily, Sandy fell asleep within less than two minutes of them heading out of St Laurent. Staff Sergeant Hopkins was an outstanding officer who Sandy was pleased to have looking after him and the team from Operation Primrose so well.

∞

It was the middle of the afternoon before Sandy woke up. He had only a vague idea of how he got to his bedroom, but sleep had been very welcome, as was the long hot shower he was now enjoying. He thought there are a number of women I need to contact as soon as I get out of the shower.

He started with Arabella, who he had managed to send a message to from Portage la Prairie before he fell asleep, saying: "George on his way to St Boniface Hospital, not looking great, get there as soon as possible". He looked at her response, which said, "What has happened? On my way now". Then a couple of hours ago: "George is in surgery, will know more in a couple of hours". So, that was probably now. He sincerely hoped they could save him.

The next one was to Hannah who had sent him a couple of messages letting him know the jury in her trial had gone out to consider their verdict. Then another one to say that they had been sent home for the night and were due back in the morning at ten a.m. He wished her the best of luck and said he would talk to her tomorrow.

Sandy quickly sent a message to his mother telling her that he was fine and would likely be home before the weekend. He thought he had better call his two bosses. Both had sent him a message to call them at any time. The time at home now was almost ten p.m., so he decided it would just about be okay. He rang Joanne O'Connor first. 'Hello, Ma'am, sorry to ring you so late. I was exhausted and fell asleep. I presume you know we have Cousins and Kelly in custody? The RCMP are dealing with them first. Peveril is in hospital.'

'Thank you, Sandy, for what you have done. You have done an excellent job. We are all really grateful.' Sandy was taken aback – Joanne O'Connor was saying nice things about him! 'I don't know if you have seen your emails or heard from Rich as yet? We have CPS agreement to charge all three with the murder of PC Joseph Foster. This is fantastic news. We have their agreement to authorise and support their extradition from Canada back to England. Your colleague, DCI Harris, is leading on this for us with the National Crime Agency. I am so grateful to the FCO for all of their help.'

This was fantastic news, Sandy knew, but didn't feel it. All he felt was that only that morning, George Peveril had just about died in his arms and he didn't know if he had been able to save him. Sandy said, 'Ma'am, have you had an update on how George Peveril is doing?'

'I rang the hospital, but they wouldn't tell me anything as I am not a family member.' Sandy couldn't believe that anyone would say no to Joanne. 'I wasn't having that,' Joanne went on to say. 'I rang a manager in the hospital, and they realised that I was not going to take no for an answer. George went straight in for surgery once they had managed to give him the start of various blood transfusions. The surgery itself went well and was pretty straightforward. It was the loss of blood that was, and is, the problem for him. They will not know until probably tomorrow morning when they rouse him from his coma if he will survive, and if so, what state he will be in. It would appear that you, with the assistance of Lofty, may have possibly saved his life.' Sandy was grateful for the update but had to smile when Joanne said, 'If he doesn't, I still have two to stand trial.' Clinical until the end, Sandy thought. 'Take your time to come back to England and see you in the Operation Primrose major incident room next Monday.'

Sandy's next conversation was with Jane Watson, his FCO line manager. She had heard what had happened, Sandy presumed via Clare, probably from Juliet, who had sent him a couple of messages saying hope you are OK and thinking about you. Jane just listened as Sandy talked. She never interrupted him and enabled him to talk about how he felt about the trauma of an armed police operation, and how someone he had got to know, if only through his family, almost dying in his arms had affected him. Maybe that was why Sandy had this feeling of being so helpless, as he had let down James Peveril and Arabella Montague. Jane was a great boss, there was no other way to describe her.

∞

Answering and sending emails was now the last thing Sandy wanted to do, although the extremely long shower had seemed to invigorate him greatly. Food was what he needed next. On arrival in the hotel restaurant, he saw that Rich and Lofty were in there. He went and sat with them. He was amazed at how fresh Rich looked. When Sandy and Lofty had gone to bed, after over twenty-four hours' working, Rich had continued working and it was now over thirty-six hours since his working day had started yesterday morning. Rich said, as Sandy sat down, 'George is still alive. I heard from one of the officers on guard at the hospital with him an hour ago, but it is still touch and go.'

'I know, Joanne has just updated me. We have just had a very pleasant chat.'

'I know, she is absolutely raving on about what you, Lofty and I have done here in Canada today. We are top of the pops back in England. I will take that praise for the moment, but we have a long, in fact an extremely long, way to go. But, for Joanne, she has two, and hopefully three, in custody for the murder of PC Joseph Foster and the CPS have already authorised a charge. Her job is almost done and then it is up to me and the rest of us to get that conviction.'

'What is happening then with Cousins and Kelly?' Sandy said, in between ordering a pan-fried walleye fillet, chips and peas. This was the fifth day on the trot he had had chips as even last night in the bunkie he had had burger and chips. At least he wasn't having a burger again. Yesterday morning, when they had been at Lake Winnipeg, he had seen signs for fishing trips to catch walleye, or pickerel as it was known locally, at the lake. This had made him not want to go fishing for walleye, as he was no fisherman, but to want to try and taste it.

Rich replied, 'They called a doctor to see them and he decided that they were fit to be detained, but not fit to be interviewed just yet. They have a lot of mosquito bites, probably from taking that fishing boat on the lake early morning or at dusk, and the doctor says they have an infection or flu as a result of excessive bites. How are your bites, Sandy?'

'Fine. Luckily, John Hopkins helped me out. What a kind man he is. As soon as I had applied the bite lotion and insect repellent, I was OK. I can understand that people like Cousins and Kelly would not bother to apply insect repellent, even though George kept telling them to, but I should have known better. So, when will they get to interview them? I presume there is no hurry from our point of view.'

'They are confident the interviews can take place in the morning. If they charge them here in Canada with any offences, we will not be able to extradite them until the conclusion of proceedings, and maybe much later in their sentence. That will be a real problem to us on Operation Primrose having to wait years for them to come back and to stand trial. That will be a shadow hanging over the force, and justice for Joseph will be a long, long way off. If Peveril dies, they will be charged with murder. We could end up waiting for ten years or more.'

'Unless we get agreement for them to serve their sentence in England.'

'I didn't think about that. I am probably too tired. I just kept thinking about a trial in ten years' time and what I would be doing then. What about Belinda Foster and her children, waiting that long for justice?'

'No, I get your point exactly. Any updates from Clare and the forensic search of the cottage?'

'Still ongoing, but I don't think there is anything for us. We have our key exhibits from the search at the room on the Peveril Estate.'

On finishing dinner, Rich was in desperate need for sleep so headed off to his room. In the morning, he was going to attend the police station to be in a room to remotely monitor the interviews. There seemed nothing left for Lofty and Sandy to do in Canada as Rich was in charge of the interview process and Clare was in charge of forensics. So, as Lofty and Sandy went out to get some fresh air and see what was happening in The Forks that early evening, they talked about planning to fly home, if not tomorrow, certainly the next day.

Chapter Twenty-One

When the morning arrived, Sandy couldn't believe the time was already seven a.m. His head had hardly touched his pillow before he fell asleep. He saw that he had a message from Hannah, telling him that the jury in her trial had asked a question of the judge that morning, about the law around consent. She sounded exasperated. She had told him on their trip to Norfolk, which seemed a lifetime ago now, that she had gone through, very carefully and deliberately, all about consent and the law and precedents that surrounded it in rape cases.

When he arrived in the restaurant, he saw that Clare was having breakfast. Sandy, for some reason, wasn't too hungry, probably due to worrying about George Peveril, but he wasn't sure what it was that was troubling him, so yogurt and some fruit was all he could manage. Clare told him they had found nothing to help them with their investigation. She was back at the cottage today and had the car that the boys had been using to take them from the estate to the cottage to look at. Clare was going to look at the car with the RCMP

CSI. Tomorrow, she planned to go back to the Peveril Estate to re-examine the boys' room there, as the RCMP CSI wanted to help, and they had lots of interesting kit, like lasers, to look for DNA and fingerprints. Clare didn't think they needed to go back, but she loved everything about forensics so wasn't going to let the opportunity pass her by. They had promised the Williams family that they would hand the cottage back to them by the weekend. It needed a major clean as the boys had left it in quite a disgusting state.

Sandy needed a purpose that day. He thought it might be useful – that is if George survived and was in a fit state to be interviewed – for Sandy to carry out the first rapport building conversation with George. He couldn't visit before the afternoon as it was this morning when they were going to try and rouse him. That was if he had survived overnight. Sandy hadn't heard anything, and Clare didn't know either.

A visit to the Birds Hill Provincial Park for a run was something that Lofty and Sandy had discussed when out walking yesterday evening around the lively Forks area. Birds Hill Park had numerous hiking and running trails all around it. However, there had been a folk festival on at Birds Hill Park all weekend and one of the hotel staff had said the place would be in full clean up mode, so probably not the best thing to do. Sandy had opted for the Winnipeg Art Gallery. Lofty had no interest in art, so when Sandy sent him a message outlining his plans for the morning, Lofty planned instead to head off and buy his wife a souvenir from Canada.

The walk to the art gallery literally only took Sandy twenty minutes, even though he was dawdling along, taking in the sights and thoroughly enjoying the warm July sunshine. The art gallery was in the centre of downtown Winnipeg. The architecture of the building was stunning from the outside and was triangular in shape and constructed of Manitoba Tyndall stone, and, as it turned out, stunning also from the inside. Sandy quite happily wandered around for a couple of hours, completely switching off from work whilst looking at, amongst other artwork, the world's largest collection of contemporary Inuit art.

The visit had done him good, and it wasn't until he got outside that his mind wandered back to Operation Primrose and George Peveril. Sandy decided not to go back to the hotel but walk straight to St Boniface Hospital. As he headed back to The Forks, he bought himself for lunch a couple of perogies, which are filled dumplings. Sandy decided to go for some cheese-filled ones. Perogies are most often associated with food from Eastern Europe and the stall he bought it from said they sold Ukrainian food. That fitted with what he knew. They were delicious and two was not enough, but he resisted the temptation for anymore.

Sandy walked over the Esplanade Riel footbridge that he and Lofty had run over a few days ago. It was not only architecturally stunning, but the great views across and back to the city were too. Sandy lingered walking over the bridge, not just because he was enjoying every part of its two hundred metres, but he was dreading what he was going to find when he arrived at the hospital, whose main entrance was now only a short distance away.

∞

As he approached the hospital room that George was in, he saw outside the room the police officer who was guarding George, as he was technically in custody. The police officer was talking to a couple of members of the nursing staff. They were laughing together, looking at something on the police officer's phone. Sandy nodded to him, at the same time showing his police warrant card. He gesticulated with his head to the room, the police officer nodded that it was OK to enter.

Sandy entered the small hospital room. He had no sooner taken more than one step in when Arabella flew from the seat she had been sitting on, put her arms around Sandy and pulled him into an extremely tight bear hug. Arabella said, 'Sandy, thank you so much for saving George's life! You will never know how grateful we are and we will never be able to make it up to you.'

Sandy, although being smothered, looked around Arabella and could see George half sitting up in the bed. He was wired up to a monitor and had what looked like two drips in one arm. His right leg was completely raised up and covered in bandages. Remarkably, he was awake with not even an oxygen mask on. George looked very weak but gave Sandy a half smile.

Arabella continued talking. 'The operation to repair his leg went extremely well. He was roused this morning and is, the doctors say, after a slow recovery, going to be fine. He might end up with a limp and need a walking stick. They say you saved his life as he couldn't possibly have afforded to lose one more drop of blood, let alone another pint.'

'Well, it wasn't just me. It was the leadership of Inspector Alan Wise and his firearms team that went in quickly after the gunshot was heard. DC Wayne Dobson helped me as there was another bleed that I couldn't cover.' Sandy, when talking about it, was immediately transported back to the trauma of yesterday morning and the cottage front room. It brought a shudder to his whole body. 'I am so glad he is going to be OK. Can I speak to him at all?'

George himself then spoke in a quiet but audible voice. 'I don't normally speak to coppers.'

To which Arabella said, 'No George, this is not the right attitude anymore.'

'Anyway, thank you for saving my life. I am not sure I will have wanted you to save it over the coming days and months. It looks like a life of prison for me, probably for many years, but at this moment I am particularly pleased. Especially as my aunty is here with me. I am going to ring my dad, mum and grandad shortly. I hope they are not cross with me for running away here, or for stealing Janice's credit card. If and when I am able to, I will pay them back. Canada was the only solution I could think of at the time. I didn't know what else I could do.' George looked at that moment like a little boy who was trying to be, but not succeeding in being, a grown up.

Sandy said, 'I am not able to ask you any questions as it might jeopardise the criminal justice process here and back in England. I just came to see how you were. Compared to the last time I saw you yesterday morning, incredibly better, I would say.'

'What criminal justice process here? We have done nothing wrong here.'

'You have been shot for one thing. Cousins and Kelly have to answer that charge.'

Without any hesitation or silence, which meant George must have thought about it, he said, 'It wasn't them, I did it. A pure accident. I was playing with the gun and it went off and hit me in the leg.'

Sandy was absolutely shocked by this comment, as this was one scenario he would never have dreamt of. He wanted to say, don't lie George, that is a physical impossibility, but instead said, 'The RCMP officers will come and talk to you about your whole time in Canada. One thing from me that I want to say is, George, do not stick up for them. You must only now think of yourself. You will not be a grass. You must tell the truth.'

A nurse had arrived to do something with George and she ushered Sandy out of the room but was allowing

Arabella to stay. She mouthed and gesticulated to Sandy that she would call him in due course.

Sandy left the hospital and thought what a lucky boy George had been. He worried about him and his loyalty to his friends. Loyalty was definitely something to be admired, but not in this circumstance. George needed to understand that. The missing boy, although not lost, was now a man and needed to make a start on getting his young adult life back on track and in the right way.

∞

On arriving back at the hotel, Sandy saw that Lofty and Rich were in the bar area drinking coffee. He went over to join them and said, 'George is going to be OK. I have seen him and had a quick chat with him.' Sandy also ordered a coffee. 'What happened during the interviews with Cousins and Kelly?'

'They were pretty talkative, but never admitted anything, which greatly frustrated the RCMP interviewing officers.' Rich took a sip of his coffee, which he was clearly enjoying. 'They both said that the shooting of George was an accident and Kelly was playing with the gun when it went off.'

Sandy wondered when they had come up with this as an excuse. They hadn't heard anything on the listening device, but to be fair he was busy trying to get into the cottage and George's screams of pain would have drowned out any other softer-spoken conversation.

Sandy said, 'George obviously wasn't in a fit state to hear what excuse they were going to dream up because he told me he shot himself accidently.'

It was clear Rich and Lofty found this as an explanation ridiculous. Rich said, 'I find that amazing. I am going to the hospital in an hour or so to be present when they interview George as a victim. The RCMP interviewer will not believe this if he comes out with it to them.'

'George seems to believe that he is being noble by not dropping his friends in trouble.'

'Pretty awful friends if you ask me. He is the grandson of Viscount Peveril, his father is an MP, and he picks friends like these. What is it they say, you can't pick your family, but you can pick your friends. Well, George blew this one didn't he, with these friends,' Lofty added into the conversation.

'What did they say about threatening the police officer with a gun on Monday morning?' Sandy asked.

'They both denied it. They knew nothing about it. They both feigned surprise. One thing that has really upset me though is that apparently, Cousins asked how George is doing, but not, the RCMP officer said, in a concerned for George manner, more concern for himself. But nothing from Kelly. He doesn't care that he might have killed his friend!'

There was no sign yet of Clare arriving back from the cottage; she was probably still very busy there. Lofty and Sandy decided to keep Rich company and walked with him over the Esplanade Riel bridge, where they parted company. Rich was heading to the hospital for the interview with George, and Lofty and Sandy had decided to walk the route that they had run on the first morning in Winnipeg. This took them up through Whistler Park and then over the bridge to head back to The Forks area for them to find somewhere to eat.

On arrival back at the hotel, they both decided to head to their rooms in order to pack ready for their trip to the airport and their flight, via a fairly long transit in Toronto, back home to the UK. They were due to arrive early on Friday morning. As Sandy was putting his clothes in his case, he couldn't believe what had happened over the last few days in Canada. He strongly felt he had had enough excitement to last for a very long time.

Just as he was heading to bed, he got a text message from Rich telling him that George had stuck to the story he had told Sandy, that he had accidently shot himself. Even a strong talking to by Arabella that afternoon had failed to change his story. The text message continued to say that the RCMP were going to have further interviews with all three of the boys during the next day, before deciding on their next course of action. The Operation Primrose team would have to wait for the chance to take over ownership of their three suspects. This looked likely to be days or weeks now, rather than, in a worst-case scenario, if they had been convicted and sentenced, years. That is, if they stick to what they had told the RCMP investigating officers already about what happened at the cottage.

Chapter Twenty-Two

The underground train from Heathrow into Central London was, as usual, packed full, with no room to move or even breath. There were people and luggage everywhere, and every language under the sun was being spoken on the train that morning as London prepared to welcome the many plane loads of tourists who had just arrived at Heathrow.

Both Sandy and Lofty felt pretty exhausted by their flights and the long transit in Toronto, but they were mostly exhausted from the emotion of their visit to Canada. Lofty was going to get a train from St Pancras back to the East Midlands and Sandy was going to head to Ely from King's Cross railway station. Both these stations are adjacent to each other, so they travelled together all the way into Central London.

There had been numerous messages that Sandy had received from Hannah yesterday. At the beginning of the day, they had started out quite despondent, because the jury were failing to reach a verdict in her court case. Then, after lunch, when the jury had been deliberating for two days, the judge said he would now accept a majority verdict. Within twenty minutes, they were back in court and the defendant had been found guilty by eleven votes to one. There are sometimes one or two people on a jury who would never be able to find anyone guilty, or they could just be against sending someone to jail for a long time. Who knows, Sandy thought, as you can't ask to find out what they were thinking, as that is against the law with jury deliberations being kept secret. Hannah was more than exuberant; she had the result she wanted, and it was the right one she felt for her victim.

Sandy suggested a celebration lunch or dinner on Saturday in Cambridge, but Hannah was not able to do this as her father, Howard Tobias, was visiting for the weekend and she had promised him that she would spend the time on Saturday with him. Sandy knew she was close to her father. Her mother had died just over ten years ago when she was only sixteen, and as an only child, the two of them had supported each other. Meeting up for lunch on Sunday in Ely was something Hannah felt would be good and suggested meeting up with his parents and Grandpa as well. Wow, Sandy thought, our relationship has moved extremely quickly to the next level, with parents meeting up. He messaged back to say he would get his mum to sort it out for them.

Katherine was excited about this prospect when Sandy messaged her. She said she would book somewhere, although she was concerned that his father, who had arrived back from Bermuda only the previous night, might be too tired. Sandy thought that his dad wouldn't be too tired; he had basically been on holiday, only needing to attend a few board meetings. It is me being tired that Mum should be worried about!

Sandy made a vow to himself to not do any work at all that day. The vow, however, didn't last very long because after saying goodbye to Lofty and boarding his train at King's Cross, within ten minutes he had started looking at and sending emails. He saw he had one from Rich, sent yesterday, taking account of Canadian time, but was early in the morning in England. All three of the suspects had stuck to their original stories. A meeting was being held on Friday when they would decide what was going to happen with the Canadian offences. Depending on what happened at that meeting, they might be able to hand them over for extradition. He would update him as soon as he knew. Rich was going to be staying in Canada for a few more days yet. The National Crime Agency and Sandy's colleague, DCI Harris, were going to be assisting if extradition became an immediate option.

When Sandy made it home to Ely, the first thing he did, after giving his mum, at her request, all of his washing, was to sit down with her and his dad to tell them about the experience of nearly having someone die in your arms, whilst doing all you could think of to save them. His parents just sat and quietly and thoughtfully listened, then sent him off to his bedroom for a shower and sleep. His dad promised to take him later to the

Cutter Inn for a few pints of the local English ale along with his father's friends and his Grandad Tom, if he could make it.

∞

The next morning, Sandy cycled to his Grandma Margaret and Grandad Tom's house. Tom hadn't made it to the pub the previous night and Sandy was keen to update him on everything that had happened in Canada. His Grandad Tom was the only person he felt able to talk freely with about his investigation. He helped his grandparents with some gardening whilst talking to his grandad, who was amazed at what had happened in Canada. Tom was exceptionally proud of his grandson and never more so than at this moment.

After finishing lunch with them, Sandy headed home on his bicycle. He decided he was going to do no work at all this weekend; Monday would come round soon enough for that. When Sandy was not far from home, his phone rang, and on looking at the name on the screen, saw it was Lofty. 'Hi, Lofty, are you missing me already?' he asked.

'Can't go a day without talking to you, can I?' Lofty and Sandy laughed together. 'When I checked my emails just now, I have seen that the memorial service for Joseph Foster is this coming Monday at two p.m. at Derby Cathedral. The place will be packed with people, but Belinda has insisted we are invited and there are reserved places for us in the cathedral. I thought I would let you know, just in case, because if you wore a uniform to police funerals you could bring it with you.'

'Thanks, Lofty. I have never been to a police funeral before and I don't have any uniform anymore either. I will bring a black tie with me though. See you Monday morning. We can try and see Belinda before the service to update her if we can.'

Just as he walked through the door of his parents' house, he had a call from Clare Symonds. 'Hi, Clare. I thought you were still in Canada. If you are, it must be early in the morning there.'

'You are right, it is six a.m. here. I am off to the cottage later this morning to hand it back to Tim Williams. The reason for the call is that I have received via email the results from the tests on the items we sent back from the room at Peveril Estate.' Sandy could tell by Clare's voice that she was really excited, so he presumed and hoped that it was good news. 'The phone had been wiped clean, but the sim card had Ruben Cousins' fingerprint on it.'

'Just his, or any of the other two's fingerprints?'

'Just his. The two blue hoodies had Cousins' DNA on one of them, and the other blue one had Peveril's DNA. The orange one is a bit more complicated, but predominately it was Kelly's DNA, but there was also one trace of Peveril's DNA on it.'

'We saw George wearing it when they arrived at Winnipeg airport.'

'The reason why it is complicated is, well, just wait for this news…' Clare was pausing for impact and Sandy appreciated it was her news, so he was letting her milk it to maximum effect. 'The bottom of the right arm still has on it a reasonable quantity of gunshot residue.'

'That is great news, Clare,' Sandy said, equally as excitedly as how Clare sounded. 'Great job! The evidence is stacking up so well. I will hopefully see you in Derby next week sometime. Have a safe trip home.'

The forensic news really pleased Sandy. He wasn't too bothered about George's DNA on the hoodie with the gunshot residue. Their case was coming together well, and Cousins was now linked in closely as the phone was right there at the time of the shooting.

Less than half an hour later, his phone rang again. This time it was Rich. 'Morning, Sandy, well, afternoon for you. I have just come off the phone to the boss and she wants you to call James Peveril, to put some pressure on him.'

Sandy wasn't sure that putting pressure on an MP and the son of a viscount was something that he had any chance of being successful with. 'Why? What has happened?'

'The RCMP are going to release the three boys soon, with their investigation to be put on hold pending any further developments. George had put a spanner in the works by saying he shot himself accidently. They will all be released and kept in custody for extradition.'

'That is good news, isn't it?'

'Yes, definitely. They are all, I understand, not going to oppose extradition and will submit to it voluntarily.' Rich went on to explain. 'The problem is, Peveril is looking for bail until we bring them back to England. This, I understand, will take a couple of weeks at the most. The British High Commission and the authorities here in Canada have only done five of these in the last five years, so it is not normal practice.'

'We can't let the three of them run off in Canada.' Sandy felt exhausted at the thought, and they would probably be back to square one.

'It is not as bad as that as Cousins and Kelly will not be seeking bail.'

'OK, the person to ring is not George's father, but Arabella, his aunty. I am sure you met her at the hospital.'

'Yes, lovely lady. She definitely calls the shots. Can you give her a call and persuade her not to seek bail for George?'

As soon as Sandy got off the phone to Rich, he immediately rang Arabella, who replied, 'Good to hear from you, Sandy. Have you got back safely to your home?'

'Yes, thank you. How is George?'

'He is doing great. They are going to discharge him either Tuesday or Wednesday.'

'We have a problem, Arabella. We can't let him have bail because if he gets bail, the other two possibly will too, and to lose them in Canada would be my worst nightmare.'

'Sandy, I do get your point, but George is my priority, and although he might be fit for discharge from hospital, he is definitely not fit to be in a prison. I am going to try to get him bail. His father and Monty are flying here tonight to support me. We will agree to put up five hundred thousand pounds as bail money, and we will agree to supervise him twenty-four-seven. Between us, and with the Williams family's help and support, we should be able to manage this.'

'I am sure it is the right thing for George, but he is looking at a long time in prison. You won't be able to protect him forever.'

'Sandy, I know this. It breaks my heart and I accept that he must face up to what he has done, but bail is the right move at the moment until he recovers from being shot, nearly dying and the operation. We have a private nurse and physiotherapist set up to visit every day. I am sorry if this is not what you want to hear.'

'No, I understand. The money and everything you are offering cannot be replicated by Cousins and Kelly, so should be much less of a worry. I am not sure my boss will agree though.' Sandy wondered, without coming to a conclusion, who was the more formidable: Arabella or Joanne O'Connor.

For someone who was not going to do any work that day, Sandy had spent all afternoon working on his phone.

Katherine had invited Hannah and her father to join them on the Sunday for the service in Ely Cathedral, which they had happily accepted. Although neither Gregor, Howard nor Hannah seemed to have a faith, it worked out well and they all enjoyed the service. Sandy loved having Hannah with him and held her hand almost all of the time.

Howard was a senior lecturer in history at the University of York. He loved the whole history of the cathedral and its beautiful architecture. He seemed absolutely thrilled to be there with them. He told them, which they already knew, but Hannah probably didn't, that Ely Cathedral was felt to be one of the seven wonders of the medieval world.

Before the service, when Hannah and Howard had taken a walk and looked around the outside of the cathedral, Howard had spotted a couple of peregrine falcons that were nesting high up on the walls. He was regretting not having brought his binoculars and camera with him. His camera phone was unfortunately, so he said to them, unable to capture the falcons' picture. Hannah and Howard had also bumped into Sandy's Grandma Margaret, who was also attending the service. Poor Howard, Sandy thought. He is getting the full family treatment. He was worried that his two sisters would pop out at any moment from behind one of the huge stone pillars in the cathedral.

They walked from the cathedral to the restaurant for lunch; this was where John McFarlane was meeting them. Howard was fascinated as they walked past the Oliver Cromwell House, and as they had a little bit of time to spare, he just had to visit it. One of his many subject specialisms was the English Civil War, which had lasted from 1642 to 1651. This was a war between Parliamentarians (Roundheads) and Royalists (Cavaliers). Oliver Cromwell, a roundhead, was a general who went on to govern England. Sandy told Howard that Oliver had also gone to the University of Cambridge, as he had, but to a different college, to St John's, the college Sandy had gone to. Howard took some good photographs of the house on his phone, no doubt for use in a future history lecture.

John McFarlane was waiting for them outside the Poets House, where they were having their Sunday lunch. The Poets House had been extended and modernised but was originally housed in three Grade II-listed properties built in the early 1900s. It was literally only one hundred yards from the cathedral. Howard and Hannah were blown away with what a wonderful and interesting place Ely was.

As they sat in the restaurant, Hannah was with, in her opinion, the three most important men in her life: her father, her mentor and her boyfriend. Sandy was pleased that she continually wanted to keep holding his hand. It was plain for everyone to see how much in love they both were. The food, the ambience of the restaurant and the company made for a wonderful afternoon.

There were no discussions about work, but Gregor told them what an incredible place Bermuda is and how much he loved his regular visits there. Sandy talked about the delights of Winnipeg and Manitoba, especially the lakes. They all burst out laughing when he told them that they had gone to the wrong lake to the one that they should have been at and the exciting drive across country to be in the right place. Everyone also congratulated Hannah for her court result. Every time John wanted to go into more detail about her court case, he was told not today.

The afternoon ended with Sandy taking Howard out for a short drive in his red Morgan Roadster motor car. Apparently, as soon as Hannah had mentioned it to him, he had been desperate to have a trip in the car. They drove quite happily together through the Fen roads, but Sandy felt utterly relieved that Howard turned down the chance to have a drive of the car. He still hadn't recovered from his Grandad Tom driving it a few days ago. He had checked it over yesterday morning as that had been his first chance to look at it, but everything seemed normal – even the roof went up and down OK. No harm had been done, but never again, thought Sandy. He wasn't in the slightest bit surprised when they got home that his sister Aileen had just happened to pop by to see them!

Chapter Twenty-Three

Monday morning was extremely hectic in the Operation Primrose major incident room. Sandy and Lofty were busy writing up reports of the activity in Canada, which needed to be submitted for inclusion on the major incident database called HOLMES. It would have been good if the database was named after Sherlock Holmes, Sir Arthur Conan Doyle's Victorian detective, but it actually stood for Home Office large major enquiry system, hence HOLMES.

Sandy and Lofty were informed that local Derby city centre enquiries had established three separate cases of people who had been offered drugs by two persons positively identified as Cousins and Kelly. All of the activity took place in Derby city centre and shortly before the shooting had taken place. One of the witnesses was the person who had made the call about the drug dealing that had led to PC Foster being dispatched by the control room to the scene. Joanne O'Connor told them that she had added this information with the CPS authorisation to the offences for extradition.

Lofty and Sandy left the police headquarters early for the memorial service. They wanted to have a quiet word with Belinda Foster before the service started, to update her on the current position of the investigation. They found Belinda waiting for them in an office at the back of the cathedral. Also present were Belinda's parents and Joseph's mother. They were all dressed very smartly, and although not wearing black clothing, they were sombrely dressed. After introductions, Sandy said, 'I hope today is not too difficult for all of you. We will be thinking about you and your family during the service.'

Belinda told them, 'We thought this was the best way to publicly mourn Joe. I understand why we are doing it, but what I am wanting is for us to have our private family funeral as soon as we can have Joe released back to us by the coroner.'

'I have spoken to the coroner this morning and as soon as we have agreement from the suspects' solicitors, he will release Joe's body to your undertakers,' Lofty said.

'The three suspects are in custody in Winnipeg and we hope to have them back in England in about two weeks or so. We understand they are not going to fight extradition, but they got themselves in a bit of bother there in Canada that we are sorting out. DI Rishabh Singh is in Canada resolving any further issues that may arise,' Sandy added, then went on to say, 'We have just returned from Canada on Friday after we were sure they were in custody.'

'What will happen when they return? I hope they won't get bail. They can rot in jail for all I care,' the very clearly distraught Joseph's mother said.

'Detective Superintendent O'Connor has got agreement that they are charged with the murder of Joseph,' Sandy said.

'That is really good news. Nice to have something positive to hear at last. When will they stand trial?' Belinda asked, before adding, 'Will I have to go to court at all? I think I would like to, but I have my two children to think about and look after.'

'We will talk about that beforehand. I suggest it would be good for you to be there some of the time. We will want to take a victim impact statement from you closer to the trial as well,' Lofty said.

Sandy said, 'I believe that they must stand trial within six months of arriving back from extradition. So, I presume the trial will be before Christmas or slightly after. Joanne has us working flat out to get everything ready before they get back.'

'I really need to apologise to Joanne O'Connor, don't I, Lofty?' Belinda said, looking directly at him.

'We will do it together, it will be fine, don't worry about it,' Lofty replied, in a reassuring manner.

'I was out of order, just a grief-stricken widow who has lost the man in her life, without any idea how I am going to cope with the future.' Belinda started to cry and her mother and father put their arms around her. This seemed like a good time for Sandy and Lofty to leave.

The cathedral in Derby had only been allowed to be called a cathedral for less than a hundred years, but the church was nearly three hundred years old with a tower dating back much longer than this. Sandy fought his thoughts of comparing it with his beloved Ely Cathedral as that would have been unfair, due to his conscious bias.

As they entered the cathedral, it was already almost full of people. There were numerous TV cameras and media everywhere. There were lots of reserved seats and Sandy and Lofty soon found theirs. The chief officers for Derbyshire Constabulary were all seated in the row in front of them and Joanne sat next to them. They were dressed magnificently in their uniforms, wearing white gloves and displaying their medals. Although Sandy didn't have any medals, as yet, it was at times like this that he wished he had a uniform so that he could stand shoulder to shoulder in solidarity and grief with his colleagues in the police.

The dean conducted the memorial service very thoughtfully. It was a service that totally honoured Joseph. The hymns were all picked by his mother, and one of his previous senior officers, a major from his former regiment, the Grenadier Guards, spoke very highly about Joseph and was quite humorous, making the congregation laugh. Joseph's shift inspector spoke about his police career and made everyone sad when talking about a life taken far too soon. The dean read out the family thoughts of Joseph as they were too upset and daunted to speak in front of so many people.

As they left the church, Sandy and Lofty agreed that it had been a suitable tribute to Joseph and had been the right thing to do, thereby allowing the family, at a later date, to grieve privately at a family funeral.

∞

The next morning, Lofty came up to Sandy smiling and said, 'I have found a teacher who knows all three of the boys well. The teacher tells me that he is fairly sure that they will be able to recognise the boys' voices and identify who has said what on the recording that I have been sent from the listening device.' Sandy started smiling as broadly as Lofty. This was another good breakthrough for the investigation.

Things in Canada were also going well. The Canadian authorities' plan was to move all three of the boys to a detention centre near to Toronto. This could be a problem for Arabella's bail application, which was going to take place later that day, as the hospital planned to discharge him on Wednesday morning.

The trip to see the teacher, Billy Buckley, at his home address in Hathersage took them less than an hour from the police headquarters. In fact, it had taken slightly longer than it needed to be as Sandy had got Lofty to drive through Matlock and then into Chesterfield so he could see the crooked spire of Chesterfield parish church. It really was a phenomenon.

'Mr Buckley, please can you tell us how well you know Cousins, Kelly and Peveril and why you know them?' Sandy asked, whilst looking at the teacher, who was probably in his late thirties and was dressed very casually, he thought, in jeans and a t-shirt. Sandy was basing this though on how the teachers dressed at the school he had attended, King's Ely. Billy had come home from school to ensure they had peace and quiet, rather than a busy school environment.

'I am the head of pastoral support at a Chesterfield secondary school. Cousins and Kelly have been pupils at the school since they were eleven. Peveril arrived at age fourteen. Most certainly, Cousins and Kelly have been two boys I have had an incredible amount to do with over those years. We managed to keep them in school until they left at sixteen. That was no small achievement, I can tell you. Peveril is a very bright boy but got into trouble early on during his time at the school. Maybe because he just didn't fit in, but Cousins and Kelly took him under their wing. I have all three of their school files with me if you want them?' Lofty nodded and said they would copy them and get them back to him by the end of the week.

'OK, we are going to play you what we feel is a key section of the recording. I am going to write in my notebook who you think said which comment, is that OK? I will then convert that into a statement for you to agree to and sign,' Sandy said.

After general nods all round, Lofty, who had brought his laptop with him, played the audio file he had been sent by the RCMP. Sandy got out his notebook and made the record. They played through the recording once so Billy could understand what was being said. When they got to the section when the shooting occurred, Billy was visibly shocked, firstly by the loud shot being fired and then the awful cry of pain. 'I know that is George Peveril screaming. Has he survived?' Billy asked.

'Remarkably, yes, he has survived, and he is due to be discharged from hospital in Winnipeg tomorrow,' Sandy said.

Lofty commented, 'DCI McFarlane acted quickly and decisively, which undoubtedly saved George's life.'

'Good on you,' a relieved looking Billy said. 'I wish we could have helped him more at school. He did manage to pass all of his GCSE exams. I have a real soft spot for George.' Don't we all have a soft spot for him, thought Sandy. 'Right, Mr Buckley, let's do this for real. I have my notebook ready to make notes. DC Dobson will stop every few seconds for you and me to catch up.

Audio file – covert listening device

'What are we going to do? Shall we make a run for it? The car wouldn't be any use, but we could take the boat.' (Cousins)

'Then what will we do, you stupid fool? Not got

217

anything on us to steal a car once we get the boat to the other shore, have we?' (Kelly)

'If you hadn't had shot that policeman, we wouldn't have been in this awful position. It is you who is the idiot.' (Cousins)

'It is that brainless idiot's fault for giving me a loaded weapon. No one cares about a dead copper anyway. I did the world a good thing by shooting him. Not sure how I hit him from that distance though.' (Kelly)

'We knew it had bullets in it; both of us were playing with it.' (Cousins)

'I didn't know it was loaded. You pulled the trigger – why do that? You are the idiot.' (Peveril)

'Don't you call me that, I will pummel you into the ground. You said no one would find us in Canada. We would be safe here, but here we are no doubt surrounded by trigger-happy cops. We could try to shoot our way out.' (Kelly)

'Why do I feel so ill?' (Cousins)

'I think you have both got the flu after being bitten by so many mosquitos when we were in the boat on the lake. I told you to put the insect repellent on. Look, I have no bites.' (Peveril)

'How come you are so clever always. You and your high and mighty family. It is as I have always thought, you always look down on us. I really am going to do you in before I am finished here.' (Kelly)

'Let's go and give ourselves up, get ourselves back

to England and let our lawyers fight it out for us.'
(Cousins)

*'Good idea let's do that. I am going to go outside
now with my hands up. You two come as well.' (Peveril)*

*'If you take one step outside, it's you who is going to
be the one I shoot next.' (Kelly)*

There was no hesitation from Billy Buckley on any
aspect of the conversation and who had said what. It was
a pretty straightforward exercise to convert the
conversation into a statement. The audio recording and
statement were now crucial evidence that Kelly had shot
and killed PC Joseph Foster.

After they had finished with Billy Buckley, Lofty and
Sandy went for a walk, so that they could get some fresh
air. The two of them set off at a good pace from the
village centre in Hathersage. They walked briskly from
the village up onto the nearby Stanage Edge. They then
walked along the gritstone escarpment and did a loop
around and walked back to the car. A stunning walk that
Sandy planned to repeat in the not-too-distant future. He
particularly liked seeing the climbers who were
climbing up the steep, but not too high, rock faces to
reach the ridge. At first, he was surprised to see them,
as from nowhere he suddenly saw a head pop up into
sight from a climber reaching the top of the rock face
and climb onto the ridge.

Chapter Twenty-Four

The next morning, Sandy was summoned into Joanne O'Connor's office. She had pointed her finger at him in an aggressive manner and indicated for him to follow her to her office. As Sandy walked there, he knew he was in trouble again. Before he had a chance to sit down, Joanne said, 'I thought I told Rich to tell you to speak to James Peveril, and for you to tell him, in no uncertain terms, not to apply for bail for George Peveril.' Sandy had already found out from both Rich and Arabella overnight that George was being given bail this morning, Canada time, when he was discharged from hospital. He also knew that Cousins and Kelly were being kept in detention.

'I am sorry, Ma'am. I did speak to them, but they wanted George to rehabilitate properly before he had to come into custody.'

Joanne pointed her finger at Sandy. 'I will hold you, DCI McFarlane, personally responsible if he skips bail and we spend forever trying to recover him back into custody.'

Sandy showed her the statement that he and Lofty had taken from Billy Buckley yesterday. As Joanne read it, he could see how her mood moved from disappointment to triumph. 'This is excellent, Alex, well done to you and Lofty. This is great news. We really have a very good case developing.' Sandy wanted to remind Joanne that he was not normally called Alex, but Sandy, due to his Scottish heritage. He thought that now was not the time in case he sent Joanne back to being in a bad mood with him again.

'Next problem for you. The National Heritage have been given a formal warning for having possession of an unlicensed firearm. They have accepted it, but it has created a right stink for them. They are reviewing all of their properties to make sure all weapons they possess, have been decommissioned and they have the necessary certificates. One thing they are saying though, is that Viscount Peveril must take some of the blame as he handed over the revolver with other family war memorabilia. I have told them we will give him a verbal caution.' Sandy knew where this was heading. 'I want you to ring him and give him that verbal warning. When the National Heritage find out that it was George Peveril who stole it, I am sure there will be further repercussions, probably with the family not allowed ready access to go all over the hall, but don't tell him that.'

When he left Joanne's office, he was aware of the fact that he had been asked in the past not to mention the gun to Viscount Peveril by his son James. However, James was in Canada with his son, and Sandy knew better than to go against Joanne, so he made the call knowing that Viscount Peveril was at that moment in his chateau near Bordeaux.

'My Lord, this is DCI McFarlane,' Sandy said when the phone was answered.

Before he could say anything else, William Peveril said, 'I understand thank you is in order, Chief Inspector, for saving my grandson's life. I spoke to him last night and he is doing well, other than being in quite a lot of bother. I told him we will get him the best lawyers that money can buy, but he will also have to be a man and face up to what he has done.'

'I only did what anyone else would have done in the same situation,' Sandy said. He was starting to feel quite embarrassed by all of the family thanks he was getting, 'I am not sure if you are aware, but a Smith & Wesson .38 service revolver was stolen from Peveril Hall a few weeks ago.' Sandy had decided not to tell him at this stage that George had stolen the gun. 'The gun was part of the family at war material you handed over to the National Heritage.'

'Yes, I know this. I handed the box over myself. It was over twenty-five years ago in 1995, to commemorate fifty years since the end of the Second World War.'

'Did you know that the gun was loaded and capable of being used as a firearm?'

'Yes, of course it was. The gun was my father's service revolver from the Second World War.'

Sandy felt he needed to get to the point as it was imperative that he didn't finish the conversation without giving the verbal warning. 'I need to tell you that you are not allowed to own a gun that is capable of being fired, and you are not allowed to pass on these guns to others. I have to give you a warning in relation to this.'

William Peveril exploded at Sandy through the phone. 'Chief Inspector, this happened twenty-five years ago, and it is not for me to check what I give over to the National Heritage, they should do it. I don't take kindly to being warned by you, young man. Good day, and don't ever mention this to me again.' He ended the call almost immediately before Sandy could defend himself. Still, he had done what was asked of him and had given the appropriate verbal warning. He thought he had better update James and Arabella when he next spoke to them about what had just happened with their father.

As Sandy was writing up the report on the gun, he suddenly had a thought. After he had finished his forensic review, he could probably take a few days off before the boys were returned from Canada. What he wanted to do was go to Florence with Hannah. Before he spoke to Joanne, he sent a message to Hannah asking if she was available to have few days with him in Florence, Italy. The answer was an almost immediate yes, but she had to be back by Wednesday evening for her to be in court at the end of next week.

With Joanne's agreement for three days' leave, he booked the flight for himself and Hannah to travel to Florence, leaving that Saturday and returning, as required by Hannah, Wednesday night.

∞

On the plane to Florence that Saturday morning, Hannah had set two ground rules: one, for Sandy to not spend the whole five days ensconced in the Uffizi Gallery or gazing at Michelangelo's statue of David; the second one was for them both to not spend lots of time on their phones, working or discussing work, but focus on Florence and each other. Sandy, if he had been on his own, may have struggled with the first rule, but was very happy to focus fully on his romance with Hannah.

Their hotel was situated right by the river Arno and very near to the medieval Ponte Vecchio, with shops built all along it. It was a lovely hotel and in a good location. They were also very close to the Uffizi Gallery that literally housed hundreds, if not thousands, of paintings, with so many of those paintings by acknowledged masters such as Raphael and Sandro Botticelli. Hannah was right, she could have lost Sandy for the whole holiday in there, only surfacing for food and for them to spend their nights together.

Hannah and Sandy visited the gallery together on one occasion. They just looked at the collections of paintings from the fourteenth century and the Renaissance period. These included some of those absolute masterpieces. Sandy, however, visited again on two occasions, whilst Hannah enjoyed a coffee or glass of wine sat outside in one of the many beautiful Florentine squares. Sandy did join her at other times, enjoying doing nothing but just drinking and eating in the Tuscan sunshine. He especially liked sitting outside a restaurant opposite the Pitti Palace, which dated from the 1300s – a magnificent building. From the restaurant he could watch all of the coming and goings into the palace with the added bonus that it was located very close to their hotel.

The whole trip was lovely, and they enjoyed their passion for each other and each other's company whilst walking everywhere. This included an extended walk out of Florence so they could look back and down at the city, to admire the scene and to take photographs of the distinctive Florence skyline with the red clay tiles of the Duomo roof dominating the view before them. It was magnificent, a truly worldwide-acknowledged beautiful city. They had visited the Duomo and climbed the stairs to look closely at the roof. They also visited the octagonal baptistery with its incredible doors that have been described by historians and art critics as "undeniably perfect in every way and must rank as the finest masterpiece ever created".

If they were asked what they enjoyed the most about their holiday together, other than each other's company,

Hannah would say the sunshine, food and drink. They had enjoyed, of course, the pizza and pasta dishes but also the Florentine steak. They drank mostly red wine, in particular Chianti. Hannah and Sandy did not miss out on having a gelato every afternoon. The ice cream in Florence was delicious.

Sandy, on the other hand, would undoubtedly say that he enjoyed most, not just the paintings in the Uffizi, which even had a Da Vinci painting in there, but Michelangelo's statue of David. Made out of one block of marble between 1501 and 1504, almost but not quite twenty feet tall and was without doubt a masterpiece, probably just about the most famous sculpture in the world. Sandy had seen it four times, so he definitely would have said that was what he enjoyed the most.

Hannah and Sandy had managed to avoid talking about or doing any work the whole trip, but whilst waiting to board the plane on their way home, Sandy saw that he had a call from Rich. He thought it must now be fine to take the call as they were heading home. 'Hi, Rich, how are you?'

'Good, thank you. I have just had confirmation that the boys are being extradited back to England next Tuesday. We have borrowed from all over the East Midlands region nine trained officers, who are flying out on Monday and will arrive back in England on Tuesday. Can we, when we meet up tomorrow, and then continue on Friday, plan for our interviews with them? The Operation Primrose interview advisor has started listing the key evidential topic areas we need to cover in our interviews.'

'Yes!' Sandy shouted, causing Hannah, who was sitting next to him reading, to turn around sharply to listen to what Sandy was talking about. 'What is happening with George?' Sandy asked Rich.

'His solicitor says he will arrive in Toronto on Monday and be ready to surrender to the team first thing, ready for the flight home.' Arabella was keeping to her promise.

'Great, I will be travelling up to Derby from Ely in the morning. Can we say ten a.m. to meet, please?'

After he ended the call, Hannah asked him, 'What are you so excited about? Is it George Peveril?'

'Yes. He, Ruben Cousins and Dean Kelly are all arriving back in the UK on Tuesday next week, ready for us to interview and charge them with the murder of PC Joseph Foster. What brilliant news.'

On hearing this news, Hannah looked incredibly shocked. 'What were those names again? How come you only mentioned George Peveril's name before? I don't think you told me who else was involved. You only called them the boys?'

'Sorry, I am not sure I was deliberately keeping the names from you. I suppose I have been totally focussing on George. Well, their names are George, then Ruben Cousins and Dean Kelly.'

Sandy had now shifted straight into work mode and didn't notice that Hannah had quickly got out her iPad, as he was busy sending emails and messages, getting himself ready for an exciting week ahead. Hannah was also now getting into work mode and sending emails herself.

Chapter Twenty-Five

On Wednesday evening at Cambridge railway station, Sandy and Hannah said goodbye to each other. They had had a wonderful time away together. They were an incredibly well-matched couple. The goodbye hug and prolonged kisses almost made Sandy miss the train as it progressed on to Ely and beyond into Norfolk. This would have been very embarrassing for him as his case was still on the train.

The preparation and planning for the interviews took a lot longer than the two days they thought it would. Sandy and Rich ended up working all weekend on it as well. The Operation Primrose accredited interview advisor was reluctant to allow both Rich and Sandy to carry out the interviews. However, Rich and Sandy outranked him and had Joanne O'Connor's backing. He was not going to win the argument. There was no way that they were not going to be the ones interviewing. The interview advisor did feel a lot more relaxed when he found out that they were both trained in investigative interviewing and Sandy had in fact completed the interview advisor course when he was in the Metropolitan Police. He was further placated when he found out he was going to be able to remotely monitor the interviews.

The CPS, in order to authorise the extradition, had already carried out something called a full code test, which in essence meant they felt the evidence was sufficient for a charge, and a public interest test was also passed. To be fair, the public interest test was always going to be passed, as prosecuting a murder should always be in the public interest. The problem Rich and Sandy had was that they needed to have everything ready for charge and then the first court appearance.

As well as the interview advisor, the team that worked together for the four days included a detective sergeant, who was the case file officer, and a disclosure officer, who was organising all of the disclosure schedules. This included what was going to be delivered to Cousin's and Kelly's solicitors in Chesterfield. It would also go to George's solicitor, who was a member of his father's old law firm where he had worked before he became an MP; they were based in Sheffield. The disclosure officer was going to personally deliver the Chesterfield disclosure files on Monday morning, and Sandy, the Sheffield disclosure on his way home to Ely before he headed on the Tuesday to the police station at Heathrow.

In terms of the interview topics and investigative areas they needed to cover, they split it up into three distinctive areas. Before the event was the first area, they wanted to cover with each of the suspects. This included how they knew each other. Then what happened during the murder itself, and finally, what happened afterwards.

For George, they knew there wasn't much they needed to cover in terms of the offence, but he was heavily involved in before, and after, the event. Unfortunately for George, he was inextricably linked to the murder, even if he hadn't been there at the time. Rich and Sandy had discussed the principle of the three of them being involved in joint enterprise. They didn't get too far in resolving this and thought they would leave it to their barrister to think through the implications of this in due course. The barrister for the Crown had been selected the previous week and was Mr Christopher Coke, Queen's Council. The suspects hadn't appointed any barristers as yet. It would only happen after charge, so either Wednesday or Thursday next week.

Late on Sunday evening, Sandy had received a message from Arabella telling him that, as promised, she and George were booked on the plane to Toronto first thing on the Monday morning. He was doing really well. She wanted advice about applying for bail for George when he was back in England. Sandy felt torn and compromised and didn't want to upset Joanne O'Connor further but rang Arabella anyway. 'Hi, Arabella, please make sure George makes that plane.'

'He will, Sandy, don't worry. I have tried to talk to

him about what happened, but he says he will not talk to me about it as he feels he has let me down dreadfully. James hasn't even tried to talk to him about it.'

'You mentioned bail for George. I am not sure that is appropriate. This is about murder, and it's the murder of a police officer.'

'I know he will go to prison, but as long as we can keep prison in the far distance, I want to do that. His solicitor, who is James's senior partner from the law firm he worked for before he became an MP, has told us not to try for bail at the magistrates' court when he first appears with the other two, but make an application to a Crown Court judge early the next week. What do you think, Sandy? I trust your judgement.'

Sandy wanted to say, he must remain in prison, it is a murder charge he is facing and to one of my police family, but instead said, 'I am sure the solicitor knows what he is doing. He is right, when all three are stood there in the dock it would be extremely hard to separate one from the other. George is a flight risk because he didn't surrender to custody, so that will go against him. Please brace yourself. He might not get bail at any stage.'

'He is not a flight risk; he will turn up for his trial. I will guarantee it.'

Sandy's experience in Canada, trying to detain George and the others, flashed before his eyes. 'What did he go to Canada for then if he isn't a flight risk?'

'Good point,' Arabella conceded.

The police station at Heathrow airport that Sandy, Rich and the team arrived at was positioned just outside the tunnel, which went to the central area where a number of terminals were situated. The boys had been separated and arrived on three different flights, all landing within a couple of hours of each other: two of them on the Air Canada flights from Toronto, and George on the British Airways Toronto flight. The Metropolitan Police had been great with organising the transport to the police station.

Sandy looked into the room where Ruben Cousins was sitting. He was in deep discussion with his solicitor. The solicitor was busy writing notes. The room was a standard interview room with the facility to digitally record the interview with audio and visual. Sandy felt extremely nervous as he knew Rich was too, but they both knew they were well prepared and ready for their day of interviewing. Rich was to wear the earpiece in case the interview advisor needed to contribute and assist them.

After introductions and Rich cautioning Cousins, the interview began with Rich saying, 'Tell us about how you know Dean Kelly and George Peveril.'

'They are my friends.'

'We know this, but how long have they been your friends for?'

'Dean, since we were about seven years old and George, for at least four years now, from when he arrived at our school.' Ruben was dressed in blue jeans and a grey cotton jumper. Even though he was dressed a lot smarter than the last time Sandy had seen him, collecting the food from outside of the cottage, he still looked very slovenly and unkempt. Maybe it was the lack of a haircut or a shave, or more probably the way he sat all slouched down in his chair.

Rich said, 'We have intelligence relating to you and Dean often being together and also being arrested and convicted for offences of drug dealing together.'

'You have the records. Use them. I am not going to tell you about what happened and the police stitching me up for those offences.'

'We don't have any records of you and George being together. Do you commit crimes together?'

'You don't really want to talk about my past, nor do I. So, why don't you just get to the point and let me go back to my cell to sleep,' Ruben said. He was starting to get agitated as he thought the interview was about the murder and not about his whole life history.

His solicitor intervened and said, 'Mr Cousins has a prepared statement ready, if it helps.'

Slightly taken aback, Rich said, 'We do need to ask our questions.' Clearly, the interview advisor said something in his ear because Rich went on to say, 'OK, Ruben, please read out your statement.'

'I don't need to read it out. It says that I never had a

gun and I didn't shoot no copper.'

Sandy asked, 'You are though admitting to being in Derby city centre on the night that PC Foster was shot?'

Cousins and his solicitor looked at each other and the solicitor mouthed the words 'no comment,' then Cousins said, 'No comment.'

'We know you were there, initially dealing in drugs; we have three witnesses to this. We have your photo on speed cameras leaving the city centre at the time,' Sandy said.

'You haven't got any evidence of me shooting no copper though, have you?'

'We have your fingerprints on the SIM card of a phone that was used in the vicinity of where PC Foster was shot, at the time that he was shot.'

'I could have put the SIM card in that phone ages before. You haven't got evidence of me with the phone when the copper was shot though, have you?'

Cousins was right, they didn't, and did not quite have ready a map that showed the phone was also at the scenes where the speed cameras took his photograph with Kelly. So Rich said, 'Our analysts are developing a map that shows that phone was with you and Kelly from the point where the car was stolen, and then plotted on its journey until where the car was burnt out.'

'You keep developing it then.' Cousins had clearly lost interest in being interviewed any longer. He started to fiddle with the cuff on his jumper and look around the room.

Sandy said, 'We know you and Kelly were dealing in drugs in Derby city centre. What do you say to this?'

'Prove it.'

'We know you and Kelly had a Smith & Wesson revolver and that was the weapon that shot and killed PC Foster.'

'I am getting bored with this. I didn't shoot that copper. How many times do you want me to say it!'

It seemed pointless continuing with the interview. They had put the relevant questions to Cousins but had not as yet spoken about the conversation that was on the listening device in Canada. They needed to establish if Cousins agreed that his teacher, Mr Buckley, would be able to recognise his voice. 'How well do you know a teacher called Mr Billy Buckley?'

'I know him very well. We were constantly in and out of his classroom since I was eleven. Why are you asking me about one of my teachers?' a curious looking Cousins asked.

'So, he would know your voice anywhere?'

'What a stupid question, of course he would.'

'You were heard saying to Kelly, "We knew the gun had bullets in, we were playing with it." You said that, didn't you?'

'Who told you that? Peveril?' a by now extremely shocked-looking Cousins said, and quickly added, 'I never shot anyone.'

The interview concluded shortly after this as Cousins was now, with his solicitor's advice, just saying, 'No comment' to anything else they asked. They left him with his solicitor, knowing now very clearly what his line of defence was going to be at the criminal trial. He didn't shoot anyone.

∞

Rich and Sandy decided the next person to be interviewed would be Dean Kelly. They had been informed by the Operation Primrose interview advisor that his research had revealed that Dean Kelly had a very short attention span and would need their questions to be short and sharp.

Before the interview commenced, the solicitor informed Rich and Sandy that his client was willing to be interviewed but he had attention deficit hyperactivity disorder, most commonly called ADHD. He did not need an appropriate adult to assist him, but what he did need was for their questioning to be as clear and concise as possible. Well done to the research completed by the interview advisor – he had prepared them well.

After the customary introductions and caution, Kelly confirmed that he knew the other two by being his friends, originally, from school, but also outside of school. Ruben Cousins, he said, was his best friend.

Rich asked, 'What were you doing in Derby city centre on the night PC Foster was shot?'

'I wasn't there, I was at home with my mum and dad.' Rich and Sandy presumed that Kelly had spoken to his mum and dad whilst at the detention centre in Toronto, and they had told him they were providing him with an alibi.

Rich showed Kelly a picture of his orange Fat Face hoodie. 'Is this yours?'

'No idea. I have one similar, if that is what you are asking. I left it in Canada.' Kelly was already rocking in his chair and his right leg was constantly moving up and down.

'We have recovered that hoodie in Canada and brought it back to England. We have had it examined.' Rich showed Kelly pictures of the CCTV and the speed camera photographs. 'This is you, isn't it?'

'The pictures are not clear enough for me to say it is me.' Kelly was right about the CCTV images but not the speed camera pictures.

'We have three witnesses who have made statements to say you tried to sell them drugs on that night.'

'I have convictions for selling drugs, so you are right.'

Rich and Sandy suddenly got very excited. Were they getting an admission? Rich lent forward and said, 'So, you admit to selling drugs on the night that PC Foster was shot?'

'No, I thought you meant witnesses from the past. I have convictions for selling drugs, so you are trying to fit me up. I was not selling drugs on that night, because guess what, I was at home with my mum and dad. All you coppers are the same. Who fits the best, well it must be them.'

They really needed to be very specific in their questioning – any slight ambiguity and Kelly didn't understand or pretended not to. He went on to say again, like a broken record, 'I told you, I was at home with my mum and dad.'

'Why did you shoot the police officer?'

'I didn't.'

Sandy said, 'Let me keep this simple. There were three people there. Joseph Foster was the one shot. Ruben Cousins says he didn't shoot anyone. So, that leaves you as the only one of the three that could have shot Joseph, doesn't it?'

'What are you on about? I don't understand.'

'Your orange hoodie has gunshot residue on it.'

Before Sandy could ask Kelly about how he thinks this came to be on the hoodie, Kelly burst out of his chair, standing up, and said, 'Other people wear that hoodie, we share it. The last person to wear it was Peveril, not me, so you ask him about that so-called gunshot thingy that you just said.'

'Please, sit down, we will try and finish our questions as soon as we can,' Rich said. 'Do you know Mr Billy Buckley?'

'Of course I do. You are just being stupid and talking pathetic now,' Kelly said, as he sat back down again. His solicitor had put his hand on his arm to reassure him.

'Would he recognise your voice?'

'Stupid question again. Duh, yes.'

'You were overheard at the cottage in Canada when talking about you shooting the policeman. You said you "did the world a good thing by shooting him". You said that, didn't you, Dean?'

'Any dead copper is a good thing, isn't it,' Kelly said, sneering at Rich and Sandy. 'But no, I didn't shoot him, I missed having the pleasure of doing that because I was at home with my mum and dad.' Kelly's solicitor shook his head at him when he said about any dead copper being a good thing. When Kelly saw this, he exploded again, this time at his solicitor. 'Don't you go shaking your head at me, you idiot. I am not having anyone tell me off, you jumped up man in a suit.'

'You weren't at home,' Sandy said, realising they probably only had an opportunity for one or two more questions. 'Your neighbour Miss Danvers said you came home at five thirty that morning with Cousins and Peveril in his Ford Fiesta.'

'She is a lying cow and hates me. Tells everyone I broke into her car. I did, but there is no need to tell everyone. What a grass. Don't you believe a word of what she is saying to you.'

Kelly jumped out of his chair again. The interview couldn't go on any longer so was terminated. Rich and Sandy walked out as Kelly was raging on at his solicitor about Eleanor Danvers. All in all, they were satisfied with how the interview had gone. Parents as his alibi was all he had.

Chapter Twenty-Six

The final interview was to be held with George Peveril. It was now early evening. George's solicitor had spent an incredibly long time with him, discussing the disclosure that Operation Primrose had shared with him. From what Rich and Sandy could see on looking into the interview room, George and his solicitor were disagreeing quite aggressively with each other. They would soon find out what this disagreement was about, as shortly after this they were told that George was ready to be interviewed.

Rich went through the initial introductions and workings of the digitally recorded interview. After the caution, Rich asked how he knew Cousins and Kelly, and the reply, like the other two had given them, was that they had met at school. They were the only two people that had shown him any friendship when he moved schools. He would always be very grateful, as this had been at a very difficult time for him in his life.

'Tell us about the Smith & Wesson revolver?' Rich asked, whilst sliding across a photograph of the gun for

George and his solicitor to view.

'I went to Peveril Hall to visit my grandfather, but he had forgotten we had arranged to see each other and was still in London.' That sounds familiar, thought Sandy, remembering being stood up himself by Viscount Peveril. 'I know the hall well and you can access it from my grandfather's private apartment. I had a look around the hall as I had not been inside there for a long while. I saw the gun in a cabinet display for the Second World War. I knew friends of mine needed something like a gun to help them, to use as an enforcer. The gun was perfect, so I snapped off a flimsy lock and took it.'

'So, you stole it?'

'Yes, obviously. However, I am not sure how the agreement works with National Heritage, but the gun is sort of owned by my family, isn't it?'

'Obviously, we know who you gave the gun to, but we need you to say who your friends are, which you have mentioned. What are their names?'

'I am not prepared to tell you who they are.'

George's solicitor then interjected and said, 'I have advised Mr Peveril to either make no comment, or, if he is going to tell you about his involvement, he needs to be fully honest and name the other two involved. I am afraid he has declined my advice.'

'George, please don't be loyal to your so-called friends; they won't do the same for you. This is an offence of murder that you are involved in, not just the theft of a gun,' Sandy said desperately, trying to get

George to name Cousins and Kelly.

'DCI McFarlane, I know you probably saved my life, but that doesn't give you any extra influence on what I am going to say. I am not going to grass on my friends. If I have anything left in my life, it is my right to be a loyal friend.'

Rich said, 'I am equally sorry, but we will not give up asking. When did you give these friends of yours the gun, and when you gave it to them, for what did you think they would use it? You said as an enforcer, what does that mean?'

'I gave it to them straight away, probably about two weeks before the policeman was shot. I thought the gun was only going to be used for threatening people with. I actually didn't know it was loaded, but I accept I didn't check.'

'Where were you on the night that PC Foster was shot? I am sure you can remember that time clearly as a lot happened after it.'

'I was at home in Losehill Farmhouse. I was in my room all night. I went to sleep quite late but got woken up a couple of hours later when I received a call. I then went to collect my friends and took them, via our family farm in Norfolk, to Canada. DCI McFarlane, you know the rest of what happened there.'

Sandy looked at George. He was dressed very smartly. He couldn't seem to get fully comfortable in his seat, clearly due to the pain and discomfort in his right leg as he kept rubbing it, moving it and stretching the leg out. He did look really well. He had been polite in all his answers, but he was very clear that he was not going to give anything away concerning Cousins and Kelly. He was an intelligent young man, but very naïve as to the extreme trouble he was in.

'What did Cousins and Kelly tell you? Did they tell you what they had done?' Rich asked.

'I am sorry, DI Singh, but you are not going to trick me. I am not saying the people that called me were Dean and Ruben, you are saying that. The friends that rang me did tell me they were in serious bother. A police officer had got hurt and they had stolen a car to get away. I met them on the route back from Derby, near to Chesterfield, along a farm track, and then took them, after collecting our passports, to Norfolk and then to Canada.'

'Why did you not dispose of the gun somewhere else, but hid it at Peveril Farm in Norfolk?' Sandy asked.

'It was my great grandfather's property and I didn't want to just chuck it in a river. I didn't think anyone would find it, but I didn't reckon on someone like you, did I?' George said, looking straight at Sandy. 'You are a big hit with my father and aunty. I say again, though, that that does not give you any extra influence on me.'

Rich showed George the CCTV photograph from Winnipeg airport. 'Is that your hoodie that you are wearing?'

George laughed. 'No. How did you get hold of that picture? I only put it on that one time as a joke. No, I won't say who owns it as obviously it is significant to you, if not you would not be asking me about it.'

'You are telling us that you were the key person to facilitate your friends; no, let me rephrase that as I am not going to call them friends as I don't think they are. You actively facilitated the evading of arrest by Cousins and Kelly. Two people who you either knew then, or knew shortly afterwards, to have carried out the murder of PC Joseph Foster,' Sandy said to George.

'I did what any good friend would do. I think I have said enough now.' His leg was clearly making him very uncomfortable.

George made no further replies and reverted to saying only no comment. Sandy thought, you are probably no longer lost as such, but definitely lost in some misguided sense of loyalty to someone who shot you and didn't even have the moral decency to ask how you were getting on in hospital.

∞

The next morning, the charging of the three boys took place as planned. There was no drama involved and none of them made any comments. Rich, who carried out the charging procedure, was informed by the solicitors that none of the boys were going to request bail at the hearing that afternoon. Rich had been tipped off by Sandy about his conversation with Arabella concerning bail and that there was a possibility of George applying for bail. The solicitor told Rich the family had agreed with his advice, to wait and apply to a Crown Court judge at the end of this week or early next week.

As soon as the charging procedures were completed, Sandy knew who he had to call first, but couldn't resist phoning his Grandad Tom instead. 'Grandad, we have just charged three people with the murder of PC Joseph Foster.'

'Sandy, well done, really well done, son. Great news. The hard work starts now though. You do know that.' Sandy's grandad often said this. Just because you have charged someone, doesn't mean to say your job is finished. His favourite phase in relation to this was always 'investigate to conviction, not to charge'. You have to work as hard to get a conviction as you do for a charge.

'I know, Grandad. You always tell me that.' They both laughed together. 'I am just about to phone PC Foster's widow so I have got to go. I will see you and Grandma soon.'

'Let's hope Mrs Foster and the family start to feel that they are beginning to get justice for his death.'

Sandy quickly rang Belinda, who answered the phone straight away. 'I know why you are ringing, DCI McFarlane, but Lofty Dobson beat you to it. He is on his way round here now, to see if we want to comment on the charging, for a press release that the police are going to issue soon. Thank you for all that you have done, and can you thank DI Singh for me as well, please.'

'I hope you feel some small comfort that, at last, someone is going to be accountable for Joseph's death.'

'Yes, we do, but I would be lying if I said it is helping with my grief; I am afraid it is not. I am also worried about having to attend court, especially if I have to say anything.'

'Talk to Lofty about this when he comes round. You have the allocated victim support homicide worker who will help you with anything to do with court. I will try and come with Lofty to take your victim impact statement, but that will probably be in a few months' time.'

'The victim support worker has already been to see me. She is wonderful and extremely helpful. I am in good hands. Did Lofty tell you I have apologised to Joanne O'Connor? Silly really, and I know Joe would have been furious with me for falling out with her. We are fine now though.' Belinda started to cry and Sandy was pleased he heard the front doorbell ring and Belinda tell him that Lofty had arrived. Sandy couldn't help wanting to cry himself.

The boys were not due in court until two p.m. This was at Westminster Magistrates' Court, which, they were told, was the dedicated court for offenders arriving back after being extradited. There was no need for Sandy to go as Rich was already attending. In fact, for Sandy, most if not all of his work on Operation Primrose was coming to an end. Jane Watson wanted him back next week as Juliet was heading off to Barbados with her family for a holiday. So, Sandy planned to tidy up a few things on the case for the rest of that day and then take the Friday off. He and Rich had been working very hard including all of the last weekend, so it would be nice to have some time off.

Sandy sent a message to Hannah telling her about the charges. Her message back said that she desperately needed to see Sandy and could she meet him in Cambridge on Friday afternoon or Saturday. Sandy felt great. It was not every day that you were involved in a case where an offender was charged with murder. It really was a good feeling. To add to this, his girlfriend wanted to see him desperately. He was a lucky man.

Sandy put on the television in the police station's staff room. The news was due on shortly. The first item was the charges of Cousins, Kelly and Peveril with the murder of PC Joseph Foster. The pictures that they showed of the boys looked fairly old ones and they looked like immature little boys in them, not the young men Sandy had been looking at over the last few days. Joanne O'Connor had given an excellent press interview and had finished by saying, 'These charges, though, do not bring Joseph back to his wife, children, family and the Derbyshire police. The pain of his loss will not be diminished by these charges but will be of help for those of us that seek justice for him.'

All of it well said by Joanne and well done to her. The strain and stress she must have been under was incredible, so today was a good day for her. One thing that Sandy did not like from the media coverage was how the media had latched on to George's family connections and photographs of George's MP father were being shown, as were photographs of Viscount Peveril.

Chapter Twenty-Seven

It was late Friday afternoon when Hannah and Sandy met up at the botanical gardens in Cambridge. Sandy had driven there in his Morgan motor car from Ely, after having arrived home the night before. The gardens are part of the university and have been at their current site, just south of the city centre, since the early 1800s. Hannah had never been there before so they had arranged to meet there to have a casual wander around, looking at the beautiful gardens before having a slow walk through Cambridge to the Oak Bistro, where they intended to have an early evening meal together.

They were walking around enjoying both the sunshine and the forty-acre site, which was wonderfully full of beautiful plants with a lot in bloom. The gardens also included a lake and glass houses. Sandy felt that something was clearly troubling Hannah a great deal, so he asked her, 'Hannah, what's wrong? You seem so out of sorts. Are you OK?'

'I need to talk to you about us, and something that is likely to come between us,' Hannah said. This took

Sandy completely by surprise, as not for one minute did, he think there was anything wrong with their relationship. In fact, he thought it was perfect. They found a nearby bench for them to sit on and Hannah said, 'Do you remember that time when we met at court in the Old Bailey for coffee?' Hannah seemed to have a large lump in her throat that she tried to clear. She looked on the verge of tears. 'Do you remember the name of the person I was defending in the trial at the Old Bailey?'

'No, I just remember how beautiful you looked even with your barrister wig on.'

'Please, don't make this any harder for me. The defendant was Ruben Cousins.'

Sandy was totally shocked by hearing this name. 'You cannot mean my Ruben Cousins, can you?'

'Well, it's actually my Ruben Cousins, not yours. I am going to be defending him at the murder trial.'

'You can't,' Sandy said, jumping up in horror. 'You must hand back your brief. You mustn't do this, Hannah. He killed a policeman.' The gardens were full of families that afternoon and a couple of them looked round to see who it was that had raised voices in the gardens.

Hannah by now was welling up with tears, which had started to appear and roll down her face. 'The trouble is, Sandy, I am his lawyer. I am not able to walk away from him. I can assure you that I have not taken on this case lightly, although it is an incredible case to be involved in. For me, it is almost career-making. It is not a case of I want to do it; it is a case that I have to defend him. Everyone must have a robust defence, in order to ensure guilt and that we don't end up in the Court of Appeal. He has asked for me personally and I am his lawyer. I have defended him twice before. You are not fully connected to the trial anyway; it is a Derbyshire Police case. There is no conflict, you have mentioned very little to me about the case anyway, just how you saved George Peveril's life in Canada.'

The tears continued to fall down Hannah's face and Sandy desperately wanted to comfort her but was so very upset himself. He said, 'Of course there is conflict. Maybe not in the legal sense, I grant you, but in our personal relationship. The conflict in my mind is insurmountable. If that is your decision and you won't change your mind, then we can't be together anymore.' Sandy didn't want to create more of a scene than what was already taking place, with even more people starting to look over at what was going on, so he stormed off, close to tears himself, leaving Hannah crying in the gardens. He knew he was being totally unreasonable, but he couldn't get the vision of Joseph, Belinda Foster and their two small children out of his mind, and the deep pain that Ruben Cousins and his friends had caused them.

He raced back to his car, which he had parked in the University Arms Hotel car park and drove at speed back to Ely. He was by now crying softly; it was the first time this had happened since the death of his grandma. He was actually crying mostly for Hannah, as he knew how much his decision had hurt her, but it was the right decision, he stubbornly thought to himself.

As he drove along, another thought entered his head. What if Hannah had said she was defending George Peveril, what would his reaction be then? Although he one hundred percent wanted justice to be done, and if that included George being convicted of the murder charge, so be it. He did, though, have a soft spot for George and his family and he might have crazily been OK with that. He was in a very emotional and confused state.

Sandy parked the car in his usual place and raced through the front door and went straight up to his bedroom. He wasn't sure what he was going to do with himself, but one thing he was sure of was that he needed to be alone.

∞

Katherine and Gregor were taken totally by surprise by the early arrival home of their son. He had told them earlier that he would be back late after having dinner with Hannah. Going straight up to his bedroom like he had just done, without saying hello, was just not like the son they knew and loved.

They both raced upstairs and Katherine knocked on the door. 'Sandy, are you OK? What has happened, sweetheart?'

'Mum, just leave me alone. I don't want to talk about it,' Sandy replied. 'There is nothing you can do anyway.'

'It might just help to talk about it though,' Katherine said, going into the bedroom to see Sandy lying on his bed, staring aimlessly at his phone. 'I take it you have had a row with Hannah?'

'Mum, you and Dad don't know what it is like to be searching for someone. You both found each other when you were sixteen years old, at the new sixth formers welcome meeting for Cambridge schools, and you have been together ever since. I have been searching for that magic, that incredible chemistry you both have all of my life. I know you and my sisters didn't think so but I have been searching, and then to suddenly find someone when I wasn't looking crash into my world, someone as beautiful, intelligent and amazing as Hannah. She is perfect for me, Mum, and I have lost her.'

Sandy started to cry softly and quietly into his mother's shoulder, who just sat there not saying a word and just hugged him. Eventually, she said, 'I am sure the two of you can sort this out. Hannah definitely feels the same way about you. It makes my heart sing when I see how she looks at you and how she is with you.'

'No, Mum, we have irresolvable professional differences. I am not going to say any more about it.'

There was then the unmistakable sound of his grandpa's old diesel Mercedes car pulling up outside the back of his parents' home. Sandy shouted at his dad, 'How could you ring him, Dad!' Katherine and Gregor were totally taken aback by Sandy shouting at his father as he had never even raised his voice to them before. Their girls had, on a number of occasions, but not Sandy.

'I didn't, Sandy. Why would I want to involve my father?' Gregor protested. Sandy knew instantly that his dad was right. It had to have been Hannah that had called John McFarlane. She was incredibly fond of Sandy's grandpa.

Katherine let John into the house and they all went into the lounge. Katherine and Gregor very quickly left Sandy and his grandpa alone together. 'I knew that you would take Hannah's side,' Sandy said.

'That is unfair, Sandy. I love you more than words can say. I would go to a world war for you and your sisters. I admit, I am very fond of Hannah though. Yes, she did ring me and she is extremely upset. What I want to give you though is an objective perspective on the situation.'

'Is Hannah OK, Grandpa? Please look out for her. I really don't want her to be upset.'

'I will look out for her, don't worry. Let me give you a different perspective. In terms of justice, Sandy, you wouldn't want anyone not to have the best legal representation that they can, would you? This absolutely helps to prevent any miscarriage of justice. For Ruben Cousins, the best barrister from his point of view is the one who has defended him in the past, which is Hannah Tobias. He most definitely shouldn't be denied her representation. That surely is the right thing to do.'

'There are other excellent barristers that could also equally represent him. What about if Hannah wasn't available due to another case commitment?'

'Yes, of course there are other barristers, but he totally trusts Hannah. If you consider for one moment in terms of Hannah's career, I am sure you are ambitious for her – being involved in any murder trial, let alone one as high a profile as this one, is an incredible experience. There will also be four Queen's Counsel barristers involved for her to learn from.'

'I understand all of your points, but do you not get my point though, Grandpa. Hannah and I are on opposite sides, and for me that is untenable. You will say why is it Hannah that has to recuse herself, why can't I withdraw. Think about my career for a moment with this case. But more importantly, I have been so heavily involved in the case and Hannah has only just started on it. So, I can't withdraw, I am afraid. That puts us against each other.'

'Hannah started with Ruben Cousins a long time ago as well. Long before your involvement in the case,' John McFarlane said to his grandson, knowing this was not an argument he could win. 'OK, Sandy, I have said my piece, I will go now.'

The two of them had a long hug at the front door before John went out to head back home. They both knew that there was weight to both sides of this argument, but it was not something that could be resolved by the two of them. Ultimately, only Sandy and Hannah could solve it.

Chapter Twenty-Eight

When Sandy arrived back at the FCO offices the next week, he found that life there was really hectic. To a certain extent, this was because it was the summer holidays and the team were missing a number of staff who were away, such as Juliet Ashton and Phil Harris. The main reason though, was because the British prime minister, Boris Johnson, had been determined that Britain would leave the European Union. Therefore, international relations and trade was the key to Britain's economic future. At every meeting Sandy went to, either with or for his boss, Jane Watson, he was told their investigations abroad must be in conjunction with the authorities there and not to jeopardise diplomatic relationships, i.e. future trade deals.

When looking through the outstanding investigation files, Sandy found that there were very few that had not been filed. Juliet had been very efficient, as he knew she would be, acting as a detective inspector in place of him whilst he had been seconded to Operation Primrose. Jane Watson had told him she would release him back to that investigation if necessary for the odd day or two, and for some of the trial. Joanne O'Connor had been pleased with this decision and had, according to Jane, been highly complementary of Sandy and his work as a detective on the investigation, so she would welcome whatever time he could be spared to work with her.

One of the deaths abroad that Sandy was disappointed had been filed was the case of John Groves and Tania Miles, who whilst backpacking in Asia, had been found dead in a hotel room in Singapore. He had wanted to look at this case in more detail, but Juliet had filed this marked "no further action". Sandy vowed that he would look back into it at some point in the future. He was wary that Singapore was very much the sort of powerhouse economy that Britain would want to be aligned with, so if he did, he would have to tread very carefully.

Another massive move in government that was happening incredibly quickly was that the FCO was being joined by the Department for International Development. Sandy had worked with them closely on a case in India so knew a few of their civil servants quite well. In only a few weeks, the new department was going to be called the Foreign, Commonwealth and Development Office. Sandy needed to start using FCDO now and to no longer say he worked at the FCO.

The fact that he was so busy should have meant he had no time to think about Hannah, but this was not true. He constantly thought about her, knowing that they could have worked through it. But he had made his decision about the relationship and he just had to get on with it. Only that morning he had been in a meeting in the beautiful Locarno Suite within the FCO offices. Whilst he normally loved being in there, mostly for the room's architectural grandeur, Sandy's thoughts had drifted back to wondering what Hannah was up to.

The weekend after they had split up from each other, Sandy had gone for a long run in the morning. He found exercise and sport were his greatest therapy. He had run from his home up through Cherry Hill Park, gazing over at the cathedral, and then on past his grandparents' house to run along a few ancient droves and tracks to a village called Little Downham, which had an interesting church, St Leonard's. He continued in a circular route back to Ely, eventually reaching the meadows along the River Great Ouse and then back home. Both of his sisters kept messaging him that weekend to find out if he was OK. Aileen had been round twice with his nephews as she knew how much he adored them. Sandy was pleased that they were both also messaging Hannah, which he found comforting as he was worried about her.

Arabella had stuck to her plan and had got a bail hearing in the Crown Court for George. This happened a week after he had appeared at Westminster Magistrates' Court. Arabella had rung Sandy to tell him that George's bail had been refused, but he already knew as Rich, who had been at the hearing, informed him on the day itself. Sandy wondered what Arabella's next move would be. She was a formidable woman, who, he was sure, wouldn't accept defeat.

When Sandy's phone rang, he was really pleased to see it was Rich calling him. 'Hi, Rich, how are you?'

'Good thanks, do you want the good news, the average news, or the bad news first?'

'Now that's a tricky one. Let's go for the bad news first,' Sandy said, worrying about how bad Rich meant by bad news.

'Eleanor Danvers has had two of her front windows smashed and her car sprayed with the word "grass" on it. Eleanor has now withdrawn her original statement and has made a new one, which says she was mistaken on the date and that it was the week before.'

'So, her grandad's birthday has suddenly changed,' a despondent Sandy said. 'You can understand it though. Single mum, living alone. Directly opposite the Kelly's. Have you put in any protection for her?'

'We have installed a camera and an alarm for her. I don't think she is going to change her statement back though. Even Joanne feels sorry for her and she hasn't even mentioned going to see her and threatening her with perverting the course of justice.'

'So, that's the bad news then. What is the average news?'

'Sorry, not finished with the bad news yet. Billy Buckley has also had a window smashed.'

'Don't tell me he is going to withdraw his statement too. That is much worse news than the Eleanor Danvers news. I could try the National Crime Agency and see if their specialist operations centre can find us a voice expert,' Sandy said, now increasingly worried that a crucial piece of evidence might not be available to them.

'Billy is still willing to give evidence so that's not currently needed. You don't need to worry. I will action the contact with the NCA.'

'Next bad news, please,' Sandy said. He knew George hadn't got bail as he hadn't heard from Arabella, so was intrigued as to what it could be.

'No, only average news next. A man has come forward saying he was threatened by Cousins and Kelly with a gun in Nottingham city centre, a week or so before the murder of Joseph Foster. His name is Gary Rawlings.'

'That is not average news, that is good news,' Sandy said, thinking this might help to make up for the loss of Eleanor.

'The reason why it is average news is that he is in Nottingham prison, serving six years' imprisonment for importation of drugs. He was no doubt supplying Cousins and Kelly. He wants a reduction of his time to serve in prison. He was only sentenced last week. I am going to see him though. Are you able to come with me?'

Sandy quickly looked through his diary and suggested Wednesday the following week. 'Any more average news or can we have the good news now?'

'Well, I think it is good news. I have been promoted

this morning to DCI in charge of the CID for the Peak District.'

'That is really good news,' Sandy said, genuinely very pleased for Rich. 'Well done, DCI Singh. When do you start there?'

'Joanne has also been promoted. She is now a Chief Superintendent, and she is still going to oversee Operation Primrose, but in essence I will be in charge and remain full time on it until the end. I will only then go to my new post. Suits me down to the ground.'

'Good for Joanne as well. Right, I will see you, I presume, at Nottingham prison next Wednesday. Shall we meet for breakfast first?'

'I will get someone to sort out the visitor passes with the prison. One more bit of good news. We have a trial judge appointed, Mr Justice Francis Kane QC. I have the plea and directions meeting with him at Birmingham Crown Court next Monday so I can fill you in on what happened when we meet. No to breakfast though because I have the school run all next week. I have already got out of doing it on Monday so dare not push my luck, but lunch on me instead.'

All in all, this was mostly good news, Sandy thought. He was thrilled for Rich and knew that he was on a journey speeding through the ranks. He had a nagging thought that Billy Buckley could still back out, which worried him. They definitely needed a backup plan. He was increasingly worried about Eleanor Danvers, not for the case so much, but for her. It must be awful living so close to the Kelly family who could watch her every move.

Chapter Twenty-Nine

The train from St Pancras train station to Nottingham took Sandy almost two hours. He had allowed time to get to St Pancras and then for the taxi to take him to the prison, which meant that he had had a very early start leaving from his London flat on the Wednesday morning. He was glad that Rich hadn't taken him up on the offer of breakfast. Sandy was very happy with the bacon roll and coffee he had bought at the station.

The plea and direction hearing had been reported in the newspapers, which had said that Cousins, Peveril and Kelly had all pleaded not guilty to all the charges. There were no applications for bail and a trial date was to be set shortly. Sandy thought some of the press reporting was awful, as there was hardly any mention of Joseph Foster, but there were plenty of pictures of both James and William Peveril. If you were a member of the public flicking through the newspapers with no knowledge of the case, you would probably believe James and William had committed the murder themselves.

When Rich and Sandy were shown into the legal visits meeting room, they were met by a young man who looked to be only in his early to mid-twenties, not much older than Cousins and Kelly. Gary Rawlings was sitting at a table, wearing a prison uniform, and lounging in his chair. He didn't look very tall and had extremely short dark hair. After introductions, Rich started the conversation.

'As you are now aware, we are from the Operation Primrose incident team. Why do you want to talk to us?' Rich was clearly more interested in Rawlings' motivation rather than what he had to say. 'What is in it for you, for you to tell us what happened in Nottingham, and why didn't you come forward at the time?'

'I am being public spirited, aren't I,' Rawlings replied in a very thick East Midlands accent.

'Let's not waste each other's time. Others, in particular Cousins' and Kelly's lawyers, will ask this: what do you want for giving us the information?'

Rawlings, now understanding that this was a business transaction rather than a straightforward witness interview, said, 'I want to be moved to an open prison and not to serve more than two years maximum.' Sandy had no idea how they got someone moved to an open prison, but quickly did the maths in his head. Rawlings had been sentenced to six years' imprisonment, you got half off for good behaviour, so that meant three years. Rawlings wanted a third of his prison time off. Was that reasonable? Yes, most probably. He hadn't asked for immediate release or anything like that.

Sandy said, 'That might be something we can achieve. Tell us if it is worth it. Don't try and embellish it, just the truth will do.'

The smile that Rawlings now had across his face made Sandy and Rich think Rawlings, for some reason, thought he now had the upper hand, when in fact it was the opposite. Let him think it, they thought. 'I met them at a pre-arranged spot, which was just by the railway station short stay car park, to supply them with a package of cocaine. We had already been paid for it. They were just the couriers.'

Rich and Sandy had a lot of questions they wanted to ask, based on the couple of sentences Rawlings had just said. The detectives in them had kicked in. Rich went first. 'Who pre-arranged it and who paid for the drugs?'

Sandy added, 'How did you know it was Cousins and Kelly you were talking about as the couriers?'

Rawlings sat up in his seat and knew he needed to be alert to not drop himself in it, or his organised crime bosses. 'I am not going to tell you any of that as it will incriminate me and others. I will though tell you that I had met Cousins and Kelly once before to carry out the same transaction, so I knew them. When I saw their pictures on the news, I thought I would say what happened to me and I admit it, I wanted to see what I could get out of it for myself.'

'So, what happened then?'

'I handed the package over and Cousins could see that I had another package in my bag, as well as a small quantity of cash, probably about two hundred pounds. He took out a revolver. He initially threatened that he would shoot me, but then he hit me over the head with it and they ran off with the bag.'

Rich and Sandy looked at each other in surprise. Sandy went first. 'Are you sure it was Cousins and not Kelly?'

'Yes, absolutely. Ruben he was called. I had to go to hospital, and they told me I had a fracture to my skull. Gosh it hurt and I still get headaches now. I was already on bail at the time and was sentenced a week or two later. I have a huge drug debt because of them, and they now have a matching debt with my dealers. They need to be very scared.'

∞

After they had left Rawlings, Rich gave Sandy a lift back to the train station. They stopped nearby at a small café for a sandwich and a coffee. They had driven into and looked at the railway station, short stay car park and there were a few CCTV cameras in place. Rich said he would get Lofty to obtain what he could, bearing in mind this alleged assault had happened a few weeks ago. He would also get someone from the team to enquire at the Queen's Medical Centre, Nottingham, to see if it could be confirmed that Rawlings had had a fractured skull.

They were both surprised it was Cousins and not Kelly using the gun, but this helped their case of murder to be strengthened against Cousins. Rawlings had admitted to drug dealing to Rich and Sandy, but when they had pointed this out to him, he had smiled and said, 'You have no drugs, and neither Cousins nor Kelly is going to admit to it, are they?'

Rich said, 'Sandy, you didn't tell me that your girlfriend was so beautiful.'

'What do you mean? I don't have a girlfriend.'

Rich was surprised by this reply and looking intently at Sandy, said, 'I mean the girl who you kept talking about in Canada, the same one you kept messaging all the time and the one you went to Florence with. That is who! Hannah Tobias. Cousins' barrister.'

Of course. Sandy hadn't thought that Hannah might have been at the plea and directions hearing.

'She asked after you and how you are doing and if you are still involved in the case. She is smart and beautiful and if you have let her go, Sandy, you are a fool.' Sandy could see that Rich wasn't joking but was very serious. It was amazing how quickly, due to circumstances, Rich, and Lofty, were now kind, caring and trusted friends of his and not just colleagues.

'Tell me about what happened at the hearing,' Sandy said quickly, desperate to change the subject and to avoid feeling sad about Hannah again. 'What is Justice Kane like? Did our barrister Christopher Coke attend as well?'

'Yes, Christopher was there, an excellent choice. There was only a junior barrister there for Kelly, the same as Miss Tobias for Cousins. I think they are trying to appoint QCs urgently. However, Peveril's QC is the one the family use, Ebony Forbes-Hamilton, another excellent choice for them. We will have our work cut out to keep ahead of her. She asked, and got CPS and our barrister's approval, to add a charge for George of assisting an offender. Justice Kane liked this as it gave the jury some wiggle room for decision-making. George still pleaded not guilty to it, which made me laugh as they were the ones that had asked for it.'

'Must be Scottish, with a name like Forbes-Hamilton,' Sandy said, and he made a mental note to ask Arabella about her.

'Yes, very Scottish, but you will be surprised when you see her.'

Sandy wondered what he meant by that, but asked, 'Any prospect of a trial date and venue?'

Rich looked very excited and said, 'Number one court at the Old Bailey, listed for up to three weeks, starting at the end of November. The defence must confirm by this Friday that they have QCs in place and are ready for a trial date as soon as this.'

Sandy was also excited with this news. A trial at the Central Criminal Court, commonly known as the Old Bailey, was a highlight to any officer's career. 'Why the Old Bailey?'

'Justice Kane thought it best to not hold the trial in the Midlands due to possible bias. But, more to the point, he has three weeks allocated for him to sit as a judge during that time in the Old Bailey, so to a certain extent, it suits him. The clerks are just arguing on which court, but it will almost certainly be number one court.'

The time had come for Sandy to run and get his train back to London. He was really pleased about the trial being in London as he would be able to keep up his work at the FCO, or as it was soon to be known, the FCDO, and still attend court as often as possible. One person he was worried for was Belinda. This location might suit Justice Kane and himself but would be very daunting for Belinda. He sent a text to Lofty asking how he was and if he had heard from Belinda. Lofty replied quickly that he was well, other than he had just had his worst time ever in the triathlon he had been training for. Operation Primrose was to blame, he thought. He hadn't heard from Belinda.

Sandy tried to, resist but couldn't and sent a message to Hannah saying he hoped she was well and that DCI Singh had said he had seen her at court on the Monday. He thought it would be OK and not insensitive, especially as Rich had said she had asked how he was.

He had almost reached St Pancras Station when Hannah messaged back to say she was fine and very pleased he had messaged her. She had added three kisses, which pleased Sandy greatly.

Chapter Thirty

The weeks and then the next couple of months seemed to go by in a flash. The work in the FCDO was extremely busy during the working week, and at the weekends, Sandy immersed himself in playing rugby for the Ely Tigers Rugby Club second team. Sandy had missed out on two possible work trips abroad. One, he would have liked to have gone on, which was to Albuquerque in New Mexico. Phil Harris went in the end. For Phil, it was a nice relief from his work with the NCA trying to get the European Union to continue with the UK involvement in the European arrest warrant process. This, he found, was very frustrating. Sandy felt he couldn't risk being involved working abroad in case it tied him up at the time of the Cousins, Peveril and Kelly trial.

He had been on a date with one of the civil servants that worked in the offices at the FCDO. Juliet and Clare had found that several of the single girls that worked there were keen on Sandy, and one in particular was especially keen and they had set him up on this date. It wasn't a disaster, but she wasn't Hannah.

The only work he had completed on Operation Primrose was visiting Belinda with Lofty and the victim support worker to take her victim impact statement. All four of them were in tears when Belinda recounted how she and Joseph had first met when he was a young, handsome, tall, and smart soldier in the Grenadier Guards. She showed them a picture of their wedding, with Joseph looking so incredibly smart and proud in his bright Guards scarlet tunic. Once he and Belinda were expecting their first child, he had applied to join the police to ensure home stability. He absolutely loved being a soldier and in the Guards, but his last posting to Afghanistan had made him think twice when he found out he was going to be a father.

Belinda had organised childcare with her parents and sister so that she could spend the first couple of days at court for the trial, and then to be back in court for the conclusion of the case. Joseph's mother planned to be there for the whole duration. Because the trial was being held in London, Jane Watson had been quite happy for Sandy to be totally involved. Everyone should have a boss like Jane, Sandy gratefully thought.

Christopher Coke had allocated the week before the trial's start date as preparation time, and he had organised a conference with the Operation Primrose senior investigation team at his chambers in Middle Temple, London, on the Wednesday afternoon. Mr Coke had sent a message to tell them to be ready for a late session. Sandy had asked Rich if he wanted to meet for lunch beforehand, but Rich and Joanne were only going to arrive in time for the conference. They were though staying overnight in London, so depending on what time they finished, a drink together at least would be nice to do.

The decision to walk to the Temple area was one that Sandy soon regretted, due to the rain that started as he walked along the Strand on that late November afternoon. However, he fought his urge to call one of London's black cabs, as he would have got to the chambers far too early and would most probably have had to stand out in the rain anyway. The Temple, which was situated between Fleet Street and the River Thames beside the Embankment, was one of England's legal centres, which it had been for a number of centuries.

The architecture was incredible and buildings had been built and added to over a period of at least eight hundred years. The alleyways to get into the Temple area from Fleet Street were like something out of a Harry Potter movie. There were also many mentions of this area in the novels by Charles Dickens. Sandy had been there several times in the past for conferences with barristers who had their chambers there. He had been to dinners in the Middle Temple on a few occasions as his Grandpa John was a member of Middle Temple Inn, one of the four Inns of Court that barristers join. He had been a member for over forty-five years and on the occasions that Sandy had been with him, John had been the after-dinner speaker on some aspect of medio-legal law relating to children. John, through his practice as a barrister and judge, and his research as a University of Cambridge associate professor, was undoubtedly an expert in this field.

Sandy especially liked the garden areas in the Temple and had often sat in there on a sunny day, but definitely not today. He had also been in Temple Church as a tourist to listen to the choral music on more than one occasion. Temple Church had been built by the Knights Templar in the twelfth century. The church featured in Dan Brown's novel *The Da Vinci Code*, and after that had featured in the film of the same name. This meant the volume of tourists visiting had swelled considerably, but this had now subsided to a normal level. Sandy had noticed that increase at the time and had avoided the church for a while.

After being shown into a surprisingly large conference room for a very old building, Sandy saw that Joanne and Rich were already present, as was the CPS lawyer and the junior barrister, but Christopher Coke QC had not yet arrived.

∞

When Christopher made his entrance, there was no doubt in anyone's mind who was going to be the star of the forthcoming trial. He breezed into the room giving everyone a stunning, charismatic smile. 'Sorry, I am late,' Christopher said. He was wearing grey, checked suit trousers and a matching waistcoat, but no jacket, along with a piercing blue tie that matched his eyes, as did his blue cufflinks. 'I have just come off the phone to Mrs Forbes-Hamilton. She tells me George is willing to plead guilty to all the charges, but not the murder.'

'No chance. We are surely not going to accept that plea,' Joanne said quickly, before anyone else could state a position.

Christopher, forever the diplomat, flashed his stunning smile. 'Of course, Mrs O'Connor, I said no. Let the jury decide, I told her. But quite frankly, we keep a lot more evidence in the trial if we keep all of the defendants in it together.'

'Would we take the guilty plea if he were willing to give evidence against Kelly and Cousins?' Sandy asked, wanting to give George a chance.

'Let's be realistic, Sandy. He is not likely to do that, is he?' Rich said, looking straight at Sandy.

'My opinion is, let us see how the trial goes and I will keep the dialogue going with the lovely Mrs Forbes-Hamilton,' Christopher said. 'OK, in terms of Mr Gary Rawlings. Not a very nice character. However, we should use him at the trial, if only to lure the defence into bringing his bad character out, which would allow us the same privilege.'

Rich said, 'We can actually confirm that he went to the QMC hospital in Nottingham and did have a skull fracture. He was kept in for two days. We also have

CCTV images.' He passed the pictures over to Christopher to see. 'I know the pictures are blurry, but you can make out that it is Cousins and Kelly in the train station car park.'

'If we haven't done so already, please serve this evidence on the defence straight away. Any updates on Miss Danvers?'

'She has told us that she is too scared to come and give evidence,' Rich replied.

'Let us treat her as both an intimidated and, what she will most likely turn out to be, a hostile witness. Poor girl, the Kelly family should not be allowed to get away with this.'

'I agree,' Joanne added. 'Let me tell you, if Kelly is convicted, I am going to go after his mum and dad for attempting to pervert the course of justice and witness intimidation.' Everyone looked at Joanne and were under no doubt that she meant every word of what she was proposing.

Rich said, 'Billy Buckley though is still happy to attend. Last September, he moved house and changed schools, and after having been promoted, he is now working at a school in Sheffield.'

'Good. Crucial evidence those admissions. We also have the NCA voice expert picking out the different boys' voices after they listened to their interviews at Heathrow. To me, Cousins' and Kelly's voices are similar, but not Peveril's,' Christopher said.

'He is a posh boy,' Joanne said, looking straight at

Sandy, who presumed she was insinuating that about him. He was proud to be a so-called posh boy!

The group spent the next hour or so talking through the order of witnesses. Christopher outlined roughly what he intended to say in his opening speech. Mr Justice Francis Kane QC was apparently a strict but fair judge. 'Who is defending Cousins and Kelly?' Sandy asked.

'For Cousins, a thoroughly dislikeable character called Charles Holloway QC. He is, though, very good, and I mean very good, at his job. Only ever defends and trust me, we will not get any concessions from him.' Poor Hannah, Sandy thought. Christopher continued. 'Then Vaughan Slade QC for Kelly, an articulate Welshman who is so laid back he is almost horizontal, but he will have to do Kelly's bidding. Each of those have a junior barrister, as does Ebony Forbes-Hamilton. Her junior is here in my chambers, so we have an inside channel.' Christopher winked at them all.

When the pizza and beer arrived, Christopher asked, 'Sandy, what is the position with the family and how are they feeling now?'

Sandy had luckily spoken to Lofty that morning and was able to say, 'We have Belinda's victim impact statement and she will be at the trial at the beginning and end. She is not in a good way. A widow at twenty-six years old, two small children and the world's media watching her almost every move. Joseph's mother and brother will be with us every day.'

They all left later that evening with high hopes for their case. Joanne was surprisingly going for a drink with Rich and Sandy, and she was offering to pay. How did Christopher describe Justice Kane? Strict but fair. Well, that summed up Joanne O'Connor.

∞

The next few days went by incredibly fast and before they knew it, the first day of the trial had arrived. Sandy had worried all weekend which tie to wear to go with the suit he had decided on. He knew this was nothing to do with the trial but all to do with the fact that he would be seeing Hannah for the first time since they had broken up in the University of Cambridge botanical gardens. He went, in the end, for the tie he had worn the first time they had gone for coffee together, coincidentally also at court in the Old Bailey.

Jane Watson had wanted Sandy to chair the team meeting that Monday morning before court, but he knew he would be too distracted so had got agreement for Juliet to do it instead. This allowed him to take the fairly short walk from his London flat to the court. Sandy set off early, as over the weekend a thought had come to him about printing off pictures of Joseph. He would need to organise this before the court started.

Just before he turned the corner, he gazed along to St Paul's Cathedral standing resolutely at the top of the street ahead. As he walked onto the street that the court was named after, Old Bailey, Sandy saw James, Arabella and Monty in the window of a café. With them was a very attractive and smartly dressed Black lady, probably about forty years old, but her short, dark curly hair was speckled with quite a lot of grey. In Sandy's view, he thought it made her look even more attractive.

Any thoughts he had of just waving and walking by were useless as Arabella waved wildly for him to come and join them. As he went in, and after Monty had gone off to get him a coffee, Sandy said, 'Not sure I am meant to be fraternising with the opposition.'

'Not a problem for us,' Arabella said, which the others all agreed. Sandy was not so sure though that Joanne O'Connor would feel the same way, so positioned his chair away from being directly in the window.

Arabella said, 'DCI McFarlane, please can I introduce you to George's barrister, Mrs Ebony Forbes-Hamilton.' Sandy now knew what Rich had been alluding to.

'It is my pleasure to meet you, DCI McFarlane. I have heard so much about you from Arabella and James. With your surname, I presume you are Scottish?'

'Yes, Scottish.' After a slight hesitation, allowing him to have a sip of the hot coffee that Monty had brought him, he said, 'Bit of both, born in England and English mother, but Scottish father and grandfather. What about you?'

Ebony had a very soft and cultured, unmistakeably

Scottish accent. 'Probably more Scottish than you.' This brought a few smiles from around the table. 'Born in Scotland, have a home in Scotland. Married a Scotsman. Two children born in Scotland.' Ebony paused for effect and smiled widely. 'But as you can see,' she said, with a flourish, 'both my parents came to live in Edinburgh from Antigua.'

Sandy asked James how he and his father were coping with the media interest in them both. James said, 'Not really a problem for me, but my father has struggled with it. I went and offered my resignation to my constituency chair and to Sir Kier Starmer, the leader of the Labour party. Both of them told me they would not accept my resignation and to just get on with the wonderful job I am doing.' An extremely sad James added. 'I am not sure how you do this, though, if your son is convicted of murder.'

As he left them and headed into the courthouse building, Sandy could see that even though there had been smiles and a bit of laughter, the strain of the situation that George was in was immense and showing on all of them as a family.

Chapter Thirty-One

As Sandy walked into the area where court one was situated, he just knew the first person he would see would be Hannah. And there she was. Standing just beyond the entrance to the court, gazing up at the dome and the murals and paintings there. They were a magnificent sight.

As he stood quietly next to her, Hannah said to him, 'It feels like we are back in Florence together, Sandy.'

'Yes, it does, doesn't it. What a wonderful holiday we had together. I would like to wish you, personally, good luck for the trial, but not Ruben Cousins, if that makes sense.'

'Thank you. I like your tie; it is the one you wore the first time we met here. I hope the Fosters get justice,' Hannah said, giving Sandy her loveliest smile, which almost melted his heart, and with that she walked off to go into court. Wearing that tie had worked, he thought.

Sandy gazed at the paintings and murals by Professor Gerald Moira, who was in his eighties when he was asked to recreate the damaged area in post-Second

World War Britain. Sandy looked at the painting of justice and the mural depicting truth, and all Sandy wanted was for that to be the aim of everyone who was to be involved in the trial as they progressed through the court case in the days ahead.

In the allocated police room, Sandy was able to print off quite easily a number of copies of Joseph in his police uniform. After walking into court, Sandy saw Lofty, who was pleased to see him, as was Belinda and Joseph's mother. Sandy could feel their nervousness. He felt the same. The first day of a murder trial was an unbelievable experience – not just nervousness, but the incredible heightened level of anticipation added to the cocktail of emotion.

Sandy had never been in court number one before and was surprised how cramped it seemed to be. At the front of the court was a raised dais with a long bench and a chair that the judge would sit at, not quite in the centre as that chair was for the Lord Mayor of London if they attended. In this case, he would be sitting alone, but there were a number of other chairs alongside the judge's chair. Directly to the right of the judge was the wooden witness box. Sandy thought it must have been made of oak. In fact, there was lots of wood everywhere in the court. Directly to the right of the witness box was where the jury would sit and opposite them was a long table. Behind this were the rows of barrister benches, or pews, as Sandy thought they looked like. The defendant's dock faced the judge. All of the barristers seemed in place and as Sandy walked over, he looked at them dressed in their gowns with the QCs wearing silk waistcoats. The barristers' wigs were firmly on their heads and he thought for a moment he may have walked into a scene from a long-ago century in history. Sandy gave the photos to Christopher Coke. He was impressed and thanked Sandy for thinking about it.

The jury selection took a surprisingly short time. Justice Kane had made the seven women and five men laugh when he had told them to put any Christmas preparation to one side or get a family member to take that on. The women in particular laughed the loudest. The focus for their lives during the next two to three weeks, he said, was for them to be on this case, and this case only.

Justice Kane asked Christopher Coke to open the case on behalf of the Crown. 'Thank you, my Lord,' Christopher said, rising to his feet to talk to the jury. He told them that they could only decide based on what they heard, either read to them or what was said in the witness box. 'Please, don't look at anything that they say in the newspapers about the case. If you did, you would think at the moment by their pictures often linked to the case that the Right Honourable James Peveril MP, or his father, one of the defendant's grandfathers, Viscount William Harrison Peveril, are responsible in some way. I can tell you now that they are not.' Sandy could see James and Arabella nodding violently in agreement. 'This case is, yes, all about the three defendants, Cousins, Peveril and Kelly, but it is also very much about the murdered PC Joseph Foster. This is a picture of him that I would like you to put into those jury bundle folders that you have on the table in front of you.' Christopher then started to hand out the photograph that Sandy had printed off.

In an instant, Charles Holloway, like a gladiator in a ring about to wield his sword, was on his feet. 'My Lord, I must object in the strongest terms. The emotion of looking at this deceased man is far too prejudicial, and you should make a ruling to not allow it.'

Christopher stopped what he was doing. He knew that this might happen and deliberately hadn't mentioned it to his opponents as he knew they might react like this. He had now, though, put it well and truly in the jury's minds, who would remember it by Holloway's intervention. Justice Kane said, 'Mrs Forbes-Hamilton and Mr Slade, your thoughts, please?'

Ebony was quite happy to go ahead, as was Vaughan Slade. 'Objection overruled. Clerk, please can you hand out to the jury the photograph of the murder victim, Joseph Foster, in his police uniform, for them to include in their jury bundles.' Brilliantly well played Christopher, thought Sandy, and well done to you yourself for thinking about it. Sandy looked round at Lofty and Belinda, who were beaming at him. Rich, who was sitting next to him, patted him on the back.

∞

Justice Kane asked Christopher to start calling his witnesses. The plan was to start with the three witnesses to the drug dealing, but before the first one could be called to the witness box, Charles rose to his feet again. 'My Lord, before this happens, I want to object that there are three prosecution witnesses that I know of – there may in fact be more – sat in this court. Arabella and Charles Montague are here and we have just seen DCI McFarlane. All of them are prosecution witnesses and should not be in here until after they have given their evidence.'

Sandy looked straight at Hannah, who gently shook her head at him as if to say it was nothing to do with her.

Ebony got to her feet. 'My Lord, can I object to the objection?' Charles looked around. He appeared furious with her. Clearly, he was thinking surely it was the three defence barristers against the prosecution. What did she think she was doing for the second time in just a few minutes? Whose side was she on! 'Their evidence is surely not in dispute, is it?' Ebony went on to say, totally ignoring the glares from Charles.

'I have no problem with them staying either,' Vaughan said. He really was so laid back so as to be horizontal.

'DCI McFarlane carried out an illegal search,' Charles argued furiously.

'Ladies and gentlemen of the jury, this will probably happen quite often, but it is unfortunate it has happened just as we were about to start calling actual witnesses. I need you to leave the court whilst we resolve this legal issue,' Justice Kane told the jury, who then shuffled out for an early lunch. 'Mr and Mrs Montague and DCI McFarlane, please can you also leave the court. Right, Mr Holloway, let's have your legal objection.'

'DCI McFarlane carried out a search of the defendant George Peveril's room. This was without the necessary authorization. Charles Montague identified Mr Cousins and Kelly through a wholly dubious photo identity parade when theirs were the only photographs shown. When they come to give evidence, I want to argue these points.'

Christopher went to stand to counter the objection, but the judge waved him to sit down. 'Mrs Forbes-Hamilton, did Mrs Montague give permission, in her house, for the DCI to search it?'

'Yes, she most certainly did, and my client was quite happy for this to happen as DCI McFarlane was doing all that he could to try and find George on behalf of his father, Mrs Montague and the rest of his family.'

'That has resolved the search in my view,' Justice Kane said. 'Mr Slade, has your client admitted to visiting Norfolk on his way to Canada?'

'Yes, my Lord.'

'What about you, Mr Holloway?'

'Well yes, but there are also the interviews of the defendants that McFarlane and Singh, who I am sure is also in court at the moment,' he said, gesturing theoretically about the court room, 'were involved in carrying out.'

'No buts. The interviews have already been agreed, please stop it. Mr Coke, you can at the appropriate time read DCI McFarlane's statement, so he can stay in court. Mr Coke, withdraw the statement of Charles Montague, as it is superfluous. All three defendants admit to being there and I am not sure what the objection to Mrs Montague is, so she can stay in court. Lunch now and return in forty-five minutes, then first witness, Mr Coke.'

Christopher was very happy with the outcome, in particular as he didn't have to do or say anything. He was however going to have to watch Holloway. He was as slippery as an eel.

After lunch, the first three witnesses were pretty straightforward. They said it was Cousins and Kelly offering them drugs, and the barristers, on behalf of Cousins and Kelly, said it wasn't them, so they were mistaken. Sandy knew that when the digital media investigator gave their evidence, this would add to the evidence that these three were saying and would be a positive for the prosecution.

The day had gone well so far, but the next live witness to be called was Gary Rawlings. Everyone was poised for the inevitable objection from Charles Holloway, so much so that the judge sent the jury out for a break before Rawlings was going to be called to give evidence.

∞

Unbelievably, there were no objections to Rawlings giving evidence and the jury returned to court. Christopher first though dealt with the theft of the gun from National Heritage. He sent round pictures of the Smith & Wesson revolver. He said, after first looking at Ebony Forbes-Hamilton for confirmation, that George Peveril had already made admissions to stealing the gun. Christopher didn't go any further to state why, or who George gave it to. Then he called Gary Rawlings to the witness box.

Rawlings was dressed in a suit and looked like a smart young man going for an interview. He hadn't gone as far as to wear a tie, but he looked much better than he had in his prison uniform. As Rawlings walked past the dock, Kelly almost snarled at him. Sandy quickly looked to see if hopefully the jury had seen this happen, but it didn't look like it. Kelly had been having trouble sitting still all day and a prison officer often had to get him to calm down. This was only the first day. How he was going to last, Sandy didn't know.

After Rawlings had given his oath, Christopher asked him, 'Where have you come from today?'

'What do you mean?'

'Where are you currently residing?'

'I would rather not say.'

Christopher, who was always in doubt of using

289

Rawlings as a witness, audibly sighed. Holloway and Slade seemed to be enjoying this and were looking forward to their opportunity to question him.

'Mr Rawlings, I want to say this first, before one of my three learned colleagues do. You are currently in prison, aren't you?'

'Why do you want to tell everyone that?'

'Because it is true, isn't it?'

'Aren't you on my side? Yes, I am in prison for dealing in drugs as those two do.' He pointed to Cousins and Kelly. Both of them stared at him in what appeared a threatening way, so that the jury now could hardly not notice. 'They both also deal in drugs.'

'It would be helpful for us all if you just answer my questions,' Christopher continued, quite pleased with the display of rage from the defendants. 'You say, dealing with drugs. Have you had one of these drug dealings with any of these defendants?'

'Yes, those two.' Again, he pointed at Kelly and Cousins. 'The last time I met them they stole my drugs and my money. He, Cousins, hit me over the head with a gun and smashed my head. They are going to get it as they now owe money to a lot bigger and more dangerous people than me.'

Christopher had decided trying to lead Rawlings through his evidence was pointless and just said, 'Can you tell us where this happened?'

'Nottingham railway station. Our drug suppliers had already done the deal and it was meant to be the handover, till they got nasty and greedy,' he said, pointing at Cousins and Kelly, who had gone from fury to laughing with each other and at Rawlings. 'You can laugh now, but you two have nowhere to hide in prison,' he said, in response to them laughing at him.

Christopher, who wanted to get this over with as quickly as possible, said, 'Can you describe the gun you say Cousins hit you over the head with?'

'Not really, other than it was an old revolver-type gun.'

Christopher abruptly said, 'My Lord, no further questions,' and sat down, which surprised the defence barristers. Ebony had no questions, neither did Vaughan. Was he going to ever get involved in the court case? Sandy thought to himself.

Unsurprisingly, Charles got to his feet. 'Just a few if I may, my Lord.' Turning to Rawlings, he said, 'So, you are a convicted drug dealer who was carrying out a drug deal and had your drugs and money stolen by two men. You then see in the news these two men charged with murder using a revolver and think you can blame them.'

'What do you mean, it was them.'

'You need to blame somebody and you saw this as your opportunity. You are no doubt in trouble from the Mr Bigs in your criminal organisation and being a chancer, you also thought you could get the prosecution to give you something to give evidence. What were you offered?'

'They have given me nothing.' This surprised

Charles as he was sure a deal had been hatched, but then smiled when Rawlings went on to say, 'I have asked for reduced time and a move in prison though.'

Charles, believing that he had landed a few body blows, said, 'No further questions,' and Rawlings left the witness box.

Christopher said, 'I have a statement from the Queen's Medical Centre in Nottingham confirming that Mr Rawlings had a fractured skull, along with a few blurry CCTV pictures that certainly could be the two defendants. But before my learned colleagues object to CCTV images, I agree they do not prove any association with the skull fracture or the drug dealing.'

In an instant, Charles was on his feet. 'My Lord, why has he mentioned the Queen's Medical Centre and CCTV pictures if he is not using them? Please can the jury be asked not to take them into account.'

'Yes, of course.' Justice Kane instructed the jury appropriately then told everyone to be back in court at ten a.m. the following morning.

Chapter Thirty-Two

The general feeling the next morning that Christopher Coke and the Operation Primrose team had, was that the first day had gone extremely well. Rawlings, albeit an extremely poor witness, had scored for them some decent points with the jury. The first witness to be called that morning was the forensic pathologist Dr Nicholas Stroud. He was at the court already and was, as usual, really pleased to see Sandy. They had been promising each other a meal out but had not yet made it due to work commitments.

Christopher read out the statements of the officers who had found Joseph in Lock Up Yard, then those of the paramedics who had tried to treat him, which concluded with Joseph being pronounced dead. There was an audible sob from Belinda, who was still in court and was visibly upset hearing about her husband dying. Sandy was especially cross when he saw Charles, and also Vaughan, frowning at her and glaring at Christopher, as if to say, can't you control your victim. Hannah also seemed visibly upset.

Christopher called Nicholas to the stand and after he had gone through his very impressive list of qualifications, Christopher asked, 'Dr Stroud, could you tell us if you visited the scene in Lock-Up-Yard?'

Nicholas, who was no doubt a master of giving evidence, turned and faced the jury. 'Yes, I did, but this did not happen until after I had completed the autopsy. I had before that been briefed wonderfully by Detective Superintendent O'Connor and been shown a three-hundred-and-sixty-degree visual recording of the scene.'

'Please tell us what happened during the autopsy and your professional opinion following this.'

'I firstly examined Joseph by looking at him from head to toe–'

Nicholas was interrupted by Charles Holloway, who said, 'My Lord, can we ask the witness to be less emotive and use the terms "body" and "deceased" rather than their first name.'

Before Mr Justice Kane could respond, Nicholas said, 'I am sorry to offend your fragile constitution,' which brought ripples of laughter from around the court, the loudest actually from Ebony. He turned and looked straight at the jury. 'However, for me they are not just a body; they were a living person. I am no different to Mrs O'Connor or Mr McFarlane as I was doing everything that I could to try to find out how and why they died. They are a person to me. In this case, that person was Joseph Foster.'

'Objection overruled,' Mr Justice Kane said. 'Please carry on, Dr Stroud.'

'The bullet entered Joseph at an upper angle through a gap in his body armour, not that the body armour would have stopped a bullet. The protection he was wearing was more like a stab proof vest. I have an entry wound there.' Nicholas pointed to a diagram that was on a screen for the jury and lawyers to see. 'With the bullet slicing through his liver and just nicking his heart, and an exit wound through his left side. The bullet caused significant trauma.' Nicholas paused to allow the jury to take in all that he was saying. 'I could find no personal physical contact with any of the offenders from the swabs that I had taken over Joseph's entire body.'

Christopher had no more questions. Vaughan Slade rose to his feet and said, 'I think you are telling us that there is no trace of Dean Kelly on the deceased. Is that correct?'

'Yes, that is correct, and before you ask Mr Holloway, nor did I find anything from Mr Cousins on Joseph's body.' He then turned to look at the jury again, and said, 'There was no trace of anyone else, so no other imagined third party was likely to be involved either.' The broadest smiles this time were from Christopher and the Operation Primrose team.

There were a couple of follow-up questions that were of no consequence and Dr Stroud left the witness box. If ever there was someone to learn from on how to give evidence, that person was Nicholas. Majestic was the best way that Sandy felt able to describe it. The judge had decided that it was now time for lunch and the NABIS evidence would follow in the afternoon.

∞

Over the lunch break, Sandy went and sought out Belinda to make sure she was OK. Belinda wasn't really OK at all. She had decided to go home that afternoon and not return until after the jury had gone out to make a decision on a verdict. The victim support homicide worker was going to travel home with her.

As they walked back into court, Christopher told Sandy that although his evidence was not in question, Charles wanted him to give his evidence in person. Sandy wondered what trap he was going to fall into as he walked into the witness box. Taking the bible that sat there in his right hand, he gave the oath: 'I swear by Almighty God that the evidence I shall give shall be the truth, the whole truth and nothing but the truth.'

'Officer, please tell us how you came to recover the Smith & Wesson .38 revolver,' Christopher said.

Sandy went through why he was at Peveril Farm, emphasising that Mrs Montague gave him consent to search, George's room and how he came to find the weapon. He then explained what happened with the gun going to NABIS and the bag for forensics. Christopher didn't need any more information.

Charles gently rose from his seat after talking to

Hannah at his side. Hannah looked straight at Sandy and their eyes locked, so much so that he didn't fully hear what Charles was asking him, so he had to ask him to repeat his question. A clearly irritated Charles said, 'I think my question, DCI McFarlane, was simple. However, how well concealed was the bag?'

'Not really concealed at all, just in the bottom of a wardrobe, but who would ever have thought to look there?'

'Just try and answer the question and not offer an opinion. I understand the gun has been examined for fingerprints and DNA. Whose fingerprints and DNA were found on it?'

'As far as I know, no one's.'

Charles looked directly at the jury and repeated, 'Nobody's fingerprints or DNA are on the gun. What about the bag the gun was found in?'

'George Peveril's fingerprints are on the outside of the bag.' Sandy hadn't been told if the fingerprint expert had agreed to say the partial prints on the inside were Kelly's, but he took a chance on it. 'And on the inside were Dean Kelly's.' As Sandy said this, he glanced at Vaughan Slade, who didn't flicker any sign of interest.

'So, there was nothing to implicate Ruben Cousins to either the bag or the gun?'

Sandy had no option but to agree with Charles, who seemed pleased to get another point home with the jury to disassociate Cousins from the gun. He didn't seem too bothered with what Rawlings had said about

Cousins and the gun. He was sure he could argue that away as a convicted drug dealer looking for a deal. Neither Ebony nor Vaughan had any questions they wanted to ask, which Sandy was glad about as he didn't know the answer to Kelly's partial fingerprints on the bag.

Sandy was released from giving evidence but told there may be a remote possibility he would be needed for the interview evidence. As he walked back to his seat, he looked into the dock and saw all three, including George, laughing together. Silly boy, thought Sandy, the jury will see you like this and think you are all in it together.

The NABIS expert gave evidence next. She was only questioned by Vaughan, who wanted to know if there was the slightest possibility that the gun, they had found at Peveril Farm wasn't the one that had shot Joseph Foster. There was a very slight possibility, she said. Sandy and Rich were confused by Vaughan asking this as Kelly's defence was that he wasn't there. Maybe riding two arguments just in case. They knew why Charles didn't want to ask anything. It was to ensure any association between his client and the gun was as little as possible; that was what he was aiming for.

The judge was keen to call the DMI evidence, but Charles said there was a legal argument he needed resolving, which could wait until the morning but would be better to take place now. Justice Kane sent the jury home for the night, with court to resume at ten a.m. with the DMI evidence.

When the court had cleared, Vaughan asked if Kelly could be excused from having to stay in court for the legal argument as he was struggling to concentrate and keep still for such a long time. As long as everyone was happy with this, the judge said that all three could head off back to prison.

All of the barristers and the judge took their wigs off. 'I am troubled, my Lord, with the evidence due tomorrow by Mr Buckley.' Sandy and Rich looked worriedly at each other. What was Holloway going to come up with now? It appeared that neither Ebony nor Vaughan were in on it, judging by their confused looks. Sandy was glad they had the National Crime Agency expert also on standby. 'In this country, we are governed by the Regulation of Investigatory Powers Act 2000. The listening device conversation would be covered by the Act as intrusive surveillance and all of the authorities required in order for that to be authorised.'

Before he could continue with his argument, Christopher said, 'I disagree, as the Peveril and Williams families would have allowed it, and so it would have been directed surveillance.'

'I see your argument,' Charles said, unflustered. 'But whichever one, it doesn't matter. Where is the authorisation? I have not been served with any papers confirming the authorisation.'

Vaughan, who had missed this point, as had Christopher and the whole of the Operation Primrose team, sat up very excitedly. This was a major chance to put a big hole into a key piece of the prosecution case, leading him to say, 'I am in total agreement with Mr Holloway. Where is the authorisation?'

On looking across at Hannah, it was clear to Sandy that she was fully involved in this legal argument and had no doubt carried out some, if not all, of the research. At last, he had proof for himself, and his family, that he had been right. It would have been impossible to be a couple who shared everything, as she wouldn't have been able to talk to him about this.

Christopher looked round at the team. They all shook their heads, and he said, 'I am sorry, my Lord, we don't know the answer. Could we look at this overnight and have the necessary answer for the court in the morning?'

The judge agreed and adjourned court until the morning. Sandy was tasked with getting hold of someone in Canada and the authorisation. Sandy knew who he needed to contact in Canada to enquire what had happened. He decided to wait until he got home to his flat.

Once there, he rang Staff Sergeant John Hopkins. 'Hello, John, it is DCI McFarlane. Are you able to help me, please?'

'Yes, of course, son. How are you? What about that boy George?'

Sandy told him how they all were and about the trial. 'We are using the evidence in court that we got from the listening device, or you might call it the "bug" or "wiretap". The defence lawyers want to see how it was authorised. I presume you need to have these devices authorised?'

'Yes, of course. Canada is extremely strong on its charter of rights and freedoms for its citizens. To authorise this, we need to use our Criminal Code of Canada, and I know it is a judge that gives the authorisation. I will check with Inspector Alan Wise and get back to you. When do you need to know?'

'Can you enquire today, please? We need to let the court know in the morning, UK time.' After they had had a general chat, Sandy turned his attention to getting caught up with his work. He had been out last night for a meal with Rich and Lofty. He needed to do some work for the FCDO so had declined meeting them tonight. He was just switching his computer off when he saw that he had a call from John Hopkins.

'Hello, John, good news, I hope?'

'No, horrendous news.' Sandy suddenly had a sick feeling in the pit of his stomach. His cry of anguish had brought his dad Gregor out of his room to see what was going on. 'Inspector Wise thought the negotiators had got it, and they had, but only for the one in the food. That was why it took so long to get the food to us. The negotiators thought the firearms team had got the authorisation for the other one, and they, as I said, thought the negotiators had got it. A nightmare, I am sorry.'

Sandy thought quickly on his feet and asked John to get sent over to his email address a copy of the original authorisation. That might just work, he thought, as it all involved the same circumstances. His sick feeling abated a little, but not entirely. He decided to wait until the morning when he had the authorisation in his hand before telling Christopher and Rich. He was glad that Joanne had gone back to the East Midlands yesterday evening.

Chapter Thirty-Three

The next morning, the Operation Primrose team and Christopher Coke held a meeting to discuss the authority that had been sent across to Sandy from the RCMP. They examined it and within it, it stated why it had been authorised. Christopher seemed hopeful that this would suffice. The one downside was that it clearly mentioned the make, model and serial number of the piece of equipment being used. This was, unfortunately, not the one that picked up the later conversation, but the one hidden in the food packaging.

When they went into court, Christopher went in on his best charm offensive with the judge. Charles, however, was not having any of it. 'My Lord, the normal practice for the RIPA Act 2000 in England, is that authorisations also stipulate what equipment is being used. If the conversation is on this named device, I am happy to accept it.' Sandy, and of course Charles, no doubt knew it wasn't recorded on that piece of equipment. Lofty had strained to find something whilst listening to the recording on that device all over again, but there was nothing until George was shot, and his cries of pain were recorded. Vaughan said he agreed with Mr Holloway; this would be a real lifeline for his client, Kelly, if it was ruled out.

Mr Justice Kane said, 'I am not going to make an instant decision but will decide over the lunch recess. I am deeply troubled by the information contained within here that has been received from Canada, that a police officer there was threatened with a gun, but there is no record of that here in evidence of similar fact, Mr Coke.'

Ebony rose to her feet and said dramatically, 'You were also probably unaware, my Lord, that my client was shot in the leg by Mr Kelly.'

'It was an accident,' Kelly shouted from the dock.

Justice Kane looked at Kelly with disgust. 'Do not, young man, shout out in my court.'

'Don't you, old man, tell me what to do. No one tells me what to do.' Kelly's solicitor ran over to the dock to calm his client down.

'Yes, Mr Slade, make sure your legal team stops any more outbursts, or I most certainly will!'

Christopher said, 'The problem we have is that the RCMP have the defendant's released under investigation, so it is not evidence we could use, as much as we really would have liked to.'

'OK,' Mr Justice Crane said, although he was clearly not OK about it. 'Let's have the jury back in court and call your next witness, Mr Coke.'

Obviously, at this moment, it will not be Mr Buckley.

So, the next person into the court was the DMI analyst who covered the CCTV evidence of Cousins and Kelly in and around Derby city centre in the places that matched the drug dealing. Charles made a point to the jury, telling them, 'The images might probably look like Mr Cousins and Kelly, but in this court, you have to be sure, beyond reasonable doubt, that it is them.' Charles was right to a certain extent. The images were very grainy, making them not completely clear.

The images on the speed cameras though were clearer and there was little doubt that Cousins and Kelly were the ones in the stolen car leaving the city centre. The analyst then showed a map to the jury of the points where the pictures had been taken, including where Joseph Foster had been shot and where the speed cameras had taken their photographs. This was then overlaid with the telephone work on the burner phone. They were able to match this exactly. The jury and everyone in court seemed impressed with this. Showing it graphically like this was very compelling. The jury were now waiting eagerly to see who that phone belonged to, but that wasn't going to be revealed just yet, but would be soon, as the next witness to be called was Clare Symonds.

Just before Clare came into court, Charles rose from his seat and said, 'My Lord, I have a legal matter I would like to discuss. Please could the jury be asked to leave the court.'

The jury and judge were clearly getting irritated by

Charles constantly asking them to be sent out of court. Although he was fighting with everything he had got for Cousins, he might just be overdoing it and starting to alienate the jury. How different the barristers were in this case: Christopher and Ebony had the jury eating out of their hands; Charles was, by a force of nature, getting them to listen to every argument he had; and the jury probably didn't even realise Vaughan had anything to do with the trial.

After the jury had left the room, Charles said, 'The key piece of evidence that Miss Symonds is going to give, from my point of view, is the phone she recovered from the room in the Peveril Estate. I would like to ask what authority she used to take possession of the phone?'

Christopher said, 'My Lord, the room it was found in is owned by the Peveril's and used by the Williams family who work for them. They gave permission for the room to be searched.'

This was true. The judge asked Ebony her view. She said she was neutral, and then Vaughan, when asked, said he questioned the authority to remove the orange-coloured Fat Face hoodie. The judge called a very early lunch and said he would consider both legal points raised and make a ruling at one thirty p.m., with the jury back in court for two p.m.

∞

Sandy and George had developed a pleasant routine of nodding to each other as they went in and out of court. This certainly wasn't happening with Cousins and Kelly, who, if they caught his eye, more often than not sneered at him.

Sandy waited as long as he could before he rang John Hopkins, as he knew it was still very early in Manitoba. 'Sorry to wake you, John.' Sandy said as soon as the phone was answered. 'I am not sure you can help, but I presume we didn't get any authority to search the boys' room in the Peveril Estate, did we?'

'You haven't woken me, son, I'm just getting ready to go to the police office. I am on duty for seven a.m. You are in luck here that you are dealing with Staff Sergeant John Hopkins of the Royal Canadian Mounted Police!' Sandy could picture John standing to attention, dressed in a RCMP scarlet tunic and proudly puffing his chest out. 'I obtained a warrant myself, albeit it was to search for drugs before we went on the Saturday. I was sure they were dealing in drugs; we just needed those local boys to tell us.'

This was excellent news and Sandy again marvelled at what a wonderful officer John was. He asked him to email a copy as soon as he got into work, which would allow him to get it to the court in time.

After they had all assembled back in court, Mr Justice Kane QC said, 'Having now seen the Canadian search warrant, not that I would have refused the evidence anyway, I am allowing the evidence seized from the house on the Peveril Estate.' He then paused, not so much for effect but because it seemed the next decision was seriously troubling him. 'I am, however, refusing the evidence obtained via the listening device. I do believe the spirit of the original authorisation would include the evidence obtained, but because it doesn't specifically and categorically, makes it in my view easy grounds for appeal for the defence. So, reluctantly, I am agreeing to Mr Holloway's objection.'

Christopher looked stunned, but tried not to let it show. There was absolutely no doubt whatsoever that this was a major blow to the prosecution case. There was clear jubilation from the defence teams for Cousins and Kelly. Even Hannah smiled. If it was her legal argument, then it had paid off handsomely.

'Please can we therefore release Mr Buckley from giving evidence, and I would like to change it around a little and call next Miss Eleanor Danvers. I may need to treat her as a hostile witness; she has been intimidated; I am afraid.'

This was a good call. Rich had told Christopher that he had spoken to Eleanor that morning, and chances of her staying in the court building much longer were slim. Lofty went off to let Billy Buckley know what had happened. The poor chap had had his window smashed for no reason. Eleanor came into court looking extremely nervous. After she had given her oath, Christopher said, 'Please bear in mind the oath that you have just taken. You have made two statements. The first one, where you describe when Dean Kelly came home with Ruben Cousins and another male, who you now know as George Peveril. The second one, after, and I stress *after,* you had your car sprayed and the windows in your house broken.' Christopher looked straight at the jury as he said this. 'Which one is the truth?'

Eleanor gulped a few times and started to cry. The judge told her to take a seat and take a sip of water, there was no rush. Eleanor, after a few moments of looking directly at Justice Kane and nowhere else, managed to mutter quietly, 'It is the first one.'

Christopher very gently said, 'OK, let's forget either statement for a moment and you just tell us, and I do need you to look at the jury whilst you do this.' Christopher gesticulated with his head at the same time towards the jury. 'What happened on the night that PC Joseph Foster died?'

As Eleanor moved her head round to her right to look at the members of the jury, she glanced at Dean Kelly in the dock, who could clearly be seen to mouth the words, 'You are dead, bitch.' Sandy was disappointed that neither the judge nor jury had seen this as they were looking directly at Eleanor. They would though have seen her visibly flinch. Sandy desperately hoped she would have the confidence to stick to what she had just said.

'I was sitting in my lounge and saw Kelly and Cousins go out, walking, at about nine o'clock the previous evening.' One thing the Operation Primrose team had been unable to find out was how they had got to Derby. They presumed it was by the next dealer up in the chain from them, but had been unable to identify who exactly that was. 'I was then woken up at five thirty the next morning when I heard car doors slamming. I sleep at the front of the house. I got up and looked out of the window and saw Cousins in the car, and him.' Not looking at the dock, she pointed in the direction of Peveril. 'There was an almighty row going on inside the house and Kelly came running out of his house and they went off at speed down the road.'

Christopher, not wishing to push his luck, said, 'No further questions,' and asked her to remain there in case his colleagues had anything to ask. Ebony shook her head, as, surprisingly to everyone else, did Charles.

This left Vaughan, who rose slowly, very slowly, to his feet, pulling his black gown up over his shoulders as he did so, and with a smile, asked her, 'Miss Danvers, you say you are now telling the truth, but how can you expect any of us to believe a word you are saying? Which is the truth: your first or second statement? I put it to you that it is the second one that is correct and that you were just mistaken on the date.'

'Why would I lie now? What could I possibly gain by doing that? You don't realise the trouble I am going to be in for this. Living where I do, being a grass as they call it, my life is now hell.'

Vaughan didn't see any point in pushing a clearly distraught Eleanor, who, when released from being a witness, ran from the courtroom, sobbing as she went. Justice Kane thought it best to start again the next morning when Clare Symonds was to be the next witness to be called.

∞

At their meal that night, Rich, Lofty and Sandy all felt depressed. The early Christmas party revellers all around them did nothing to lift the mood. The loss of the listening device evidence was a major blow to their case. Christopher, who seemed to be ever the optimist, told them not to worry, these things were all part of the course of a trial, in particular, a murder trial. Sandy's feeling of doom had not improved as he arrived in court the next day.

Shortly after ten a.m., Clare made her way into the witness box. Dean Kelly hadn't made it to court yet as he was currently refusing to leave his prison cell. A short discussion between the judge and Vaughan had agreed that they could proceed with the next witness, but not any further than that without Kelly. His solicitor was hotfooting it across to the prison to cajole his client to attend.

After Clare had given her oath, Christopher said to her, 'I want to ask you about a few of the items recovered from a room being used by Cousins, Peveril and Kelly in the Peveril Estate in Manitoba. Tell the court about the hoodies that you seized, and could you tell us were any of the defendants' DNA found on them or inside them?'

'Yes, I took possession of three hoodies; two of them were blue. The only DNA found on these blue ones was individually that of Ruben Cousins on one and George Peveril on the other one.'

'So, there is a strong likelihood that those belonged to them?'

'Yes, the orange one though had a small amount of DNA from Peveril, but the DNA was predominately from Kelly.'

'So, we can take it that this hoodie belonged to Kelly?'

Before Clare could respond, Vaughan was on his feet. 'Objection, my Lord. How can the witness know if Mr Kelly owned the hoodie?' Vaughan was clearly trying to get in a pre-emptive strike to show that someone else could own it and wear it, not just Kelly.

'Let me rephrase the question,' Christopher said, whilst nodding at Vaughan. 'From the DNA found within the hoodie, is it safe to say that Mr Kelly must have worn this item of clothing?'

'Yes, he must have worn it frequently, if we take account of the amount of his DNA inside.' Vaughan went to stand but sort of stopped halfway up, thought better of it and sat back down. Sandy wondered what had sprung him into life, but then realised when he heard Christopher's next question.

'What was found on the right sleeve?'

'Gunshot residue. Quite a lot of it.' The jury, on hearing this, started scribbling away on their notepads. Kelly, who had just at that moment arrived in the dock, was shouting some unintelligible abuse at the prison officer who was trying to get him to sit down. Pure theatre thought Sandy. Wonderful.

Vaughan was itching to get up this time but had to wait his turn until Christopher had finished his questioning with Clare. Christopher's last question for the moment was, would the gunshot residue fit with being very close to where a gun had been fired? Clare, of course, said yes.

'You are unable to say that this gunshot residue comes from the Smith & Wesson revolver, are you?' Vaughan said, now on his feet. He should really have waited until Christopher had finished his questions, but the judge and Christopher were allowing it.

'No, we can't say exactly which gun it came from.'

'Exactly,' Vaughan said, nodding encouragingly at the jury. Neither Ebony nor Charles needed to ask anything.

Christopher continued with his questioning of Clare. 'Tell the court about the phone you found in the room in Canada where the three boys were staying. This is the same phone that we have connecting to phone masts in and around Derby city centre and present at the very time that Joseph Foster was shot, is that correct?'

'Yes, that is correct.' The jury and others were seen to write in their folders the information that they had been waiting for.

'When you had the phone examined, were any individuals' DNA or fingerprints on it?'

'No DNA, but the fingerprint of Ruben Cousins...' Again, there was furious writing by the jury on hearing Cousins' name. Clare paused for a moment and then said, '...was found on the SIM card inside the phone. The outside had clearly been wiped.'

Christopher had no further questions. The first, as always, to rise to their feet was Charles. Justice Kane played with him a bit and said, 'Sorry, Mr Holloway, but I wondered if Mrs Forbes-Hamilton had anything to ask first?' Ebony, with a smile, knowing exactly what the judge was doing, said she hadn't.

Charles, who had stubbornly remained standing, said, raising his voice, 'What you are unable to say though, Miss Symonds, is when Mr Cousins touched that SIM card. It may have been days or months earlier?'

'I agree, we are unable to date a fingerprint in this situation.'

'So, it is fair to say then, that although you can associate Mr Cousins with the phone, you can't say that it was on the night in question, can you?'

'You are right in one respect.' Charles had no further questions and having made his point, quickly sat down. Clare hadn't finished though and continued talking. 'Through other investigative means though, we can. The jury have seen the map placing the phone at the same time and place where Mr Cousins' photo was taken on that night.'

Charles was swiftly back to his feet. 'My Lord, can you make an order so that the jury disregard the last bit from Miss Symonds' evidence?'

Justice Kane looked down on Charles and peering over his half-rimmed tortoiseshell glasses, said, 'No, you said associate him to the phone on the night in question. The photographs of Mr Cousins that are in the same place as the phone are an answer to your question.' Everyone could see that Charles was furious, most probably with himself, for at last taking a wrong step in the trial.

Vaughan, who was probably sleeping again after exerting himself so much earlier, had nothing to add and Clare left the witness box. The rest of the day was taken up with the readings of various statements. Rich gave evidence of the interviews, which took up most of the time, with Mr Coke's junior asking the questions and Rich giving the answers, which, although made some sense, was in fact back to front on what had happened in reality, where Rich was the interviewer.

At the close of the day, Christopher told the judge that the prosecution rests its case. Justice Kane informed everyone to return on the Monday for the beginning of the defence case. This would start with Mr Cousins, then Peveril and finally Kelly.

Chapter Thirty-Four

After his game of rugby and feeling brave after having a couple of drinks in the bar on the Saturday night at the rugby club, Sandy couldn't resist sending Hannah a message: "Hope you are not working too hard this weekend!"

He had an almost instant reply: "Lol! What do you think? Working with Mr Charles Holloway QC, I have no alternative but to work hard!"

Over the weekend, Sandy had a chance to look through a lot of the media reporting relating to the case. He was pleased to see that as soon as the court case had begun, there was little that featured Viscount and James Peveril. Most news outlets had shown pictures, and not just on the first day, throughout the trial of Joseph in his police uniform, and a couple showed him in his Guards uniform as well.

On the Monday as he arrived in court, Sandy was looking to see if he could spot Hannah to smile at and say hello to, when Viscount Peveril walked up to him. 'Good morning, DCI McFarlane, really good to see you, young man.' He had seemingly forgotten the last time they had both spoken, thought Sandy. 'I thought I would be at court today to support George as he is going to give evidence.' Viscount Peveril suddenly realised that he shouldn't have told Sandy that. 'Disregard my last comment, dear boy. He may give evidence.' And with a wink, he was gone.

Sandy noticed that Janice Peveril was present, no doubt as a witness for the defence. Christopher had agreed with Ebony that she was better to use Janice as a witness than the prosecution. A very persuasive lady was Ebony Forbes-Hamilton. There had been no sign of George's mother, Helen, at the trial at all, probably too difficult emotionally for her. The two Montague's and James had been present for every minute though.

Dean Kelly's mum and dad had also been present throughout, not in the court room itself, but outside, as they were sure to be his alibi witnesses. Every time Rich or Sandy walked by them, Kelly's parents' glares at them were extremely unpleasant. When Sandy caught sight of Hannah, she was talking to a lady, who, Sandy presumed, must be Ruben's mother. This was her first attendance.

'My Lord, I intend to call no evidence for Mr Cousins and he will not be giving evidence,' Charles Holloway announced at the start of court that morning. This surprised everyone, in particular Christopher Coke, who threw down onto the table the list of questions he and his junior had spent time working on. Charles continued. 'I would like to remind the jury that Mr Cousins doesn't have to prove his innocence. It is the prosecution, and the prosecution alone, who have to prove his guilt. I will expand on this when I make my closing speech.' Had Hannah double-bluffed him, Sandy wondered, or had she been working at the weekend for that speech.

'Very well,' Mr Justice Kane said. 'Mrs Forbes-Hamilton, are you going to call any witnesses?'

'Yes, my Lord, please can I call Mrs Janice Peveril to give evidence.'

When Janice had settled into the witness box and outlined her relationship with George, Ebony said to her, 'You told the police that on the evening before PC Foster was killed, George was in his room. You heard him go out in the middle of the night, come back early and then leave again, and you didn't see or hear from him until after he returned to England from Canada. Is that correct?'

'Yes, that is correct,' Janice said, who didn't seem in the slightest bit nervous or flustered.

'What time did he first go out in the night?'

'It was two a.m. I know it was that time because I checked the clock beside my bed.'

'So, this was after the time that PC Foster was shot and killed? George was in his room until then, so he couldn't possibly have been in Derby city centre thirty minutes before this?'

'Yes, that is correct.'

There were no more questions. George's alibi had been firmly established. Charles got to his feet and said, 'You never saw him though, did you, at any time during the evening, in the middle of the night, or early before breakfast?'

Quick as a flash, Janice said, 'I heard him in there though. Who else would it be in my house or driving George's car backwards and forwards?' This made the people in court chuckle.

'Then he stole money from you in order to complete his getaway, isn't that, right?'

Before Janice could answer Ebony was on her feet. 'My Lord, George Peveril is not charged with theft of any money and I wouldn't want for one moment to have to explain the law of theft to my learned colleague. George always intended to give the money back, but his father has given it to him.'

Charles withdrew the question and as Vaughan had nothing to add, Janice left the witness box, smiling at George as she went out of the court, having delivered exactly what he needed her to do.

The next witness to be called was George himself.

∞

As George walked to the witness box, it was noticeable that he had a slight limp, but it appeared that he had recovered well from his leg injury. He was dressed very smartly in a suit, which made him look a bit older than he actually was.

Ebony, as she started questioning him, was exceptionally soft and encouraging. 'George, have you any previous convictions?'

'No.' This was a truthful answer, but he had been arrested more than once for possession of cannabis.

'Why did you take the gun from Peveril Hall?' Clever use by Ebony of the word "take" rather than "steal".

'It really belongs to my family and I was borrowing it.' Ebony, or her junior, had clearly spent time with George going through his answers – borrowing, not permanently depriving, as the law of theft required. Clever. 'My friends wanted something to help them in their work where they were often threatened.'

'Can you please tell us who those friends are?' Ebony said, trying to get George to state in open court the names of Cousins and Kelly.

No doubt in their consultations he had been adamant he wouldn't, and he said, as predicted, 'I am not prepared to name them.'

'It is obvious though who they are, as they are your co-defendants,' Ebony said, elaborately pointing to Cousins and Kelly in the dock.

'Obvious or not, I am not going to name them,' an adamant George replied.

'You then went to your friends' aid in *their* time of crisis and took them to a farm owned by your family in Canada, is that correct?'

'Yes,' agreed George, who realised that Ebony had weaved in Cousins and Kelly again as the friends in question. Although he was smart, he was no match for her.

'Is there anything you wish to say to the court, George?'

Although it was clear for all to see that this was a planned response, George did come across as surprisingly sincere, when he said, 'I would like to personally apologise to the family of Mr Foster, for the pain caused by any action that I took, which might have in some way contributed to his death and their sorrow.'

Christopher rose to begin his cross-examination and paused before he started and said, unscripted, 'Thank you, Mr Peveril, for those comments. Can I just keep you on that honesty track?'

'Not if you want me to use my friends' names, no, you can't.'

Christopher shook his head and smiled. 'No, it's OK, let's deal solely with you. When you say, "borrowed the gun", did you ask permission from say National Heritage or your grandfather?'

George shook his head, then said, 'No.'

'Whether you realised it or not, the gun was a live one and it is a crime to possess it without a licence. You have stated that you supplied it to your friends, to, in essence, help them to commit crime with?'

'Yes, I realise that,' George replied quietly, but loudly enough for everyone, including the jury, to hear.

'Did you know what your friends – I am not naming them – had done when you went to fetch them and make good their escape to Canada?' Everyone smiled at the way Christopher included the comment about his friends' names.

'I was at home; my step mum Janice was not lying.' George looked round at the jury as he said this. 'I didn't know, not at first, but I did soon after and definitely on the way to Norfolk. It was the only place I could think of to leave the gun. I wasn't going to throw it away; it had belonged to my great grandfather.'

After Christopher had finished with George, who had now, in essence, in the witness box, admitted his involvement, Vaughan stood up to ask questions. 'You wear an orange Fat Face hoodie, don't you?'

'It belongs to one of my friends and yes, I have worn it.'

Vaughan had no more questions. Ebony asked for clarification, 'How often have you worn that hoodie?'

'I think only once when we arrived in Canada,' George replied.

'After the shooting had occurred,' Ebony said, nodding to the jury. She had nothing else to add to George's defence. After lunch, it would be Dean Kelly's turn to stand in the witness box, that is if he could manage to stay still for longer than one moment.

∞

The first person that afternoon that Vaughan called was Dean Kelly's father. He was asked, 'We are only interested in the night that PC Joseph Foster was killed. Do you know where Dean was that night?'

Mr Kelly seemed unsure about what he was being asked. 'You mean when we said he was at home all night with us?'

'Yes, that night. Did Dean go out at all?' Vaughan asked, trying to slow down his speech and make his question easy.

'No, he was at home all night with his mum and me. He never left our side,' Kelly's dad replied.

'We have heard from a Miss Danvers that he went out with Ruben Cousins and didn't come home until five thirty in the morning. What have you got to say to that?'

'She said she got the date wrong and it was another day.' Mr Kelly obviously hadn't been updated about what Eleanor Danvers had actually said in court. 'She told me she had made a mistake.' After you had trashed her car and smashed her windows, Sandy thought. 'There was no way Dean could have done that to the policeman as he was at home with us,' Mr Kelly shouted.

Vaughan told him to stay there as there may be further questions. Christopher asked him if he knew what perverting the course of justice and perjury meant. He said he wouldn't do any of those things. Rich and Sandy whispered that Mr Kelly hadn't got a clue what Christopher was on about.

Ebony said, 'Mr Kelly, Dean must have at least left at five thirty in the morning, as we know that he went to Norfolk and then flew to Canada. So, Miss Danvers must be telling the truth about that, mustn't she?'

Mr Kelly now didn't know what to do: stick to the original story or go with the logic of Mrs Forbes-Hamilton's question. 'Oh yes, those two boys,' he said, pointing to Cousins and Peveril, 'turned up and they, including Dean, went off together.' He quickly added, 'On a planned holiday.'

No one saw any point in continuing with Kelly's father or to call Mrs Kelly, as it was blindingly obvious, they were only sticking up for their son.

Dean Kelly was then called to the witness box. There was a real feeling of anticipation buzzing around the court as he ambled into the witness box. He couldn't read the card that had the oath on it so had to repeat it after the clerk. Sandy had a quick thought and slipped a note with Christopher's permission to Ebony, as it fitted for her to ask this question better than Christopher. Sandy had been worried before the case that it would have been three QCs versus just one for the prosecution, but it had turned out Ebony had been much more on the prosecution's side.

Vaughan said, 'You have been present in court throughout your trial, and the prosecution are alleging that on the night in question, you were in possession of a gun and went out to deal in drugs, and when threatened by a police officer, you shot him dead. Are they correct?'

Kelly seemed to get cross very quickly. 'They are lying, my dad just told you I was at home, so it is not correct.'

'The prosecution has shown pictures of you around Derby city centre on that night, including one of you in an orange Fat Face hoodie. Are the pictures mistaken?'

'George Peveril used to wear that hoodie, not me.' Rich and Sandy looked at each other. How could you stoop so low when George had refused to name him. 'It was his gun that was used as well. It wasn't mine.'

It appeared that Vaughan actually hadn't wanted Kelly to give evidence, so he sat down quickly, hoping Kelly wouldn't drop himself in it. Ebony rose to her feet. 'So, Dean, it looks like you are now claiming that George was wearing the orange hoodie and shot the policeman?'

'I didn't say he shot him, did I? It was him wearing the hoodie and it was his gun, is what I am saying.' How was that different, Rich whispered to Sandy.

'Are you left- or right-handed?' Ebony was now asking Sandy's question, which they both knew the answer to.

'Right-handed, why?' a very confused Kelly replied, and promptly picked up the glass of water in his right hand.

'Did you know George Peveril is left-handed?' Ebony slowly asked, to make sure the jury got the significance of why she was asking this. 'And the gunshot residue was on the lower right arm. Do you understand what this means?'

'I haven't got a clue what you are going on about.'

As much as Christopher wanted to tear into Kelly to get him to lose his temper and show the jury what a horrible person he was, he resisted the temptation as there seemed no point. Ebony had nailed him for being someone who would drop a friend in it to save his own skin. Just as Kelly was about to be released from being a witness, the temptation was too great and Christopher rose to his feet and said, 'Mr Kelly, how can you blame George Peveril for what you did? Be a man and own up to it.'

'What are you saying? That I am not a man. How dare you!' Kelly snarled at him.

'The truth is, you and Cousins went armed to deal in drugs, and whoever got in your way, both of you would have resorted to serious violence. It is a fact that if you fire a gun, it has only one purpose. To kill.'

For a moment, everyone in the court thought Kelly was going to throw his glass of water at Christopher, but in the end, he just shouted at the top of his voice, 'You shut up. I am not answering your questions.' Kelly's fury was there for all to see. Christopher was glad that he had got up to speak.

Justice Kane adjourned for the day, with closing speeches to be commenced in the morning. All in all, the Operation Primrose team felt they had had another good day. It was a shame that they couldn't have had a chance to question Cousins, but they knew that would count against him, when the judge advised the jury of what it meant.

Chapter Thirty-Five

The closing speeches started the next morning. Christopher was noticeably short, sharp and to the point. Ebony, in her speech for George, was honest about what he had done, but stressed, extremely strongly, what he had not done. Vaughan, on the other hand, for Kelly, was very much along the lines that his client wasn't there at the shooting and there was no actual physical evidence that could make the jury sure, beyond reasonable doubt, that he had committed murder.

Charles Holloway, no doubt due to the hard work of Hannah to provide him with material, but also the fact that Cousins hadn't any witnesses and had not given evidence himself, waxed lyrical for an inordinate length of time. However, a key piece of what he said made Sandy and the jury take notice.

'Members of the jury, I now want to turn to something that you may have heard of. It is called joint enterprise. History is littered with literally hundreds of cases of miscarriages of justice.' This was not really true, Christopher wanted to say, but couldn't interrupt.

He knew Justice Kane would resolve it in his summing up. 'This so-called joint enterprise means that two or more people can be convicted of the same offence, in this case the murder of PC Joseph Foster. This is even when they have had quite different levels of involvement. The prosecution for the Crown, in this case, is quite clear that they believe Dean Kelly had the gun and fired the shot that killed PC Foster.' Gosh, these two defence barristers were quite happy to throw the other's client under the bus, Sandy thought.

Charles continued. 'I agree with them. I want you all to know that Ruben Cousins didn't do this. He is not the murderer. It doesn't matter whether Cousins had the foresight or not that something like this might happen. I back up what I am saying by telling you that the UK Supreme Court, the highest court in the land, heard two appeals against joint enterprise convictions for murder. Both appeals were allowed. It was stated that the common law on joint enterprise had previously taken a wrong turn. Don't take a wrong turn here for Ruben Cousins.'

Incredibly good, thought Sandy. If Hannah had prepared this for Charles, she had done very well, and on one hand he was proud of her, but on the other hand, he was far more nervous that the jury might buy the argument.

Mr Justice Kane QC in his summing up went back through the evidence, and slowly but surely, recapped for the jury what evidence they had heard and needed to pay attention to. In relation to the joint enterprise argument, he commented, 'Mr Holloway was not entirely correct when he talked about miscarriages of justice. A number of these are perceived but not actual legally agreed miscarriages of justice.' Christopher was right, the judge hadn't missed the point. 'That case he mentioned doesn't stop more than one person with a different level of involvement being convicted of the same offence. There have been many cases where this has happened since that appeal court ruling. Just because Kelly had the gun on this occasion, Cousins may have had the gun on another occasion. You heard what Mr Rawlings said about Cousins and the gun. You have to decide, as stated by the prosecution case, if you think that Peveril, by providing the weapon, and in essence, also the means of escape, has met that standard of also being guilty of the offence of murder. You have to decide whether Kelly was there and fired the shot that killed PC Foster. You have to decide from the prosecution case against Cousins whether he and Kelly went out to sell drugs, armed with a gun, which they would use to stop, or cause serious harm to, anyone they encountered who would prevent them from carrying out their criminal intent. It matters not that on this occasion, it was Kelly.'

Although this was all within the bounds of what he could say, it was quite clear what Justice Kane thought it terms of who was guilty. He sent the jury out saying he would only accept unanimous verdicts on all of the charges. All of the Operation Primrose team felt extremely nervous. After saying hello to Belinda, who had returned to court that day, Sandy went out to do some early Christmas shopping. He knew he probably shouldn't have done so, but he bought some earrings for Hannah, which he would pass on to his grandpa to give to her. He wondered how nervous she was feeling. He had seen Arabella and Monty earlier and they were worried that the judge might have sealed George's fate. James was tied up in a vote in the House of Commons but was ready to return to court at a moment's notice. The Viscount had gone home to his palatial house in Eaton Square.

∞

The jury spent the rest of that day and then all of the next day locked in their discussions to consider their verdicts. Surprisingly, there were no questions of clarification asked by them. Joanne O'Connor had arrived not long after the jury had started their deliberations. Joanne, the CPS lawyer and Christopher Coke had firmly decided and agreed on having a retrial if it turned out the jury couldn't make a decision. Sandy, when he heard this, felt he couldn't bear the thought of a retrial, but realised what he felt was of no consequence compared to how Belinda Foster would feel if that happened. Belinda and her wonderful victim support case worker had gone off, both to do some shopping but also to do some sightseeing. She had visited London quite a few times when Joseph had been in the Army and was stationed at Wellington Barracks.

At the end of the day, Justice Kane called the jury back into court. After asking them if they had reached any verdicts on which they all agreed, he was told yes, on all of the counts except one. He then asked them if there was a majority verdict for that one and was told no. He asked them to come back in the morning and try for just one more hour to see if they could reach a majority verdict for that offence.

The Operation Primrose team went out for dinner and Joanne paid the bill. It was a pretty subdued meal. Joanne though was determinedly buoyant; she was an incredibly vibrant and driven individual. In her mind, this was a good result. She reasoned with the team that as there was only one charge outstanding, the others must be guilty verdicts, they must be, she said louder in a decisive tone. For example, how could George Peveril not be guilty of the theft of the gun or supplying the gun? Her infectious enthusiasm lifted everybody.

The next morning, the judge had a note telling him the jury were unable to agree on the final count on the indictment. They came back into court. Sandy could feel his heart thumping so hard he was sure Rich, who was sitting next to him, could hear it as well. Probably how Rich was feeling as well.

The clerk asked for the foreman of the jury to stand. She was a smart-looking woman in her late fifties. He went through each of the charges against Cousins. All unanimous. Guilty. Guilty. Guilty, the foreman of the jury said. The main feeling for Sandy now was one of complete and utter relief. He wanted to look at Hannah first but caught Belinda's eye. She was crying softly into the shoulder of her victim support worker and Lofty was holding her hand. The charges against Peveril were read out. Guilty. Guilty.

'How do you find the defendant on the count of murder?' the clerk asked.

'On the count of murder. We are unable to agree,' the foreman said.

The clerk, without pausing, went on and said, 'On the count of aid and abet?'

'Guilty. That was the decision of us all.'

Kelly, who was the only one of the defendants who when asked to stand by the judge had refused to do so, was asked again, but again he disobeyed.

Guilty. Guilty. Guilty. The verdicts of the jury rang out in number one court in the Old Bailey. Kelly started to shout and scream at the foreman of the jury and then at the judge. The prison officers pulled him away fighting until he was out of sight.

Justice Kane thanked the jury and asked Christopher to take a moment to consider whether the Crown would seek a retrial in relation to the murder charge against George Peveril. He would return for sentencing at two p.m. and would like an answer by then as he may need to put it off if a retrial were required for the charge against Peveril. Christopher asked for one moment, which was all he needed, and Joanne, who was now by his side, and the CPS lawyer descended into a whispering huddle. Sandy looked at Lofty and Belinda, who were both shaking their heads. They wanted no retrial. Sandy desperately tried not to look at Arabella and James, who were imploring him to intercede. Sandy quickly joined the huddle and told them Belinda's view. 'That was just what Detective Superintendent O'Connor's view is. I will withdraw the charge against Peveril.' Christopher got up and told the court of the decision. Justice Kane was content with this course of action and formally discharged George from this charge.

∞

That afternoon, when everyone, including the defendants and the jury, who had asked the judge if they could remain in court for sentencing, was settled, Christopher Coke QC outlined the previous convictions for Cousins and Kelly. There were nods to each other from the members of the jury. He then informed Mr Justice Kane QC that Mrs Belinda Foster had asked DCI McFarlane, on her behalf, to read to the court her victim impact statement. Sandy, with the statement in hand, looked directly at the judge. He knew in order to get through this he should not waiver his gaze. How any family member could do it, he had no idea.

'I am unable to tell you in person what the loss of my husband has done to me and my children, as I am too scared to do this in front of you all. I would not be able to emotionally cope. I also knew I wouldn't be able to look at the people who have taken everything away from me and my children and our hopes for a future.' Sandy had to gulp a few times to get rid of the lump in his throat. He could just make out the quiet sobs of Belinda at the back of the court. 'I met Joseph when we were both eighteen, on holiday in Greece. Me, after my studies and Joseph, on leave from the Army. Gosh, he loved being in the Army so much. To be a Grenadier Guard was to him an honour beyond his wildest dreams.' Sandy took a sip of the glass of water that Christopher had given him. 'I thought it was just a holiday romance, but he kept visiting me in Derby every time he was on leave. He would turn up with flowers. He was absolutely dedicated to me, and he asked me to marry him. We were so young, but how do you turn down someone you love so much, and who is so in love with you too.'

Sandy needed to pause for a few moments to just look at Belinda and smile. 'When I gave birth to our oldest child, Joseph was away serving in Afghanistan. Every day whilst he was there was a torture of worry. When he came home, Joseph had nearly completed six years in the Army and he joined the local police near where we lived in Derbyshire. It broke his heart to leave the Guards, but his love for me and our child, and our

335

soon to be born youngest child, was enough. As it turned out, he thoroughly enjoyed being a police officer. Derbyshire police are a good and caring police force and he felt part of their family.' Sandy could hear the odd sob from others in the court now rather than just Belinda. 'When you are woken in the night and you see the distraught face of your husband's sergeant and a detective stood in front of you, you just know the worst has happened. I cried so much, screamed in rage so much. I have so much emptiness and despair, I still, to this day, don't know what to do.' Sandy took another slow sip of water in order to catch his own emotions. 'I am not able to sleep, the medication doesn't work. There is not one day free from tears. I have no idea how I, and my family, will cope in the future without our beloved Joseph. I would like to ask the defendants why you took the life of this beloved, gentle and gallant man. Thank you for listening to me.'

Before he took his seat, Belinda and Sandy hugged, and Arabella, her eyes wet with tears, nodded at him. Justice Kane felt the court needed one moment, he said, to absorb what had just been said. Then mitigation started for all three defendants. For Kelly and Cousins, their adverse childhood experiences; for George, a boy from a privileged background, who had lost his way. The judge took it all into account when he sentenced them.

Dean Kelly did stand this time. The sentence for the murder was life imprisonment, to serve a minimum of thirty-four years. Cousins, the same, but only a twenty-four-year minimum tariff. Holloway had been superb in his mitigation. Finally, George Peveril was left, and was sentenced to a total of eight years. A long time, but incredibly a lot less than if he had been convicted of murder.

The after-court party in a private room above a pub in Fleet Street was a really great occasion. Christopher had taken care of the drinks bill. Christopher Coke QC had been utterly magnificent throughout the whole trial. Sandy was having a great time, but he couldn't help thinking about Hannah, and in particular what sort of night Belinda would be having. They revelled in celebrating the court result and the commendations that Justice Kane had given to the team, which included one for Sandy. Joanne's press briefing outside the Old Bailey had also been excellent. Somehow, Clare, who was at the party, had taken photos of Lofty and Sandy in their totally ill-fitting white CSI suits on the banks of Lake Manitoba, and this was displayed on a loop on a screen, which everyone, including Lofty and Sandy, found extremely funny.

Chapter Thirty-Six

Almost two months later, after Christmas and New Year had come and gone, Sandy eventually agreed to Arabella's persistent requests to go and see George in prison. Sandy drove to Swinfen Hall Young Offenders Institute via Leicester. It was a really cold, late January day and he was wrapped up well in his Morgan Roadster. There was no chance of having the car roof down on this trip. As much as he loved to drive like that, that was still likely to be some months off. He was remarkably busy at work at the FCDO but had no planned further exciting investigations abroad to look forward to.

Sandy waited in the car park for Arabella to arrive and had to admit, he was pleased to see her when the big black Range Rover pulled in. Arabella had told him on the phone that she had struggled for months, both before and after the trial, to get motivated again as the CEO for Peveril's, but her drive and enthusiasm was thankfully returning.

As soon as George turned up in the visitor area, he

hugged his aunty, then after looking Sandy up and down, deciding what to do, hugged him as well. 'Thank you for coming to see me, DCI McFarlane. I know I have already thanked you for saving my life, but I am really thankful.' Sandy looked at George. Although he was in prison, he seemed to have a focus to him and he looked well. 'I don't know if Arabella told you, but I am due to take my A levels this summer then spend three years completing a degree in environmental and sustainable agriculture.'

Arabella wanted to contribute and said, 'George is predicted three A stars.' Arabella, as always, the proud aunty continued. 'He is due for release after half his sentence so taking account of his time on remand this is in almost exactly three and a half years' time so will be able to complete his degree whilst here. They have in fact been marvellous in organising everything.'

'Well done, George. I often said when looking for you that although you were missing, you were not lost, as we knew you were in Canada.' It had in fact been Lofty that had first said it, but that didn't matter now. 'I did though after a while think you had lost your way as a young man. You no longer look, and sound lost in that way, so well done. The challenge is to keep it going in here – three and a half years is a long time still to do in prison.'

'I know. The reason I wanted to see you was to firstly say, truly, thank you, and then I wondered if I could write to you? Just to talk about any topic under the sun that makes me have to research a reasoned response back to you. Would you do that for me?'

Arabella could not resist contributing to the discussion again. 'Sandy, he wants you to mentor him. Please say yes, that you will?'

'I am not sure I am such a great choice, but I would be honoured to try and help you, I really would. One of my grandparents does research and drafts papers on ethical medico-legal cases, in particular relating to children.' Sandy didn't mention the fact that he was a retired judge. 'I can ask him for a couple of topics to start us off. Things like, should a hospital stop treatment when the parents want it to continue. Has your grandfather been to see you in here as yet?'

Arabella started to speak but George put his hand on her arm and said, 'He has said he can't bring himself to visit me in here, but we have a phone call every two weeks and we write to each other once a month. Dad comes regularly and my mum has been once, as has my stepmother and my sisters. So, it's all fine, other than this one.' He tapped his aunt's arm. 'She keeps turning up all the time!' They all laughed together. 'One final thing. I just can't put out of my mind what you said on behalf of Mrs Foster. I wondered if you could tell her I am truly sorry for what happened. I know she won't believe me, but I did not know the gun was loaded.' Sandy thought, we knew that as we overheard you talking on the listening device.

'I can tell her, but I'm not sure she will accept it. Are

340

you still friends with Cousins and Kelly?'

'No, they showed their true feelings to me throughout all of this.'

As Sandy and Arabella said goodbye, they promised to keep in touch and Sandy told her he really would write to George and would also tell Belinda Foster what George had said.

∞

Derby, and where Belinda Foster lived, were, in fact, only about thirty minutes away from where he was at the prison, so Sandy made a decision to go and visit Belinda. He had not spoken to or heard from her since the day the trial finished, but he knew that Lofty did from time to time.

As Sandy parked his Morgan Roadster outside the Foster's home, he hoped Belinda was there. He hadn't thought to ring first. He was pleased when Belinda answered the door and even more pleased by her extremely positive reaction to him arriving. 'How are you, Sandy?' Belinda asked. Even though it was the early afternoon, she looked to still be in her night clothes, and looked a lot older than her twenty-seven years. Grief does this to you, Sandy supposed.

'I am well, but more to the point, how are you?'

'Not too good at all. I haven't left this house since the day I arrived home after the trial. Everyone told me that after you get justice, you will have closure and a

341

chance to move on. Not true. It was an anti-climax. In fact, the trial gave me something to focus on, and then it was gone. The children are with my mum and dad but visit most days. Dad has insisted they come home this weekend so that I develop a will to live for them.'

'I am so sorry to hear this, Belinda. I always wondered what is meant by the term "move on", but why would you want to move on from Joseph? Surely a better phrase is to move forward, but with the memory of him with you, not to leave him behind.'

Belinda became more alert when he said this. 'That is the most positive thing someone has said to me. I can almost understand that,' she said.

'For example, Joseph had, I know, a huge affinity with the Army, and the Grenadier Guards in particular. Why don't you set up a charitable organisation for veterans in Joseph's name in Derby? I am sure DC Dobson and the Derbyshire police would help.'

Suddenly, in an instant, Belinda became brighter. 'I get it now. I have been desperately sad being like this because I don't want to move on from the love of my life. The way you describe it, I am not moving on but forward, but also with Joseph with me. He would have loved to have been involved in something like this.'

'I will ring Lofty today and see how we can start the ball rolling. I also saw George Peveril today.'

'How is he? I felt sorry for him in the end. I came to the conclusion he was a bit of a victim as well,' Belinda said. 'He will still be so young when he comes out of prison though; he can start his own life again, not like Joe.'

'He asked me to apologise to you on his behalf, for the part he played in Joseph's murder.'

'You tell him thank you, but if he has anything to do with those other two again, he will have me to answer to.' They both laughed together. 'I can't forgive *them* though. They are monsters.' Belinda couldn't even bring herself to use their names.

As they said goodbye at the door, Belinda told him how much she liked his car, but Joe would have called him a poser for having a car like that. Again, laughter. This, it seemed, had been a good decision for him to visit Belinda.

∞

As Sandy drove home, he received a call from his Grandpa John asking him to pop by as he went past Cambridge. Sandy's mum must have told him he had gone off to the Midlands today.

After about thirty minutes, he thought he would phone Lofty to see how he was and talk about his conversation with Belinda. Lofty, though, beat him to it and rang him first. 'Sandy, well done with Belinda. She has been on the phone to me. I have just spoken to our welfare department and we are going to set up a charity in PC Foster's name. The first charitable event will be a triathlon, where people can do all of it or a section of it.

I told Belinda you would do all of it. You have two months to train and your challenge is to come within thirty minutes of me, or you personally double the sponsorship you raise.' Lofty laughed. He was fired up and determined to lead on this for Belinda and Joseph.

'I will try then to raise as little sponsorship as possible!' They both had a good laugh. Lofty was an outstandingly good man.

Sandy arrived in Cambridge in a very good mood. He parked outside his grandpa's house. Sandy wondered what he wanted. As he was shown into the lounge, his grandpa turned around and walked straight out again, shutting the door. Sitting there in the lounge was Hannah. Sandy felt his knees go weak and he sat down. 'Sandy, please hear me out and don't be cross with John,' Hannah said. That was the first time he had heard her use his grandpa's first name rather than judge, or Judge John. 'I am so sorry for any hurt or conflict I caused you.'

Sandy needed to stop Hannah apologising. Looking at her and moving to sit next to her on the sofa, he said, 'No, Hannah, it is me that should apologise. Not for one second did I listen to your side of it. I had only the vision of the Fosters in my head.'

'I know you think I did it for my career,' Hannah said. 'I really didn't. I was Ruben's lawyer. Not anymore though, and he is not going to appeal. Charles Holloway told him he got off lightly with his sentence as he should have got the same as Kelly. How is Mrs

Foster?'

'Not at all good,' Sandy said. 'I have just been to see her today. She is going to set up a charitable foundation in Joseph's name and apparently, according to Wayne Dobson, the first fund raising event is a triathlon, or individual parts of it, and I am being entered.'

'Could I do it with you?' Hannah asked, with pleading eyes.

'You can do everything with me now if you would like?'

'Yes, please,' Hannah said, smiling widely. They heard a very loud shout in the hallway: 'Yes!'

'Grandpa, have you been listening to our conversation?' Sandy said. He and Hannah laughed. When John walked into the lounge, he saw them both kissing passionately so promptly turned around and walked back out again.

'Grandpa, can you call mum and tell her I won't be home for dinner? Hannah and I are going to the Oak Bistro to start again.'

Author's Note

I spent over thirty years as a police officer and the majority of these years were as a detective. I served as a detective in every rank, finally spending my last six years as the detective chief superintendent (head of the detective branch) of the Cambridgeshire Constabulary. As a detective, I led over a hundred major crime cases, a number of which were homicides or suspicious deaths. I absolutely loved this opportunity. The rank I enjoyed most though was the rank that Alexander McFarlane holds, that of a DCI. I am best known for my work as a detective around the UK for my role, over many years, as the national policing lead for the investigation of child death, as well as for my role as the senior investigator at the deposition site for the recovery and forensic investigation into the deaths of Holly Wells and Jessica Chapman, two ten-year-old girls from Soham, who were murdered by Ian Huntley.

In October 2019, my wife Debbie and I had a chance encounter in a remote hilltop village in the Atlas Mountains (Morocco) with a couple from Melbourne –

Professor Anne Buist and her partner Graeme Simsion. They are both authors and were working on a romantic comedy novel together. Graeme authored the bestselling novel *The Rosie Project*. When I told him I had a detective crime novel in mind, he proceeded to give me a fifteen-minute masterclass on how to write a novel. Coincidently, both Professor Buist and I were to be keynote speakers at a conference two weeks later in Melbourne, relating to children who had been murdered by a parent. This chance meeting cemented my thoughts to write the novel I had been talking about for years.

This didn't occur, however, until the first lockdown arrived due to the COVID-19 pandemic. Even though I was still busy with my safeguarding work and writing a number of reviews, I decided to write a first draft of a novel during this period. That novel, *Greed is a Powerful Motive*, has now been published by my publisher Cranthorpe Millner.

A number of years ago, I was working in Derbyshire for the constabulary and talking about wanting to write crime fiction. DS Gary Lunn (now retired), who I was working with, told me he had a story for me that would fit. He had spearheaded a campaign to get the murder of a Derbyshire police officer formally recognised. This police officer was PC Joseph Moss, who was murdered whilst in the execution of his duty in 1879. He was shot by a "gentleman", Gerald Mainwaring, who had been out drinking with a female friend. After being arrested, he was in the police station and shot not just PC Moss, but another PC, who survived. He was convicted of murder and sentenced to hang, but it was changed to life imprisonment. He served fifteen years and then returned, it is believed, possibly to Manitoba.

All of the characters in the novel are fictional. I have, though, used a number of themes from the original case: out of honour to Joseph Moss, my PC is also called Joseph, and I made them the same age and both had been in the Grenadier Guards; the place the person came back from, but in my case went to, was Manitoba, Canada; the weapon used was a revolver; the PC was murdered during the execution of his duty; and the location of the murder was Lock-Up-Yard, now in the open air near the market place in Derby city centre. There is a remembrance plaque in the flagstones there to Joseph, marking the exact place he was shot.

I look forward to continuing DCI Alexander (Sandy) McFarlane's story in the future with his investigation into a suspicious death in a chateau near Bordeaux, France.

Acknowledgements

To my wife Debbie, who is and has always been my greatest supporter in all that I do. Debbie was the first to read this novel and then painstakingly helped me to carry out a first edit for every page of it. For this and everything, I am truly grateful.

To all my family: my mother Florence, my children Daniel (who also helped greatly in the editing of the book), Rebecca and Matthew, my father-in-law Sydney Barton and sister-in-law Ruth Chaplain-Barton for reading and commenting on the story.

Also, to my close friends who have taken the time to read the novel and to give me feedback. So, thank you to Judi Richardson, Lorri and John Kendall (my Canadian family), Joanne Procter, Andrew Harrison (my writing and sourdough buddy), David Marshall (my work buddy), Angela and Mark Craig (my friends, but also my daughter's mother- and father-in-law), James Bambridge, Jane Ashton, Glenys Johnston, Mike Richardson, Mark Birch and Wendi Ogle-Welbourn.

I would also like to thank Detective Superintendent

Fran Naughton for her knowledge and experience to assist me with my research into joint enterprise. And of course, Gary Lunn for telling me the fascinating story of PC Joseph Moss.